Witch's Knight

by

Evelyn Silver

The Bloodline Chronicles, Book One

Witch's Knight

Cover Art by *Debbie Taylor*

The Wild Rose Press, Inc.
PO Box 708
Adams Basin, NY 14410-0708
Visit us at www.thewildrosepress.com

Publishing History
First Edition, 2022
Trade Paperback ISBN 978-1-5092-4437-9
Digital ISBN 978-1-5092-4438-6

The Bloodline Chronicles, Book One
Published in the United States of America

With a delicate touch, the vampire pinched the plastic tube with her nails and severed it. The end still connected to Sarai's body spurt with each beat of her frightened heart, while the other end dropped limp and began to drip onto the floor to mingle with the blood of the dead scientist. The vampire brought the end of the connected tube up to her lips like a straw, and Sarai's gut twisted as she felt the liquid pulled from her body at a much faster rate. It made her fingertips feel cold.

"Do you mind not sucking my blood while I'm trying to have a conversation with you?" Sarai demanded. "It's rude."

The vampire paused, blinked, and then laughed as she lowered the makeshift straw. "Please do forgive me, little witch," she said, her voice heavy with mockery. "I wouldn't want to be accused of rudeness. If we're being so polite, why don't you tell me who you are?"

Sarai pursed her lips. "Let me out of this chair, and maybe I will."

Dedication

This book is dedicated to Evan, Ashley, and Rachel, who have all supported me and my writing so much over the years.

Author Note

This book is intended for adult audiences due to subject matter pertaining to sexual situations, mention of child loss, violence, attempted assault and lots of very delicious blood. Reader discretion is advised.

Acknowledgements

To everyone who has supported me over the years, I can't begin to thank you. Reading my rough drafts and helping me hone my craft was a favor that puts you near and dear to my heart. For all my beta readers and supporters out there, you mean the world to me.

I'd like to thank Ashley and Rachel, my non-related sisters. You've been with me since first grade and are the best friends anyone could ever ask for. You've read my work at its worst and its best and always been fantastic. Whether Ashley's telling me I messed up commas or Rachel's throwing chocolate from a safe distance when I'm PMSing, I'd be nowhere without the two of you.

Thank you to my spouse, Evan, who has always supported my writing endeavors as well as my numerous started and forgotten projects that never went anywhere. You're amazing, and I'm so happy to have met you and be raising a family with you. Our love started with a shared love of literature, and I'm so happy that I can now put my book on our home library shelves, thanks to your support. Also, thanks to my in-laws for raising him and being beautifully open-minded towards your weird daughter-in-law/sister-in-law!

Thank you to my parents for all the love and support given over the years. I truly appreciate you valuing my education and you attending my poorly written plays in high school. It's a good thing I got better, and now I'm in print! I know you don't always "get" my shenanigans, but I also know you'll always love me, and I'll always love you.

Thanks to my brother for being supportive, despite

thinking this whole book is a gross kissy thing he wants no part of. You're not bad, for a little brother.

Thanks to the good teachers over the years who helped me grow as a person and a writer.

Thanks to my voice actors for the audio book. You guys were amazing, despite me having no idea how to put together something like this, and I'm so grateful for your patience and for you lending your voices to my characters.

Thank you to my editor, Callie Lynn Wolfe, at The Wild Rose Press. As a queer person, it means so much to me that an ally in the publishing world wanted to take a chance on my writing. You were willing to help me take that important step towards bring a queer and polyamorous love story into the light. You're a great person, and a great editor. Sorry about the whole em dash situation, I'll hopefully get better in book two!

Last but not least, thank you to the communities I've been a part of over the years who've helped me grow. I hope that this book in some small way gives back by providing you representation and I look forward to being with you for many more years to come.

Chapter One: Zombie Rat

Sarai Reinhart hated onion day. She had spent the better part of two hours chopping onions in the back of the small, family-owned Indian restaurant where she worked, and knew that it would take two or three days for the smell to disappear. That was with wearing gloves. At least she only cried a little; she'd learned weeks ago that wearing sunglasses while chopping protected her from the worst of it.

"Hey, Sarai!" the owner, Rohan, called as he walked through the cramped kitchen. He was a tired, overworked man with a British accent who paid her under the table and didn't let servers keep tips. Sarai didn't mind the last part too much since he paid her a full two dollars above minimum wage, and the tiny restaurant only had ten tables.

"Hey," she replied, waving at him with the knife before bringing it down on an onion. She missed and ground her teeth as it went through the tip of her finger, but she hid the pain. Within a moment, it had healed thanks to her unique gift, and she used the corner of her black skirt to wipe away any evidence of the wound.

"Can you run out and clear table nine for me?" he asked.

"Mmm hmm." Better than chopping onions. She finished the one she was cutting, put the knife to the side for when she returned, and stuck her head out from the back to see how bad the situation with table nine looked. Just a few plates and a half-eaten basket of naan. Excellent.

She went out and started stacking bowls that smelled of aromatic curry. Her stomach growled, but she told herself to be patient. Rohan let her have a free serving of chicken curry or channa masala to go most nights, especially if it wasn't busy. The chicken wasn't kosher with its dairy and meat combination, but she hadn't ever kept strictly kosher. She didn't care much as long as there wasn't any pork, shellfish, or visible blood in her meals. The only reason she did any of it was a way to connect to the Jewish mother she couldn't remember. And strict kosher rules went out the window when the curry served as her meal for the day.

I need to learn more spells, Sarai thought to herself. She knew that somewhere in the world an enchantment existed that could charm a pot to fill with whatever sample of food was put into it. But enchantments on objects like that were difficult. Many modern witches never learned more than basic spells, never progressed beyond mastery of their one innate gift. Her father's coven hadn't focused much on mundane skills good for surviving, like making food. She'd learned basic wards, but anything else would have to come from a more experienced witch or a grimoire, neither of which she had access to. No 'good' witches wanted anything to do with a Reinhart.

Sarai glanced around and saw no customers at the nearest tables, so tore a large piece of the bread and stuffed it in her mouth, letting her curly golden-brown hair fall around her olive face to obscure what she was doing. There was a noise behind her, but she ignored it as she scarfed down a second piece.

There it was again, more frantic. Clicking? No, snapping. With a sigh, Sarai turned to face a plump blonde woman with short hair snapping at her.

"Are you eating?"

Sarai raised an eyebrow and swallowed. Without thinking her words through, she blurted, "Is that a trick question?"

"Excuse me?!"

"Um, no I didn't eat the naan?" It was worth a try.

"That is disgusting!"

If you don't want to see people eat, don't go to a restaurant, Sarai wanted to say. Instead, she said, "Sorry you feel that way, ma'am."

Sarai turned back to finish stacking the plates but stomping and huffing alerted her that the woman hadn't finished. Rolling her eyes, she turned back around to look up at an average-height woman towering over Sarai's petite frame as a swollen finger jabbed into her chest.

"I demand to speak to your manager. You're going around infecting food and putting your hands in everything, who knows what you did to my food with your incompetence. I want my meal taken off my bill, now."

Sarai stared. "I'm bussing. I haven't touched your food."

"Don't talk back to me; you're just a server. Some teenage idiot. I'm sure you put your filthy hands all over it, you degenerate. I want to speak to the manager!"

Her blood boiled. She wasn't a teenager. Sarai was twenty-four years old, but her short stature didn't do anything to discourage the assumption. With someone so aggressive, there would be no correcting her. Of all the days, the woman had to pick onion day. She plopped the plates back on the table; there was just one thing to do.

"I'll go get the manager."

Technically, the restaurant didn't have a manager, since the owner was the head chef, but all this woman wanted was someone to shout at so she could get a free meal. Sarai didn't feel like being the target.

"Hey, Rohan, there's some lady that—"

"I heard," he muttered, wiping his hands on his apron. "Just... just go take your break."

Fine by her. She went out the back door to the North Carolina air and let herself slump next to the dumpster. It smelled worse than the onions. She hated customers who acted so superior. If the woman knew what Sarai was capable of, the death she could cause, she'd cower. Anyone with sense would, especially a mundane human. She buried her face in her onion-scented hands and tried to press the tears back into her skull. There was no point in putting up with it all, yet she did. She was capable of more in life, but she was trapped cutting onions, living in poverty, and with no end in sight.

Wiping the stinging water from her eyes, Sarai took several breaths to calm herself. That was when an opportunity climbed onto her shoe.

The mouse was small and almost cute. Braver than most mice, to get so close to a person. She snatched it up by the tail, watching it wiggle at the end. Mice were pests. They carried diseases and could be bad so close to a restaurant. It was good to get rid of the mouse. That was the justification she could come up with for killing something that hadn't done anything to her.

Magic sparked in her fingertips and snaked down through the squeaking rodent's tail. Power travelled through its body, coursing through its veins, then stilled it when the magic reached its brain.

Sarai wasn't a true necromancer, a proper one who could raise the dead back to life or resurrect a soul: her limit was creating obedient zombies. But any necromancy was considered dark, feared, and coveted by magical communities. It kept her running from her father's abusive coven, hiding from the many witches, witch hunters, and other power-hungry monsters who wanted her to use her gift on their behalf. Considering all the drawbacks of such an ability, the least she could do with it was to teach a rude customer a lesson to make herself feel better.

The mouse twitched, then stiffened again, blinking its calloused and dead eyes at her, awaiting commands.

"Just hide in my sleeve for now," she instructed, and it scampered up to obey. "I'll tell you when I'm ready for you."

Collected and focused, she went back inside. Her heart felt faster and the tingling in her fingers felt… good. Every day was a drudge, and now she would do something about it. For the first time in years, Sarai felt powerful and in control.

"Here," Rohan said, thrusting a mango lassi drink into her hands. "On the house. Take it out to that pig and apologize to her."

She couldn't have planned it better. "Fine." Sarai plastered a smile on her face and went out to face the woman again, but not before whispering into her sleeve,

"Go for her fingers when she finds you. Get in."

With a plop, the mouse was submerged in the yellow-orange liquid, hidden from sight. She stuck a straw in and went out to enact her plan.

"It took you long enough," the woman puffed.

"So sorry, ma'am. I'm very sorry you had a bad experience, and I won't ever do it again. We hope you'll like this drink, on us."

"I bet you don't even have a GED. Not scavenging trash right in front of us like some bum. If you bothered to make something of your life, you wouldn't eat garbage. What's the highest degree you've ever achieved?"

Any reservation about what she was doing flew out the window. "I never graduated preschool, ma'am." It was true. She'd never gotten any traditional schooling since her father's reclusive coven relied on witch tutors of their own for their dark education. "Please enjoy your drink."

She frowned. "What is this? Is it alcoholic?"

"No, it's a mango lassi. It's a yogurt drink. Very sweet, like a milkshake."

"I want my meal taken off my bill," she growled and grabbed the drink, pursing her lips like a cat's anus around the straw. As she looked down, two dead rodent eyes peered back at her.

The drink went flying, and the rodent lunged for her hand, latching onto a ringed finger with a vengeance as a shriek high enough to shatter glass broke the eardrums of every customer and staff member in the building.

The woman managed to fling the mouse into the wall next to her and stumbled away. Its dead flesh burst, blood oozing from the grotesque tear, but it still obeyed its master's command as it dragged its mangled corpse forward toward the woman. She climbed on a chair and pointed her wounded finger. "ZOMBIE RAT!"

Well, she was half right.

"I think it's a mouse," Sarai supplied. A rat wouldn't have fit in the glass. Deciding enough was enough, she picked up a dirty curry bowl and covered the mouse with it, catching it before it could do more damage. She lifted the bowl to grab it in her hand, and let the spark of her magic dissipate, leaving it limp with death.

"It's okay, ma'am. I think it's dead."

"It-it was in my drink!" Her screaming became unintelligible, and Rohan ran out to try and figure out what happened. Sarai just stood there, her dead minion oozing mango sludge in her hand as customers stared at her.

"I'll just get rid of this," Sarai muttered, trying not to grin as she rushed out the back to toss the mouse into the dumpster. It was the rush she'd needed, the feeling of action she'd craved. Weight had lifted off her shoulders and the dumpster didn't even smell too bad. She could almost cry tears of joy; Sarai should have used her powers against rude customers years ago. It was the freedom she needed. Freedom to use her birthright, to be seen. They were feelings she repressed just to survive in the mundane human world, hiding from witch hunters and abusers who would kill her, or worse.

As she came back in to wash her hands, shouting grew from the front and her feeling of relief dissipated.

Attacking a customer with a mouse had been a terrible idea. Rohan didn't deserve the abuse being flung at him from multiple customers. Helplessness and regret burned in her chest, and she went back to chopping onions, her hands shaking. She needed to make it up to Rohan somehow. Maybe use a little of her next paycheck to get him something. She'd been saving up for a newly portable CD player, but considering the trouble she'd caused, Rohan deserved it more.

Rohan stormed back, glaring.

"What the hell was that?" he asked, his voice as even as his anger would allow.

"I-I'm sorry, I don't know how—"

"You put a mouse. In. My. Drink." He closed his eyes. "I had to comp every meal out there. They're going to call the health inspector and…"

Crap.

"I, I'm sorry."

"Get out. Right now. Don't come back."

Sarai didn't argue. There was nothing to say to defend her actions, how petty and immature they had been. He deserved better. "I'm sorry."

"Out."

She gathered the plain canvas tote bag she used instead of a purse and walked out. It was too early to catch the bus. She'd have to wait a while, alone with her thoughts.

One of the customers, a burly man in his thirties with a patchy mustache, was waiting outside, his arms crossed over his chest, staring at her.

"Zombie rat, huh?" he asked her.

"Mouse," she corrected in a numb monotone. "No zombie or rat, just mouse."

"Sure. How'd you get it to drown itself like that?"

"Didn't do anything. I'd never serve a valued customer a mouse. Zombie or otherwise."

"Uh huh. Guess she wasn't a valued customer."

Sarai shrugged. "You got a point to make, or are you going to let me get fired in peace?"

"By all means." He gestured for her to walk ahead, and she did, glancing back to catch sight of him still watching her as he pulled out a new model flip phone. Sarai made a point to take several unnecessary turns to lose sight of him on her way toward the bus stop but couldn't shake the distinct feeling of being watched. To protect herself, she slipped her hand into her tote bag and found her most prized possession; a red, fingerless glove that functioned as a wand, but was much more practical since a traditional wand or staff would stand out to anyone hunting witches like a massive forehead pimple on a bride. With the glove as her focus, her abilities expanded from the use of only her gifts to a full range of spells.

Muttering protective wards under her breath in Hebrew, her first language, Sarai glanced at a video rental store as she neared the bus stop. If only she had a VHS player that worked; the one she'd scavenged on a bulk pick-up trash day had, unsurprisingly, turned out to be trash. She thought about taking the bus down to the local library to get new books. A little entertainment would help.

Sarai arrived at the bus stop and slumped in a seat. The weight that had lifted to give her that moment of bliss returned tenfold, crushing her. She had to go back and beg for her job, that was certain, but not until Rohan had time to cool off. Or… she could leave it all behind, try to find a witch coven to join. Nausea twisted her gut at the thought, and she dismissed it. She did have other options. Protection spells could be used to keep her safe while pickpocketing, which would ensure she had enough money until she could get another job. Another depressing job with no light at the end of the tunnel. Survival for the sake of surviving. She needed something more, desperately. Maybe a new hobby, or a romance.

Movement flickered in the corner of her eye, and a stranger sat down on the opposite end of the bench. A stunning and beautiful stranger wearing the latest low-rise jeans, a flowy black top, large sunhat, and rhinestone-studded sunglasses that obscured half her face. Sarai's heart skipped a beat, and she couldn't help but openly stare at the perfection of the woman's red lips against her pale complexion, her sharp jawline, and her elegantly tied-up black hair. The woman looked far too put-together to be waiting for a bus and would have appeared more natural stepping out of a limousine. She felt compelled to interact with the beauty.

"H-hey," Sarai said.

The woman turned her head, and the young witch wished she could see something in those sunglasses other than her own awkward reflection. Sarai wanted to see what color eyes the woman had; she already knew her own were brown.

"Yes?" Her voice was sultry, and the way the corner of her lips curled in amusement was an invitation. Sarai stared her mind blank as she struggled to think of something to say.

"Um, do you know the time?"

The woman pushed her sunglasses up as she

looked down at the thin watch on her delicate wrist. Sarai tried to catch sight of the woman's eyes but couldn't see from the angle. "It's five thirty."

As the woman looked up, Sarai was captivated by the most brilliant sky-blue eyes she'd ever seen. The moment of beauty evaporated in an instant as blue flickered with red.

Sarai jumped to her feet as if the bus bench had turned to hot coals as the woman flicked her sunglasses back down over her eyes and sat there like nothing had happened.

"Th-thanks." She turned on her heel and started walking away as fast as she could. She'd never met one before, since they weren't likely to be out during the day, but every witch knew only vampires had red eyes. Vampires were not friends to witches and had a reputation for killing known necromancers on sight.

She couldn't leave fast enough and started the two-mile trek home. At least the day couldn't get much worse.

Chapter Two: The Vasi

Glancing nervously back every few seconds until she was certain the beautiful vampire hadn't followed her, Sarai walked until she reached her apartment. Though, calling it an apartment was generous. It was more like a large closet with leaks. If the wind blew too hard or cars drove by too fast, the walls rattled, and cold air would gust in. Her personal things were all discarded items rescued from other people's trash. Everything from her second and third hand clothes to a stained mattress and splintered table with a single folding chair had been thrown away by someone else at one point. Her instincts told her that the mattress was a plague carrier, but with her healing ability she never had to worry about sickness.

Her most important possessions were the repurposed witch supplies stacked in a corner. They weren't much–yarn, salt, candles, and whatever herbs she could find–but she knew how to work with them. The salt lined all her apartment's windows and the front door, spelled to keep anyone from being able to scry her home. Knots in red string tied in just the right way hung like silent wind-chimes as a secondary form of magical protection, matching a few that hung under her clothes and off her tote bag. It doubled as colorful decoration, making the depressing apartment slightly less miserable. For good measure, she'd taped a rolled-up paper to her doorway with the words protect my home in Hebrew, *shomer beiti*, scribbled there. It was her rudimentary low-budget witchy version of a mezuzah, which was a special blessing Jewish homes were meant to have in their doorways. She envied the fancy cases of proper mezuzahs, but what she made served its purpose. Every time she passed in or out, she would brush her hand against it, a spark of magic on her fingertips as she refreshed the protective spell. No simple magic would ever find her.

Sarai plopped onto her mattress, the wall behind her trembling when her head hit it. Her stomach growled, and she sighed. She had really been hoping for some chicken to take home, since it was a Friday night. Still, she had something. Getting up, she fished the last of her cereal out of her cabinet and stared out the window as she stuck her hand into the box and stuffed her face. The sun had nearly set after her long walk, so she pulled two tealight candles out from her pile of witch supplies.

Channeling her magic through her focus, she cleared her mind and whispered, "*Esh*," with reverence. Creating fire was tricky to Sarai, as it wasn't her innate gift. The spoken word in a language she viewed as special helped shape her intent in casting the spell and the twin flames flickered onto the wicks of the candles after several moments of magical struggling.

The purpose wasn't magic or protection like the salt and knots around her. In fact, she wasn't entirely sure what the purpose really was. She knew it connected to her mother, and there was some sort of religious significance, but the religion didn't matter to her as much as having that thread of connection to her dead mother.

"Miss you," she said softly, and swallowed a mouthful of dry cereal. It was half a lie. She missed the idea of her mother. She couldn't miss what she couldn't remember. As she stared at the low light, something beyond it shimmered, with the tangibility of the glow around a full moon. A translucent Sephardic woman with black, curly hair and a white dress sat across from her. Sarai's eyes widened. She knew this woman but hadn't seen her in years. Liora was an imaginary friend Sarai's mind had conjured as a child to bring her comfort when she'd been locked in a closet by her father.

"What..."

The woman evaporated when Sarai blinked.

She was overworked and overstressed, Sarai decided. Between the rude customer, being fired, seeing a vampire, and walking two miles in North Carolina's humid summer heat, she had to be delirious. Likely dehydrated and hallucinating. She chugged tap water from a chipped ceramic mug, then used the cup to snuff out the candles so she could reuse them. Something told her she wasn't allowed to blow them out, so she always let them die 'naturally' from oxygen starvation under a cup.

Drained from the day's events, Sarai curled up on her mattress. As she drifted into unconsciousness, she almost swore she could hear Liora's faint voice, whispering something unintelligible.

In her sleep, the voice didn't disappear, and her dreams found her trapped in a dark, small space. It stunk of her father's cologne, lingering on clothes in the closet. The artificial scent gave her nothing but panic, and fear kept her body from responding.

"*You need to get out,*" Liora said, materializing before her in a white sundress that almost made her glow in the darkness. "*You need to leave, now.*"

"I can't leave," Sarai whispered. "I'm trapped."

"*You can. You have to wake up. You have to hide.*"

Sarai's eyes flew open, and she stared around her still room, heart racing. Moonlight streamed in through her open window, and a wind whistled through the cracks in the walls. Slowly, she willed her arms to move and sat up. There was no closet, no Liora. No need to be afraid. The creaking noises of the building around her were just a normal part of poverty.

And then the front door burst into splinters as a small army of armed, masked men in black body armor broke into her sanctuary.

She opened her mouth to scream but was rushed and brought down hard to the floor, the breath knocked out of her.

"This her?" a gruff voice asked.

"Yeah, that's the necromancer from the restaurant. I'd recognize that mane of hair anywhere."

Sarai's eyes widened in horror. They knew what she was. Her mind raced. The apartment was warded so they hadn't used magic to find her. There didn't seem to be a single magical focus or weapon among them. That meant one thing: witch hunters. Humans bent on enslaving or destroying anything occult.

"Please don't hurt me!" she blurted out. "I'm pregnant!"

It was a lie, but they didn't know that. She hoped even hunters retained enough decency to hesitate before hurting a pregnant woman. She just needed a moment to touch their skin, to sink her power into their worthless brains… but they were covered from head to toe in protective clothing.

As they looked at each other, apparently unsure what to do with the new information, she yanked the ski mask off the man who held her down on the floor and unleashed her power. He screamed as his veins surged with death, but she didn't have a chance to finish. A blow to her head sent the world in a spin, and something clicked around her neck. She tried once more to reach for his skin, but something went wrong. As she reached for the well of her magic, there was nothing, like a wall had been erected in her soul.

Numb terror spread throughout her body as she realized what had happened. They put a silver collar on her, the precious metal keeping her from accessing any magic. She thrashed against her assailant but stilled as something cold pressed under her chin.

A gun.

"Please don't kill me," she whispered.

"Maybe. If I were you, I'd think carefully about your next move, witch," the man growled, half of his face twisted as if electricity had scorched his veins. "Get up."

Trembling, she obeyed.

"Now be quiet and come with us."

She tried to think of something, anything, she could do, but there was nothing. Without her magic, she was helpless. She had to do whatever they said with the gun against her.

"I'm pregnant," she reminded them, pushing out her malnourished abdomen as much as she could so that hopefully they would think there was some truth to her lie. "Please, I'm–"

"Shut up." The metal of the gun pressed harder against her chin, and she kept silent. He hadn't shot her. That gave her hope they wanted her alive. If she played along, she might live.

She followed them out of the apartment building, praying someone with a landline would hear the commotion and call nine-one-one, but no one peeked out of their doors or even seemed to stir from their slumber. In the street, they clambered into a windowless, unmarked van. Once inside, a gag was forced into her mouth and a blindfold over her eyes, while a zip-tie bound her hands.

They drove for what felt like ages. The road became bumpy, and she could hear gravel under tires, but otherwise had no idea where they were. It might have been bearable if it weren't for the blindfold. Tears soaked it as she tried to think of anything other than the darkness. Tried to be brave. When the panic nearly became too much for her to hide, Liora's voice floated through her mind: salvation.

"*Numi numi, yaldati, numi numi nim.*
Aba halach le'avoda... halach, halach, halach..."
Go to sleep, my little girl.
Father's gone to work. Gone, gone, gone...

While the lullaby was comforting and helped her cling to some sanity, the words made her feel alone, abandoned. Anyone and anything who might protect her was gone, gone, gone...

Her father never protected her, her job was gone, her magic was gone...

"*Halach, halach, halach...*"
Gone, gone, gone.

When they finally stopped, Sarai was forced out of the van. With the movement, she was able to rub the back of her head against the metal vehicle just enough to get a glimmer of sight back.

Her surroundings had changed drastically. Instead of suburbia and buildings, there were trees and a dirt path. The path led to a fenced warehouse that was the only structure in sight, with a few more hunters at the entrance. Witch hunters with this level of organization could only mean one thing: Vasi. They were an organization every witch knew to fear, notorious for not only wiping out covens and hunting vampires, but for torturing witches into signing binding contracts, forcing them into magical slavery that compelled them to hunt down their own kin.

If she went inside the warehouse, Sarai would have no chance of escape.

She jerked out of the grip of the man holding her and punched him hard with both fists. He shouted as his nose crunched and dripped blood, but she didn't wait to see if he would recover. Sarai made a break for the fence.

"Stop her!" someone shouted behind her.

"Pyro, get her feet!"

Flame and pain erupted around Sarai's ankles, and she stumbled, screaming as the heat scorched away her socks and blistered her sensitive soles. Tears streamed down her face, and she shrieked curses in every language she knew, wanting the pain to end. It was all-consuming. Her ability to heal always ensured she never had any lingering pain, even from the worst of injuries. With the silver collar suppressing her magic, the pain stayed.

She looked up in hysterics as two of the men dragged her forward, her knees skinning against the gravel path.

"Try that again, and I'll order her to roast you up like a proper witch bonfire," one of them snarled. Sarai was in too much pain to think of running and looked up at the source of the fire.

It was another witch, with a fireball dimming in her palm. Her eyes were like windows to an abandoned home where the electricity had been cut for years, and her skin was covered in scars.

Sarai wanted to tell the witch she was sorry, that she understood why it happened and didn't blame her, but all she could do was sob from the pain as she was dragged by the two men into the dreaded building, down the stairs, and to a sterile lab.

It was an icy room that gave her goosebumps, with a surgical table in the middle and bloody tools in trays. Liora's voice echoed somewhere in her mind, her lullaby on a loop as if it could take away the fear.

Sarai wanted to tell them she would never relent, never sign a contract. But all she did was whimper as she was forced into a chair and straps were tightened over her wrists and blistered ankles. She bit down on the inside of her cheek; she had to be strong, hide her pain and fear from them.

"I'm not signing a contract," she told them. She wanted to sound strong, but her voice cracked to betray her.

They ignored her. Somehow that infuriated her more than being burned. She clenched her fists, trying to stop the trembling.

"Did you hear me?" she snapped. "I'm not signing

a contract."

"You will," one of the armed men said, a blond with greasy hair, rolling his eyes. "Little thing like you? I give it a week. Bet I won't even need to turn the electricity all the way up before you break."

Sarai didn't reply. Maybe it was better when they didn't talk to her.

The other man grabbed her hand, analyzing her red glove. She immediately clenched her fist. They couldn't be allowed to take it from her.

"Think it's her focus?"

"Probably. Nothing else interesting on her."

With a satisfied nod, the blond man snapped, "Open your hand up or I'll call the pyro back to burn it off."

Sarai hesitated, then to her shame, she complied. Her focus was stripped from her hand and locked away in a cabinet. At least she knew where it was.

After giving a quick, constricting tug on a wrist restraint to ensure it was secure, the man said, "Dr. Stearne, she's all yours. Try to process her quickly, she's a necromancer. We need her to deal with your other subject. She said she's pregnant, but I don't think she looks like it."

The alleged doctor, a scrawny man with uncombed brown hair, adjusted his glasses and used a cotton swab and rubbing alcohol to clean the tip of Sarai's finger. "I'll run a test for her later. Could be early, so doesn't make much of a difference for now." He pricked her fingertip with a needle. It didn't hurt much, at least. Not compared to the pain in her feet.

The doctor looked at the blood on a slide under a microscope, then looked up in confusion. "You said she's a necromancer? How do you know?"

"Harold saw her do it. Control a dead thing at a restaurant," one of the men replied. "Can you hurry–"

"Shh, shh. I need more from her... twenty milliliters should do." The doctor seemed excited and scampered over to tie a tourniquet above her elbow and prep a spot-on Sarai's arm while she squirmed, then jabbed it with another needle. She whimpered. It hurt more than the first. Between the knowledge of a needle in her arm and the pain in her feet, she began to feel nauseous. Part of her hoped she might vomit on them.

"Oops," muttered the doctor, and removed the needle. Then he stuck it again, this time deeper, and got his target. Her blood raced down a clear tube. She tried to take deep breaths to keep down her panic and shut her eyes. She could hear him clinking glass bottles, moving around the room, whispering to himself.

Finally, he snapped at her, and she winced from the sound. It was so much like the evil woman at the restaurant. "Witch girl, you're a necromancer?"

Sarai opened her eyes, seeing him once again by his microscope. She didn't reply.

"We already told you," one of the men said in exasperation.

"I know, I know. But her blood is... the way it's reacting with... Maybe she's a healer? A really strong one."

"I'm not a necromancer," she said, seizing the opportunity. If they thought she was less dangerous, maybe they would want her less. Or be less cautious when imprisoning her. "I don't know why you think I am. I'm a healer. That's all, I just heal."

"No, she's a necromancer," insisted one of the

21

men, and pointed at the scars her magic left in his skin. "Look at my face, she did this. She tried to kill me."

Oh, right, they'd seen her in action. She cursed under her breath.

"She can't be both. Witches only do one thing," added another man.

"It's rare, but…" The doctor began muttering to himself once again, and the words that Sarai was able to catch made her feel cold. Particularly, 'bone marrow extraction'. He picked up a phone, toying with the cord after dialing, and talking excitedly with someone on the other end.

She felt…violated. It wasn't right for them to do this to her, to snatch her from her home, strip her of her focus, and steal her blood. She wanted to hurt them. She wanted an army of zombie mice to swarm and chew out their eyes so they couldn't see her cry.

"Keep her here for now," the doctor said as he hung up the phone. "One of you go tell Tom about her. I have work to do."

Chapter Three: Escape

The next hour consisted of Vasi members coming in and out of the room to speak with the doctor as he continued to excitedly mutter to himself and scribble notes in binders. Sarai contemplated trying to talk with any of them but decided against it. There wasn't anything she could think to say that would help her situation. As the doctor stuck yet another needle in her arm to withdraw more blood, she began to worry how much he wanted to take from her. There had to be some limit. She knew from previous experience that one wasn't allowed to donate (or, in her case, sell) plasma in the human world more than once every month. With her healing abilities, it wasn't a problem for her, but the silver suppressing them as more was stolen from her began to make her feel dizzy.

Suddenly, there was a loud noise from above. Sarai looked up to see the ceiling rattling and dust drifting down in the florescent light.

"What the hell was that?" asked Dr. Stearne.

"Sounded like... an explosion?" the blond man replied.

The door crumpled off its hinges. A figure in dark camouflage appeared in the room, standing with its back toward her, a leather gloved hand lifting a Vasi goon off his feet. His face drained of color as he realized what was about to happen, and his shriek filled the air. Red liquid gushed from his throat as the intruder used its jaws to tear it open. The man's shout turned into a choked gurgle as he drowned in his own blood. He was dropped to the floor, a chunk of his throat still held in the monster's mouth. It spit the chunk of flesh to the floor and kicked the dying wretch as he flailed.

The creature's face was pale, where it wasn't drenched in blood, and feminine. It was framed by a few loose strands of black hair otherwise tied in a strict bun, accentuating an elegant neck. If it weren't for the crimson irises, the color of the blood it licked from its wanton, sensual lips, then its features might have been described as angelic in a terrible way.

And yet… also familiar.

It surveyed the other two panicked Vasi, and a second creature darted into the room. He was a tall, terrifying man with long, braided black hair and similar red eyes, but with a less pale, light brown complexion. Blood was slick on his clothes, as if he'd stuck both his arms elbow deep into bodies.

"Take one in for questioning," the first intruder said in a voice like velvet.

"Which one?"

Dr. Stearne's armed guard snapped out of his terrified daze and pulled a gun from his belt. Before he had a chance to fire, the pale intruder darted forward at speeds no human eye could follow and there was a sickening crack coupled with the sound of torn flesh. The man fell to the floor. At least, most of him did. His head followed his body a few moments later, eyes wide and unseeing.

"The one that's left."

The monster caught Dr. Stearne's wrist in his grasp

and looked back toward the woman he took orders from. "What about the girl?" He jerked his head toward Sarai.

If her mouth had retained any moisture, Sarai would have gulped. Despite everything wrong in her life, she wasn't ready to die just yet.

"I'll take care of her. Bring this one back to the others, I'll join you soon."

The taller one nodded his head in respect, threw the squealing doctor over his shoulder like a prize hog, and disappeared.

They were alone.

"You're not the one we're looking for," the woman said as she pulled out a black square of cloth to wipe the blood from her lips and chin. "But you don't look like you're on their side either."

With the blood somewhat cleaned away, recognition dawned on Sarai; the vampire was in fact the beautiful woman from the bus stop. But now, her eyes held no hint of blue. Only red.

"I-I'm not on their side. I'm on my side."

The vampire pulled off a single glove and touched the silver collar with the tip of her finger. Flesh hissed from the contact, proving her vampirism in one more definitive way as it burned, but the woman's expression didn't so much as twitch. Could vampires feel pain as mortals did?

"That's not working out very well for you." Her red gaze trailed down to the clear tube stealing blood from Sarai's arm for use in experiments.

"I... saw you. Before. I asked you the time," Sarai said.

She smiled. "I was tracking the Vasi, and you

flushed them out very nicely for me. I suppose I could thank you for that."

With a delicate touch, the vampire pinched the plastic tube with her nails and severed it. The end still connected to Sarai's body spurt with each beat of her frightened heart, while the other end dropped limp and began to drip onto the floor to mingle with the blood of the dead scientist. The vampire brought the end of the connected tube up to her lips like a straw, and Sarai's gut twisted as she felt the liquid pulled from her body at a much faster rate. It made her fingertips feel cold.

"Do you mind not sucking my blood while I'm trying to have a conversation with you?" Sarai demanded. "It's rude."

The vampire paused, blinked, and then laughed as she lowered the makeshift straw. "Please do forgive me, little witch," she said, her voice heavy with mockery. "I wouldn't want to be accused of rudeness. If we're being so polite, why don't you tell me who you are?"

Sarai pursed her lips. "Let me out of this chair, and maybe I will."

"I suppose that would be polite, wouldn't it?" The vampire was amused, which Sarai decided was a good thing. Cold fingertips brushed against her skin as the needle in her arm was removed. She'd expected a vampire's touch to be... harsher. Especially since she'd just seen the beast kill two men.

Then the vampire drew a dagger from her waist and smirked. Dread washed through Sarai's body as she shut her eyes, tensing in expectation of the worst. But instead of pain, there was a snapping sound and a release of pressure from her wrists. The lack of pain surprised her. She expected a lot more of it. As she opened her eyes and looked down, she saw that the vampire had cut the straps binding her in place.

Huh, she thought to herself. Asking had worked.

"Now, tell me who you are, little witch." The vampire knelt and cut the bonds over Sarai's ankles, hesitating at the sight of the burns there.

"I'm…" Sarai frowned as she thought about how to answer the question. These were vampires, so they had nothing to do with her cruel father's coven. But, if they recognized her prominent last name, or even had a clue as to her true nature, they could kill her on the spot. Vampires were not known to be fond of necromancers. She had to give a fake name.

"Sarai… Smith." She cringed at the only fake name to come to mind. "No coven. I'm a nobody."

The vampire frowned, then sighed and shook her head. "If you're going to lie to me, you better believe what you say. Your body betrays you. For one, blood as sweet as yours doesn't belong to 'nobody'."

Sarai grimaced. If her blood gave away anything, she couldn't speak to that. She had no experience with blood drinkers of any kind and wasn't sure what a vampire could taste.

The woman shrugged off her dark camouflage jacket to reveal a slimming black, sleeveless top and long cargo pants covered in pockets. Her arms were pale and flawless like the smoothest, most delicately carved alabaster. There was something so elegant about her exposed skin, from her collarbone to the lean muscles of her upper arms, down to those graceful fingertips. Sarai had the sudden urge to lean forward and touch them, to see if they were as smooth as they looked.

Looking away from the enchanting arms, she saw a utility belt at the vampire's waist sporting several guns. Funny that a vampire would use guns. There didn't seem to be a point to their strength and speed if they were going to use common human weapons.

"Here." She draped the jacket over Sarai's shoulders, who clutched the sides and pulled it around her to cover her singed and now blood-splattered clothes. It was unnerving that it was cold. The jacket had just come off a body, which should have made it warm. Except the body it had come off of was a walking corpse.

"Thank you," Sarai said reflexively, and put the jacket on.

"What gift do you have? If you want my assistance in leaving this place, you'll tell me that much."

"Healer," she said. It wasn't a real lie, so maybe the vampire wouldn't notice the half-truth. "Nothing dangerous. I'd like to get the collar off to heal my feet."

"A useful trick." The vampire darted forward, making Sarai flinch, but she held herself firm. She wasn't going to show fear to this thing. Though, with the way the woman's hourglass shape stood out against the sterile environment–voluptuous and violent, dressed in black and adorned with her weaponry–it was impossible not to feel intimidated. "Nonetheless, I think you'll keep that lovely collar on a little while longer. We'll take things one step at a time."

Sarai scowled. "They hurt. I can't walk on them."

The vampire lifted her thumb up to her own fang and scratched it open. Sarai's eyes widened as ruby drops swelled there.

"A little will help you. Or you can stay as you are."

She held out the digit.

Sarai knew what vampire blood could do. There were dark rituals as well as healing potions that involved vampire blood, but she never thought she'd be faced with the ingredient herself. It wasn't something found at the local drug store. The thought of drinking it made her skin crawl, and it was absurd to think half the reason she was so averse to it was the fact that it was very much not kosher.

"You want me to just..." Sarai barely had a moment to protest before the thumb brushed past her trembling lips to touch her tongue.

It tasted... good. Sure, it tasted coppery like any blood would, but there was something else. Something that sparked a fire in her throat and her core. That made the hairs on her arms and the nape of her neck stand on end in a good way. Her deep brown eyes closed in bliss as she wrapped her lips around the wounded thumb and sucked every drop she could. When she opened her eyes to meet the vampire's red gaze, she shivered, but not from the cold. Sarai couldn't make herself stop until the cut had closed and there was no more of the elixir to drink.

"Better, little witch?" the vampire chided. She pulled her thumb away, lingering against Sarai's lower lip as if painting it.

Speechless, she nodded. Her cheeks felt flushed, her body tingling from the back of her head down to the tips of her toes. The sensation faded. Sarai had never done drugs before, but she imagined that they felt similar.

She glanced down at her feet and was shocked to see how quickly so little had affected her. It wasn't perfect healing, not like her gift, but the blisters and worst of the burns had disappeared, leaving only a light tenderness. If only her socks hadn't been destroyed.

But her socks weren't all that had been taken from her. Panic settled in her chest, and she jumped to her feet, slipping on the bloody floor. The vampire caught her.

"Careful," she teased.

"My focus," Sarai said, yanking her arm away from the vampire's light hold, and stumbling toward the row of cabinets. "They took it, put it in one of these." A door to one of the cabinets stuck when she yanked; locked. That had to be where they kept things they didn't want their witch slaves getting into.

"Keys. I need the keys."

They jingled like metal from heaven, and Sarai snapped her head around to see the vampire holding up a ring of keys. She stepped forward reaching for it, only for the vampire to raise an eyebrow and pull them back.

"Give them to me," she demanded.

"Correct me if I'm mistaken, but one of these will release you from your collar, won't it?" the vampire said. "I wasn't turned yesterday. I think I'll hold onto them." She put them into one of her many pants pockets. Sarai wondered if it was possible to pickpocket her. No, vampires were infamous for their heightened senses, among other abilities. She'd never be able to get the key unless this creature handed it over.

The vampire strode to the cabinet, grasped the handle, and yanked, ripping it off its hinges, metal squealing as if in pain. Sarai gulped at the show of strength, but at least she got what she needed. Inside was the familiar leather glove. She snatched it up and slipped it onto her hand. Home, almost. She felt the weight of the repressive silver on her neck more than ever, and the aches in her feet reminded her that her connection to her gifts and all magic was cut off.

"Why won't you let me take it off? I'm no threat to you." That you know of, she thought to herself.

"I don't trust witches. You might be a healer, but you might also be a very capable spellcaster." She grinned, showing off bloody fangs. Sarai took a step back. "Now, you've been rude to me. I asked you to tell me who you are, and you didn't make a proper introduction, so let's try again. I am Knight Commander Marcelle de Sauveterre. And you, little witch?"

She'd been caught in a blatant lie before, but she couldn't give the complete truth. Her life could depend on a believable lie. Why couldn't her heart stop racing? The damn vampire had to be listening to it.

"I'm Sarai Meir." It was her mother's last name, the mother she had no memories of. The largest population of Meir magic users were a group of Sephardic Jewish witches who lived in a hidden desert coven in the Negev, with origins in the surrounding countries they'd fled to escape persecution in decades past. If the vampire did recognize the name, it wouldn't raise any red flags, as the Jewitches weren't known for anything other than secluding themselves away from outsiders, with only the occasional young member leaving to explore the world as her mother had regrettably done. Since the name had belonged to her mother, it wasn't a complete lie for Sarai to claim it, even if she hadn't grown up with it. "So, what now?

Are you going to keep me here or let me go? I'm not contracted to the Vasi, and I can't hurt you."

Marcelle gave a crooked smile. "I won't abandon you to die when we blow up this building, and I won't kill you now. I never said I was going to let you go. Frankly, you haven't given me a reason to." She moved closer and reached out to brush her chilled fingertips against Sarai's cheek, eliciting a shudder. "I want to know why you're so sweet. I've tasted witches before. They're better than humans, but you're in a class all your own, even if you do smell like onions. Not to mention, the Vasi went out of their way to target you, quickly. I want to know why."

Sarai didn't answer, then caught her breath; Marcelle wrapped an arm around Sarai's waist, pulling her in close, like a snake pressing up against a frantic rabbit, then scooped her up into her impossibly strong arms. Sarai could feel them against her own skin now. They were smooth. Freezing, but so beautiful and smooth.

"Close your eyes and hold on tight, little witch," she teased. Then, they were flying. That was the only way to describe it. The moment it began, Sarai shut her eyes to protect against the speed of the wind lashing around her like a whip. When everything stopped, her stomach lurched forward as dizziness overwhelmed her, but she managed to keep from vomiting. Thankfully, she was in Marcelle's arms and not responsible for holding herself up.

"Here we are."

Chapter Four: Apple Juice

The clearing outside the Vasi's warehouse in the woods had been turned into a killing field. Blood watered the grass and gravel in a downpour, looking like black tar in the red light of a slowly rising sun. Bodies lay in pieces, their chests ripped open and hearts removed, their throats torn out, their arms pulled from their bodies. One or two twitched. It was a massacre, just like what had happened to the scientists, but a thousand times worse. Vampires were everywhere, their mouths latched onto human necks as they feasted.

Sarai couldn't tear her eyes from the sight. She'd seen death before. She'd hurt people before, both against her will and willingly. But what she saw before her was so much worse. She took a step back, right into Marcelle.

"You're all right. We won't kill you. These people earned their deaths for what they've done to our kind. You've done nothing wrong, so I promise there's nothing for you to fear," Marcelle murmured. "There's a car right here, you can get in."

The car turned out to be one of several black, windowless vans. Funny; for some reason, she'd imagined that vampires would ride in horse-drawn carriages or packed into coffins on the back of wagons. She tried to ignore the sound of cannibalistic feasting behind her, but that was a feat easier said than done. If she got into the van, it could be her fate. Or it could be her fate if she didn't get into the van.

Her knees trembled, reminding her of her weakness. Running was out of the question due to the absurdity of Marcelle's speed. Into the van it was, though she did have thoughts of warnings most children were given about getting into windowless vans with strangers who would steal them away. She never got those warnings; her father's family were the ones driving the vans.

"Let's see…" Marcelle knelt in front of a mini fridge wedged between benches along the sides and pulled out a juice box, tossing it into Sarai's lap as she sat down. She stared in confusion as to why, of all things, there was a box of apple juice even in the van in the first place. "It's no meal, but that should give you energy. Drink up."

"Why do you have apple juice?" she asked as she freed the straw and punctured the seal.

"We keep it for our humans if their blood sugar ever gets too low," the vampire explained. "Can't have them fainting on us."

Right… blood loss would do that. Though she imagined a few drops from the tip of Marcelle's thumb did better than a box of juice. That being said, she didn't know if vampire blood helped with blood sugar or just healed wounds and gave a high.

Hunger curled in Sarai's gut, and she sucked the juice down to the last drop, sated for the moment. As she finished, a pale hand reached out to take it from her, and she pulled back. Maybe the vampire hadn't hurt her yet, but it was still engrained in almost every witch not to trust something like her.

Marcelle sighed and closed her eyes for a moment. When she opened them, Sarai was startled to see that they had changed from red to the enthralling ice blue she'd seen at the bus stop. And when she opened her mouth to speak, her fangs had disappeared. "Is this better?" she asked.

The vampire looked so different with those minor changes. So human. It was almost easy to forget that it was a monster before her, something capable of ripping a man's head off his shoulders. That her inviting red lips were painted with blood, not lipstick.

"I promise none of us have any interest in their experiments. And I don't torture someone without a very good reason. You're safe for now. I'm sure you'll feel better when you have clean clothes and a good meal—"

The vampire's attention snapped away, and Sarai turned her head to see what was happening. Noises from outside changed. There were two humans standing in the doorway of the compound. One was a terrified Vasi, brandishing a gun. The other was the fire witch. Two fireballs growing in her palms. The dead look in her eyes flicked with awareness as she acknowledged the massacre before her. Even if a fire witch was better equipped to handle a vampire than, say, a healer, no one had a chance against so many. And bound by a contract, there was nothing to be done to save her.

The pit of her stomach clenched, and Sarai wished the vampires would give her a quick, clean death. It was better than the life of a slave.

"Give the girl back and I won't burn all your undead asses, understand?!" shouted the Vasi in desperation.

A small girl with red eyes stood among the vampires, her front drenched in blood. She dropped the dying human in her grasp and stepped forward, but several other vampires gathered around her protectively.

"If you think, for a moment, we would ever surrender one of our own," began one of them.

"No, the girl! Give me the witch!"

Absolute dread gripped her heart, and her hands shook. As much as she did not like the thought of being stuck with vampires, they were better than the Vasi. The worst a vampire could do was kill her. She hoped.

Sarai felt Marcelle's gaze and looked up to see her eyebrow raise. She tried her best to keep the fear from her face: Marcelle could not find out. She didn't know what vampires did to powerful or useful witches, but she refused to be subjected to it.

"You just keep getting more and more interesting, little witch," Marcelle mused. "Between a pureblood princess and a nobody healer, he asks for you. You must be special."

"I'm not," she snapped. She silently tried to cast a spell for protection. She knew it wouldn't work, and even if she had access to her magic, it would have been difficult without speaking to help her harness her intent, but the situation made her desperate. She tried to feel her power, to connect to the red glove that was her magical focus. Nothing. She cursed under her breath, hating that she was dependent on vampires for protection.

"Forgive me if I don't take your word for it. Stay put for now. I'll be right back."

"Wait!"

Marcelle froze and turned back to her. Those ice blue eyes chilled Sarai, making her shift as she tried to push down the soul crushing fear they caused.

"Yes?"

"Don't... Don't let them take me."

Marcelle smiled a little. "I wouldn't dream of it." As relief washed over Sarai, the vampire woman climbed out of the car and walked forward casually. "I'm curious as to why she's so important to you," she said, addressing the Vasi.

"Give her to me!"

Marcelle snapped her fingers. Vampires dropped from the trees above, descending like demons onto the waiting humans. The fireballs shot out from the witch's palms. One missed its target, the other singed its target's arm, causing him to scream as he rolled on the ground in an effort to put out the flesh-melting flames.

In the time it took Sarai to blink, Marcelle had darted forward and grabbed the fire witch. The witch dropped dead after a sickening crack; the poor girl's neck had been broken. It was a much cleaner death than any of the other humans had been granted. Sarai was grateful for that.

Vampires forced the Vasi to his knees in front of Marcelle, and he shouted in pain when his wrist was snapped to make him to let go of his gun. A wet spot grew at the front of his pants as proof of his fear.

"Pack him up with the others for questioning," Marcelle ordered.

Sarai wished they would kill him. Anyone who would force innocent witches into battle with such vicious beasts deserved to die.

Alone in the back of the van, an emotional dam

broke. Sarai screamed into her fists and slammed her forehead against her knees, rocking in her seat. She grabbed the collar and pulled with all her might. Her fingernails scraped against the silver, but not a bit of it broke. It had to come off, there had to be some way to be free of it. It just had to. If it didn't, she wouldn't be able to handle it.

"So dramatic," muttered a low voice.

Sarai froze, and slowly raised her head. It was a male vampire, his eyes bright red with bloodlust and framed by dark brown hair that fell around his pallid face.

He'd slid into the van like a reptile to watch her, making her feel like a child caught running with scissors, her hands still gripping the collar. "You're the one he wants? And here I thought Marcelle was just bringing me a snack for the road."

"*Caution*," whispered Liora in her ear. That made her blood run cold. She'd learned her lesson well and would never again ignore the imaginary friend's voice in her head.

"Sorry, but I'm off the menu," she told him.

"I can do more than bite, if you'd rather."

In a whirl of motion, he'd pushed Sarai onto her back on the floor, both wrists captive in a single, iron hand with probing fingers moving under her prized red glove as if to push it off. His other hand slid under both the jacket and her shirt, like a human ice sculpture against her skin. A cold, wet tongue flicked against her cheek.

"I will kill you if you don't get off me now," Sarai bluffed, her body shaking in terror and betraying her.

"You smell like fear. I can almost taste it. Some

say it makes blood too bitter, but I find it tastes better that way." His chilling hand slid up her body, resting just under her breast. That wasn't meant for him, yet there he was, so close. Another hand slid threateningly along her inner thigh... and it was wet with blood. Human blood of the Vasi and witches he'd slaughtered that day. Yet, she couldn't move. She could just look up in petrified horror, her threats dry and useless. His nose wrinkled, and he frowned. "You also smell like onions."

"Get off her, Nicolas."

Marcelle stood in the entrance to the van, her arms crossed as she glared at him. Nicolas looked up.

"You know I don't mind sharing." He grinned, showing off his fangs. "She's a witch we found with the Vasi, no one will care. Probably contracted, right?"

Marcelle snarled, her eyes flashing back to red and fangs bursting forth in her mouth as she lunged forward and pinned him to the wall by his throat, the vehicle rocking from the force.

"Do not touch her. Have I made myself clear?"

"Yes," he gasped. "My apologies."

Sarai was ready to faint, trying to remember how to breathe without hyperventilating.

Marcelle pushed the other vampire to the opposite side of the vehicle and looked down at Sarai. She pulled the lab coat closed around the witch's body and pulled her closer, a protective arm around her shoulders.

"You're all right," she murmured.

Sarai didn't reply. She wasn't sure if the grip around her body was comforting or anxiety-inducing.

After using the jacket to wipe the blood from Nicolas's hands off her skin, she shrunk into herself and tried to find comfort in the slim warmth provided by the borrowed clothes, tried to ignore the situation she was in as more vampires climbed into the van. In her search for comfort, she realized one very important thing was missing. In the commotion, Nicolas had slipped the glove off her hand.

"My focus..."

Nicolas smirked, holding up the fingerless glove while licking blood off the fingers of his free hand. "This thing?"

"Hand it over," Marcelle ordered. "I'm not in the mood for your nonsense."

He laughed. "How about I trade it for a little taste?"

"How about I rip out your heart and show it to you?"

"Mm, you know just the sort of dirty talk to turn me on."

"When we get back, you'll spend the day in silver. Would you like to make that a week, or is one day enough for you?"

Nicolas's face fell, and he froze, still holding the glove.

"Marcelle, she's just some stupid... I wasn't going to do anything! You can't be serious."

"Dead serious."

One of the other vampires, a black woman wearing significantly less human blood than Nicolas, looked with disgust at him. She rolled her red eyes and yanked the glove out of his grip, then extended it out toward Sarai.

"It wouldn't kill you to be decent for just one car ride, you know," she said to Nicolas. "I don't want to listen to your bullshit."

Shaking, Sarai reached out and took her beloved possession out of the palm of the strange vampire, pulling it back onto her hand. Everyone seemed to disapprove of Nicolas, so perhaps his behavior was the minority. That was comforting, especially with Marcelle using her authority over him. Still, there was no way to be comfortable while riding in a car full of vampires.

The ride was silent and lasted a long while as they sped through roads and cities for what seemed like ages. Completely exhausted, Sarai had no choice but to drop into sleep.

When she awoke, she found herself curled in a fetal position with her head resting on a lap. A cool, gentle hand had its fingers in her hair stroking her while someone whispered something in her ear. She was still tired and considered going back to sleep before she realized it was Marcelle's fingers in her curls and shot up like startled prey bounding away from a fox. The vampire woman chuckled.

"Relax, little witch. I haven't hurt you."

Maybe not. But waking up to find comfort in Marcelle's touch was disturbing.

"I'm not that little," she retorted, in denial about her four-foot-ten-inch status.

The scenery outside the window had changed, and they'd come to a halt. Outside was a mansion surrounded by a forest. There were beautiful stone walls, large windows, and a grand front door at the top of an elegant staircase. Flowers and trees grew in abundance around the building and along the sides of the long driveway, making it look as if she'd been transported to some corner of the world time had forgotten.

It was beautiful. And while it was better than the Vasi's torture warehouse, Sarai feared it was to be her new prison.

Chapter Five: Interrogation

"Come with me," Marcelle ordered the witch as the others all climbed out of the vehicle, Nicolas gripped between two of the others as he was taken out like a prisoner.

Between the van and the large truck was the little girl the vampires had rescued. As Sarai stuck by Marcelle's side, she overheard her speak in a high-pitched whine.

"But I want to eat them. They hurt me, it's my right. I command you to let me."

"We need them for information, my lady. Your brother's commands are law over yours," one of the vampires with her said.

"Fine. Keep them gagged and away from me." The girl pouted like a spoiled child denied candy and stomped up the stairs into the mansion.

Marcelle looked at Sarai. "I won't let them hurt you," she assured her. "But do try not to get into Artemisia's path if you can avoid it. She'd likely not do anything, but she's a pureblood. They tend to do what they want. I'd like to keep you safe for now, but even one as young as her could overrule me."

The use of the phrase 'for now' didn't escape Sarai's notice. She clenched her fists in determination. Her first priority was getting the collar off. She needed to be able to defend herself for the inevitable moment the vampires decided their interest in her ran out.

She did her best to keep her face stoic as she followed Marcelle up the stairs and into the mansion. How many mortals made it to the mansion and lived to see freedom? Had any witch ever even seen the place? It was a secret place hidden away in the forest, where the rays of the sunset turned green as they reached through leaves to illuminate the vampire's mansion like light through the windows of a church, painting whatever it touched. It was so deceptively beautiful. Fitting, considering vampires themselves could be described exactly that way. Deceptively beautiful.

Sarai stared out at the forest, not wanting to walk into the building. She inhaled and for the first time since she'd been "rescued" she felt some sort of relaxation. She smelled wet earth and grass, as if someone had mowed the lawn just before the rain. She didn't remember hearing or seeing rain, so it must have been ahead of them.

"Sarai? Is something wrong?"

Marcelle's voice broke the spell, and Sarai looked down at her bare feet.

"I shouldn't track in dirt," she muttered. Even as she said it, she knew it was a ridiculous excuse to postpone the unavoidable.

"Don't concern yourself with it. Come."

The grand double doors opened. Inside was ostentatious splendor, marble staircases and pillars, statues, paintings, and all sorts of art. It made Sarai feel small. Her father's coven liked grandeur, in particular the psychopathic woman who called herself Sarai's stepmother, but Sarai felt safest in her little abandoned house, with no luxury at all. Her older half-sister often agreed with Sarai's preference, helping her build blanket forts that hid away anything fine in their rooms as they pretended to go camping. Camping in the wilderness or squatting in an empty building always felt safe as a result.

At the center of all the elaborate architecture, the little girl called Artemisia stood embracing an older pale man and a Mediterranean looking middle-aged woman. There was something different about them compared to the other vampires. While he had bright red eyes, his face showed clear signs of age. Wrinkles and crow's feet, deep furrows and laugh lines. Gray hair almost erased the streaks of red growing from his head in a mess around his shoulders. The woman didn't stand out as much next to him, simply because she was just as beautiful as the rest and didn't look old. Sarai had never heard of a physically old vampire.

Next to them was yet another of the red-eyed creatures, but he wasn't focused on the little girl. He looked up and made direct eye contact with Sarai. He was taller than the older looking one, but there was a similarity in their features. His hair was bright red, pulled back into a ponytail. His shirt covered most of his skin with its high collar and long sleeves, but muscles were obvious underneath. Instinctively, Sarai wanted to hide from him. His stare was too intense, it made her want to become one with the paintings on the walls, something no one looked at but just passed by. He turned his head to look at Marcelle and gave her a curt nod. She nodded in return; her head bowed deeper than he had as if in respect.

"This way," Marcelle said, and walked past the vampires congregated in the entryway. Sarai kept her eyes down on her feet as she walked. She was too afraid of having to look into more pairs of red eyes to risk looking anywhere else, and only raised her head when Marcelle stopped in front of a wooden door. "Here we are."

The door opened to reveal pure comfort. There was a large bed with soft blankets and pillows, a folding screen to change clothes behind, a dresser, table and chairs, and a few other pieces of miscellaneous warm brown wooden furniture. There was an open door through which she could see a large tub, the ultimate cherry-on-top.

It was unreal. She'd spent six years living out of a small room with just a tough mattress and some light furniture gathered from curbs on bulk pick-up trash days. The thought of being anywhere near anything so comfortable and lavish did not seem plausible. The one bedroom was nicer than her entire home, yet she, a captive, would stay there? It had to be a joke.

"Why don't you wash?" Marcelle suggested. "Your blood smells sweet, but the rest of you smells like... well. I could do without the onion stink. When you're done, I'll have some real clothes for you, and we can discuss this situation over some food."

Sarai didn't need to be told twice. She took a step toward the bathroom but stopped. Questions raced through her mind, and she wasn't sure where to start. She decided on one of the more important issues, and turned to face Marcelle, tapping her finger against the silver collar.

"What about this?" It was a stretch, but she dared to hope. Maybe, if she kept out any blatant lies, she could convince her. "I'm a healer. I won't do anything to you." *As long as you don't do anything to me.*

The vampire laughed.

"I'm not an idiot. Count your blessings and don't push too far. For all I know, the moment you're free, you'll start obliterating vampires with spells. I know you're in no pain from it since silver burns vampires, not you. And I gave you my blood, so if all you wanted to do was heal then there should be no problem. Right?"

Sarai ground her teeth. Damn this monster.

"Fine." She turned on her heel and stomped to the bathroom, slamming the door behind her with a satisfying bang. She was going to take the longest bath that she could and make the vampire wait for her.

And what a bath it was. The tub was massive, deep, and wide enough easily for two people to fit. A far cry better than the tiny shower stall in her apartment; the water pressure there was so poor that her usual showers involved sneaking into a local gym's locker room without a membership. Functional hot water had always been a fifty-fifty shot, even at the gym. She couldn't remember ever having access to something as expensive and luxurious as the bath before her.

As Sarai waited for the tub to fill and steam to fog up the room, she looked over an array of bottles on the sink countertop. Eau de toilette: toilet water. She ignored that one and went over the bottles with English labels, picking one to fill her bath with bubbles and sweet, relaxing scents. With the water up to her shoulders, it was enough to ease her body and let her relax for the first time in ages. Once she scrubbed her olive-toned body and rinsed her still uncombed hair, she found it hard to convince herself to leave. But when the water grew cold, she knew it was time to face the monster in the other room.

As she stepped out and chose one of the large, fluffy towels that hung from the wall, she caught sight of her foggy reflection in the mirror and blew a rogue curl out of her face. Her golden-brown hair was an absolute mess. An overgrown "Jew 'fro" mane that bounced down just below her shoulder blades, it was a trial to maintain at the best of times, let alone after being dragged about against her will by witch hunters. It would need spells to sort out, or hours of work she was too drained to think of tackling. Throwing it under a towel turban was the best option for the moment.

Back in the room, Marcelle sat at the small table, a plate across from her at the empty chair. There was a bowl full of oatmeal that smelled of cinnamon, some bread, cheeses, sliced fruits, eggs, sausage, and a glass of water. Sarai almost bee-lined straight to the food, but her eye caught the clothes laid out for her on the bed: undergarments, sweatpants, tank-top, jeans, sweatshirt. All were much better options than towels.

"I wasn't sure what you'd want to wear, so I brought you a few options," Marcelle said and leaned back in her chair. The vampire herself had changed clothes as well, and now wore a blue, loose, and silky sleeveless top along with comfortable looking black pants. It was so different from the dark, militaristic camouflage uniform she'd been wearing that Sarai had to do a double take. The woman looked stylish now. Not just her clothes, but Marcelle's black hair was different as well. it had been in a bun, and now it was loose, flowing in elegant waves down the vampire's back. Sarai couldn't look away. She'd never seen hair so long it brushed against the floor like that before. It was almost longer than the vampire was tall, at least five and a half feet.

"There's the changing screen there, or you can go back to the bathroom if that makes you more comfortable. If there's something else you'd prefer, within reason, please do speak up. I don't mind seeing to your needs."

"You want to see to my needs," Sarai repeated.

"Don't ask for anything too scandalous, but yes." Marcelle smiled. "Need help changing?"

Sarai blushed at the insinuation and scooped up a comfortable looking pair of sweatpants and sweatshirt along with the underwear. She checked the bra size and was uncomfortable to see that it seemed right. How had Marcelle known, and how long had she stared at her breasts to figure it out?

"I'm fine." She hurried behind the changing screen to dress herself, then came out and plopped herself into the chair across from Marcelle where she could inspect her food.

"I hope the food's to your liking," Marcelle said.

Sarai didn't care too much, as long as she got free food. And it was good food. Ignoring the fork, she stuffed her mouth with diced pineapple and suppressed a moan of pleasure. It had been so long since she'd tasted fresh fruit.

"I have an offer for you," Marcelle said. "You tell me all about yourself and why the Vasi are interested in you. The full truth. In exchange, I provide you shelter, food, and my personal protection from Vasi and vampires alike. Does that sound fair?"

Sarai put down her bowl and stared into the fruit.

No matter how nice Marcelle seemed, she was still a vampire. The deal sounded too good to be true, so it had to be a lie.

"*Trust her.*"

Sarai blinked at the words from her imaginary friend. She looked up at Marcelle, then beyond her at the hallucination. Liora wanted her to trust a vampire. What twisted part of her own subconscious did her imaginary friend come from to think that trusting a vampire was a good idea?

"I've got a hard time believing you can protect me," Sarai said. "What if the purebloods decide they don't like me?"

"I am the knight commander of the realm of New Ulster, and the purebloods–those ones with the permanent red eyes–gave me permission to keep you here as we walked in," Marcelle said. "That's as safe as you can be, assuming you don't do something stupid. To be blunt, I think you'd be safer here than on your own. Vasi have been doubling down on their witch hunts, with more force than we've ever seen. We've been considering offering alliances to any we can find, but your kind are quite good at evading us. Spells against the undead and whatnot."

"Yeah, well, your people have a habit of sinking their teeth into us," Sarai retorted.

Marcelle shrugged, as if it didn't matter to her. "Mostly just the ones contracted to Vasi nowadays. Your kind are not as lucky in avoiding them, it would seem. I've seen the aftermaths of recent raids on several covens. Many seem to be captured, but the ones who resist too well leave corpses. They'll be after you again, sooner or later. My protection will grant you safety from them. I assume you don't want to return to their prison?"

It made sense. Sarai had proven terrible at keeping herself safe from Vasi, mostly through sheer carelessness. Maybe Liora was right.

"All right. Deal." Sarai licked her fingers clean, then picked up a fork and knife to start in on the eggs. "So. Ask me whatever."

"Let's start with who you are. You are not no one. And do remember that I can detect lies," Marcelle warned. "Living bodies give away subtle hints that are like Vaudeville lights to trained eyes as to whether or not you're telling the truth. Don't test me."

It made sense that vampires could function as walking, talking lie-detectors with their heightened senses. It had already been tested and Sarai lost that round.

She took a deep breath and locked eyes with the vampire. "My real name is Sarai Reinhart."

There was silence, and Marcelle's ice blue eyes narrowed. "They're rather prominent in Virginia, the Reinhart coven. Aren't they…?"

"Literal Nazis? Yeah, that's them."

There was silence so still Sarai felt self-conscious simply breathing. More than that, she felt self-conscious of the polluted blood in her veins. It was wrong she was biologically linked to such a vile coven, one that was so cruel to others including her own mother. Less obsessed with 'racial' purity than their human Nazi cousins, the witch coven was obsessed with powers and breeding the strongest bloodlines they could into their perverse family tree. If they wanted someone who didn't want to join them willingly, they were no better than the Vasi. And once they got what they wanted… once Sarai's mother no longer had any use… Their closets were littered with skeletons.

"So, are you going to kill me now?" She didn't think so, considering Liora's advice, but her heart beat a little faster, nonetheless.

"It's not your fault you were born into their coven. You can't be fond of them if you're using fake names to hide your identity."

"That's a way to put it."

"Did you hide it because of the reputation, or… you said you're a healer?"

"I *am* a healer."

Marcelle leaned forward, staring at her. Sarai shifted uncomfortably, feeling very much like an insect under a microscope.

"And what else?"

Sarai clenched her fists. How had Marcelle figured it out so fast? She couldn't possibly know about such a rare witch phenomenon. She was a vampire.

"Witches only ever have one power."

"Except when they don't. If you want the deal to stand, you won't lie to me. Understood?"

Sarai nodded. Still, telling a vampire what she could do was terrifying.

"And you're not going to kill me if you don't like the answer?"

"I don't like the answer if the answer is incomplete or untruthful," Marcelle said. "You want to fix that for me, and we'll go from there?"

Not the answer Sarai was looking for. "It's hard to explain."

"Try."

Sarai bit her lip. "It's…" *Necromancy. Just say necromancy.* Yet, she couldn't. "I don't even know if it works on you. Vampires, I mean. I… I can put my power into bodies, and it kills them if I don't stop. And I can control them."

"Do you control them before or after they die?"

Sarai bit her lip. "After."

Marcelle's eyes narrowed. "Necromancy."

"Not the kind that's really serious though," she said, as if there were any form of necromancy that wasn't serious.

"Are there other necromancers in the Reinhart coven?"

"Not really. Well, yes. My dad's the source. He can cause necrosis with his power, but it just kills people. With me, the power got stronger. And with my sister. Well, half-sister, Alma. But she can't keep control of them for as long as I can, so you don't need to go after her or anything. She's a good person. Helped me get away when it got too dangerous for me. Stayed to look after her mom." A stupid decision, in Sarai's opinion, considering her mom was a manipulative and horrible woman, but there was no point in dwelling on the past. On how she wanted to pull Alma with her to freedom. None of that mattered anymore. Alma chose her mother. "And our power only works on people we kill ourselves, people we infuse with our power. I can't just control you or other dead bodies like a real necromancer." Not that she'd ever tried to control a vampire, but now wasn't the time to say she might be capable of more.

"Good to know." They stared at each other in silence.

"So what now?" Sarai asked.

"You'll be keeping the silver collar for now, if it's all the same to you."

That was expected, if uncomfortable. She slipped her finger under the collar and rubbed the skin a little to soothe the irritation. "Anything I can say to convince you to give me the key?"

"Not at the moment."

Sarai glared at her, then lifted the cup of water up to her lips and gulped down every drop, taking her sweet time before putting it down with a hard clang.

"So, what do you want from me? Everyone wants my powers. I'm not signing a contract."

"We wouldn't ask you to. We don't have slaves."

"Good to know the murdering, bloodsucking vampires don't have slaves," Sarai muttered, rolling her eyes and trying hard not to think about the bloody massacre. "I wouldn't want to think you were immoral or something."

Marcelle cocked her head to the side like a curious cat. "Do you think the Vasi we killed tonight deserved any less?"

Those ice blue eyes were too unnerving, and Sarai couldn't meet them as she thought of the answer. From what she knew of the Vasi, the answer was that they deserved everything they got. Possibly more. The scars and evidence of torture on the late fire witch who'd burned her feet were a testament to that.

"Well, it's not just them, is it?" she snapped back. "Everyone knows what vampires do. We grow up hearing stories about it. About vampires like Nicolas."

"Nicolas is an idiot who is being chained in silver as we speak for his disrespect," Marcelle said. "We have laws about who we're allowed to do what with. Enemy combatants are one thing, a rescued uncontracted witch is quite another. Speaking of... while I will be keeping them for a while for interrogation, I would like your opinion on the Vasi we captured. Specifically, the one I found in that room with you. Since their crimes are significant enough to warrant execution, our laws give the injured party a right to his life. Obviously, our own princess has priority, but witches have endured more at their hands. You're the only witch available to represent the others, so it's possible our leaders may decide you also have that right."

Sarai frowned. "You mean, you want me to decide if he gets executed or if he gets let go?"

"No, no. You misunderstand. He'll die, that fate is sealed. I'm asking if you want to kill him."

It was one thing to fantasize about undead mice attacking her captors, another to be told something so drastic. Sarai knew she could kill in self-defense. But to kill a man who was a helpless prisoner in a premeditated decision was something different. It was something her father or stepmother would do. She couldn't be them. Still, there was so much witch blood on Vasi hands, and she had a chance to make one of them pay for what he'd done.

"I don't know," she whispered. "I need to think about it."

Marcelle nodded. "While you're here, I have a request. I want you to wear this." She pulled a gold ring with a fleur de lis emblem on it from the ring finger on her right hand and held it up for Sarai to take. "Wear it on your left hand. If anyone troubles you, show them this ring and they will not touch you."

Sarai raised an eyebrow. "Are you proposing to me?"

The vampire laughed, her voice like wind-chimes in the breeze. Why did it sound so beautiful? Then she went down on one knee, holding the ring out as if it were an actual proposal. Sarai's eyes widened in shock.

"Sarai Reinhart, won't you please be my ward?"

Her mouth opened, then closed, gaping like a dying fish. The malicious laughter in Marcelle's eyes didn't help at all.

"I, I'm not–I don't even know what that means!"

She chuckled and got back up. "Relax, sweet witch. Under these circumstances, it means anyone who hurts you has to deal with me. There are very few willing to take that risk. I said you were under my protection, and I meant it."

"Fine, fine. Just don't do that again, please. It's weird," Sarai said, waving her hand. Marcelle caught it and slipped the ring on as if it were an engagement ring. It felt heavy, antique.

"You make me so happy," the vampire teased.

"Shut up."

Marcelle laughed. "I'll leave you to your own devices for now. We have a library and some gardens if you'd rather not stay in this room. If you need anything, don't hesitate to ask anyone who's around. If they're wearing gloves, they work for me and will help you."

"I'll stay here." The thought of wandering around a building full of vampires was out of the question, even with her apparent ring of protection. Who knew if there were more like Nicolas who hadn't been silvered for the night? Liora said to trust Marcelle, and that was as far as she'd go for the time being. Still… it was just a boring room free of any entertainment. "Maybe I'll go to the library."

"I'll be back for you some other time then. *Au revoir, ma petite sorcière.*"

And with that, Sarai was alone. The stress melted away as she dropped backwards onto the soft bed. Overcome by its coziness, her eyes drooped. Liora began to hum and, to the tune of the imaginary woman's voice, Sarai finally felt safe enough to get real sleep.

Chapter Six: Sources

Sarai woke to the sound of something rapping against the bedroom door and wiped sleep from her eyes. When had she pulled the blanket over herself? She must have done it in her sleep.

"Hello, Miss Reinhart? Are you in there?"

She cringed at the sound of her name, mentally kicking herself for telling it to Marcelle regardless of the circumstances. She hated when people called her Reinhart. She had a perfectly good first name and more people needed to use it.

"Who's there?" she called back.

"I'm just here to bring you some lunch, Miss. I'm not one of them, a vampire, if that makes you feel any better. I just work here. My name's Rosaline. I can come back later if you're not hungry?"

Lunch? Had she been asleep that long? Her gurgling stomach confirmed it. Smoothing out her messy hair that still hadn't gotten any kind of proper combing, she jumped up from the bed. She paused, as to not reveal how frazzled she felt, then opened the door a crack to look the visitor over. She was without a doubt human; there was a stark difference between the girl before her and Marcelle. Vampires had an ethereal beauty and grace, and the awkwardly smiling brunette girl before her lacked that as she stood there dressed in something like a hotel maid's uniform, acne scars on her face unsuccessfully covered with makeup. She was also struggling to keep a plate up in her hands.

"Mind if I come in? This thing is a little heavy."

"Oh, yes, of course." Feeling like an ass, she opened the door, and the girl trotted herself in, setting the covered platter on the small table, which had been mysteriously cleared of her previous dishes. "Were you here earlier?"

"No. I think Nadine stopped by? She said you fell asleep on the covers, so she tucked you in right," Rosaline said.

"Oh. Okay." It sounded nice, but Sarai wasn't crazy about the idea of people watching her sleep.

"You all right?"

"Uh, fine. Just, not used to people tucking me in. Or strangers coming in while I'm sleeping. Thanks for knocking, I guess."

"I can tell her not to next time," Rosaline offered. "We're just here to help out. It's always weird, someone's first night here. With vampires." She smiled when she said the word. "If you ever want to hang out with us mortals, you're welcome to stop by our quarters."

"Mortals? You mean, more humans?" If Sarai had been told to guess what a human captive in a vampire palace would look and behave like, Rosaline wasn't it. "Are you prisoners here?"

"Oh, no, we're not here against our will," Rosaline giggled. "There's a good number of us. Runaways, druggies, lots of both. Generally, people who won't be believed if they go running to the press screaming about vampires. They call us 'sources'. You know, as in 'source of blood?' It's a hell of a great job we've got here. Do some basic housekeeping, donate a bit of blood. Then we get to stay in this place. All sorts of great food, comfy beds. Even have a salary." She lifted the cover on the food for Sarai revealing chicken, shrimp, mashed potatoes with gravy, and broccoli, and Sarai bit her tongue to keep from licking her lips like a slobbering cartoon.

"You're here... willingly?"

"Definitely. Get the best high I've ever felt when they heal us. Enough to make even the worst druggies give up everything else just to stay here and get a little taste. They're practically running a rehab house. Lure us in with that first taste, then make us work for it by getting clean. We taste bad otherwise." She snorted a little at that and rolled her eyes. "Once that's done, it just gets better whenever they heal us. It's just... damn, it's good."

Sarai blushed at the thought of the blood she'd sucked from Marcelle's fingertip. If that was what Rosaline was referring to about the healing process, Sarai knew exactly why the humans stayed. But she wasn't staying because of some sort of addiction like Rosaline. She'd made a deal.

"Hey, so, this is a weird question, but..." Sarai paused, then blurted it out. "Am I a prisoner? The room is nice, but I get the feeling that if I tried to waltz out, they'd stop me."

"Girl, I just work here, you know? They don't tell me about that stuff," Rosaline said. "I don't remember them ever keeping someone against their will. Well, except those vampire hunter types. You're my first witch I've ever even met. But they do have an actual dungeon and you're not in it, so that's good, right?"

"I guess." She was still wearing a collar.

Rosaline looked at her sympathetically. "Why don't you eat up, then come hang out with me for the day? I've got an appointment in a half hour, but I can show you around and stuff."

"That would be nice, yeah." She sat down and started to eat the food, pushing the shrimp away from the rest of the food so that they didn't touch. Rosaline spotted the removal, and her eyes widened.

"Oh, I didn't even think. You're not allergic or anything are you? I just picked out some things I know I like."

"No, just don't like seafood," Sarai said. Marcelle might have noticed the lie, but she didn't feel like going into an explanation. "Everything else looks great, don't worry." That placated the girl, who got to work making the bed. It felt awkward to watch. "You don't have to do that."

"It's my job, don't worry about it," she dismissed with a smile. "I get paid good bucks for this. Which I should since I know how to fold a fitted sheet."

"And they call me a witch."

Both women laughed.

"So, uh," Sarai swallowed a mouthful of chicken. "You said you have an appointment? Like, a doctor's check-up?"

"Oh, no. Vampire blood keeps me healthy as a horse; I haven't seen a doctor in years. Got an appointment with one of the knights here. You know, ah, for dinner. Or lunch, breakfast... whatever. They keep me confused with that. Still surprised they don't burst into flames in the sunlight. Apparently, all it does is hurt their eyes, so most of them sleep through the day unless they have some specific job to do during the day."

"For... oh." It clicked. Rosaline had an appointment to have her neck bitten. "Does it hurt?"

"Well, yeah, a bit. But not as much as you'd think when they do it right. Doesn't even leave any scars because of the blood they give us in return to heal," she said with a shrug, and looked around the room. "Ug, those old-fashioned suckers. I keep telling them they should put TVs in the guest rooms. When most of them were born before electricity was invented, they end up neglecting things." She rolled her eyes. "We could get you a TV, some music. There's a mall they let us go to not far from here. Could get some things for you. CDs, some VHSs."

"That would be nice. I don't even know whose clothes these are," Sarai said.

"Can't take you myself, but I can come get you after my appointment if you want to hang? Give you a good tour and all that."

Morbid curiosity won out, and Sarai replied, "Well, I don't mind going with you. If that's okay? As long as I'm not expected to, you know. Are they nice to you about it?"

"Oh yeah, *super* professional. You don't have to worry about a thing."

Sarai finished up her meal, and the two girls were off down the halls. They were old halls, and Sarai wondered how long the mansion had been standing. Perhaps longer than the United States had been a country, considering how long vampires lived. Maybe the original builders still roamed the halls? But there were more important questions on her mind.

"How does it work? This appointment stuff."

"Super simple. We have sign-up sheets, and the vamps check who's available, put their name down. We get veto power though. And anyone who acts up can get in some serious trouble. Most of us have regulars we're used to."

"That's... good." She still had a hard time imagining vampires feeding as anything other than monsters from stories.

Soon enough, they were in front of a plain wooden door. Rosaline rapped on it with her knuckles, and it opened to reveal a familiar face. The last time she'd seen him, he'd been accompanying Marcelle in the hunters' compound, killing people.

The man was too tall, Sarai thought to herself. He was a Native American man with long black hair, light brown skin, and oddly enough a few tattoos on his arms in geometrical patterns. Could vampires even get tattoos? Perhaps he'd gotten them when he was alive. Tattoos aside, the oddest thing about him was the ragged band T-shirt featuring a yellow submarine that he wore.

"Oh." He looked at Sarai with surprise, and she immediately felt awkward. It had been a bad idea to join Rosaline.

"She's just tagging along with me so she doesn't stay alone in her room," Rosaline said with a smile.

"I'm not your appointment," Sarai blurted.

He smiled a little. "Don't worry, I didn't think you were. The name's Bear."

"That a name or a nickname?"

"Both. You wouldn't be able to pronounce my other names. Come on in."

Well, it was a fitting name, Sarai thought. He was massive like a bear.

"Sarai," she said and followed Rosaline inside. "I'm Sarai."

The room, however, was not at all fitting for a vampire. Maybe a teenager somewhere. There was a lofted bed, like a bunk bed but with a computer desk underneath. One of the walls was plastered with posters of various bands, while another had a full black bear's skin hung, and another had a stone fireplace. The bunk bed had what appeared to be a handmade blanket hanging off the edge. She wondered if he'd made it himself, or if someone else had. It was a very confusing room.

"Nice to meet you under better circumstances, Sarai. You're looking a little better."

"Yeah."

"Get a chance to explore yet, or is Rosaline giving you a tour now?"

"I guess this is part of the tour?" she glanced at the human, wanting her to say something. To take the attention off her.

"Probably a good time now. Most of us like to sleep during the day if we're not jumping in to surprise Vasi, so no one should be up to bother you."

She crossed her arms in front of her chest, holding herself as she watched Rosaline roll up one of her sleeves. "I saw you yesterday. Didn't get enough to drink then?"

"Very little. I don't take time to feed on missions like that," he said. "It feels unprofessional."

"Hungry, big boy?" Rosaline teased, waving her wrist like an appetizer as she sat down in a large comfy chair like some kind of queen on a throne.

Bear gave her a little smile. "You know it." He sat down on the chair's arm and took Rosaline's hand in his, turning her wrist upward. "Are you sure you want to stay and watch?"

"I'm here, aren't I?"

"Suit yourself." His eyes turned red and his fangs extended. Sarai wanted to take a step back but rooted her feet; she wasn't going to let him think she was afraid. She couldn't help but flinch when Bear sunk his teeth into Rosaline's wrist. Though, she didn't look too bothered. Her eyes closed and she leaned back in her chair as Bear gulped down mouthful after mouthful of her blood. It reminded Sarai that this was a drug addict; she looked like she was getting a fix.

When Bear was satisfied, he pulled his teeth away, keeping pressure on the wound with one hand while scratching his own wrist just enough to draw a thin line of blood that he put up to Rosaline's lips. She latched on like a baby on a breast and the wound on her wrist healed almost instantly.

"You look a little sick, Sarai. Are you all right?" Bear asked.

"Fine. Why wouldn't I be fine?" The faster they left, the better.

Rosaline just smiled, rubbing her healed wrist as she got up. "Well, I'm feeling great. Sure I can't get just a little more?"

"The idea is for me to feed on you, silly, not the other way around," Bear joked.

Rosaline rolled her eyes. "You suck, Bear."

He laughed. "That's not even funny. That's terrible."

"I'll see you in a few days, dude," Rosaline said, and stuck her tongue out at him as he helped her to her feet. While the source girl took her time, Sarai couldn't close the door on the room fast enough. As soon as it slammed shut, Rosaline asked, "You sure you're okay, girl?"

"Yeah... fine." She sighed. "Maybe I shouldn't have come. I think I just... Maybe I need a little more time to process this."

"Don't worry, I get it. I was freaked out the first time too. Want to go back to your room?" Rosaline asked.

It sounded nice but confining. What else had Marcelle mentioned there was? "Actually, I think I'd like to check out the library. See what vampires read."

"Sure, I can show you," Rosaline volunteered.

The library wasn't too far from the knight's quarters. It was behind a pair of large wooden double doors, and any witch or bookworm's wettest dream. Two levels of floor to ceiling books were available before her, hosting thousands of books. More than thousands.

"There's some private reading rooms to the side over there," Rosaline pointed out a row of doors. "They're sound proofed, I think. Lots of the rooms around here are since they have sensitive hearing and all that jazz."

"There's so many books," Sarai said in awe. She could smell the old paper already. "I mean, I've been in libraries before, but this... I'm going to be here for a while."

Rosaline smiled. "All right. You know how to get back to your room?"

Sarai nodded. "I think so."

"I'll leave you to it then. I'll come by your room later with food, okay?"

"Thanks." The girl might have been an addict to the vampires and their feeding, but she was kind, and she was mortal. Rosaline could be a good friend to have.

Chapter Seven: The Key

Thankfully, the library was empty, with most vampires asleep throughout the mansion, so Sarai took her time picking titles about things she never would have been able to read in a human or witch run library: vampire history. If she was to be stuck in a place surrounded by them and disarmed of her magic, then she had to arm herself with knowledge. It was tactical as it was fascinating. She even found herself ensnared by some of the more fanciful depictions of vampire history, such as a mural with a plaque dedicating it to a battle between a King CuChulainn and a Queen Medb. The first was a man with demonic wings and red hair, the other a woman with silver hair and angelic feathered wings. A fiction, though she had to wonder why any vampire would use angelic and demonic characters to depict their own kind. Those were such human attributes to use since, neither angels nor demons existed in any such form; vampires couldn't even fly. Perhaps the painter had been human.

She settled herself into a comfortable reading chair in one of the private rooms, cozy and quiet. It was the perfect place to learn, and the best starting point seemed to be Volume I of a series titled, *A Complete Hiftory of the Kingdom of New Ulster*. She could tell it was old not just by the feel of the book itself, but the way the "s" in history had been written to look like an "f."

Chapter One started with an Irish family of purebloods, and Sarai thought of the men she'd seen when first entering the mansion. Two of them with the pureblood girl, both with red hair. That was a typical Irish trait, wasn't it? They had to be members of the family. And the demonic man in the painting also had red hair. Perhaps he was an ancestor?

She glanced at the table of contents and found one entry listing a family tree. That could be useful. She flipped to the page and was greeted with a painting of a family portrait from hundreds of years past. It was a family of red-haired aristocrats, including a woman with a crown, a younger boy and girl, and the two men she'd seen in person. Her fingertips brushed against the image of one in particular, the one who'd looked at her. His gaze from the page was less intense, but still left her feeling uncomfortable. How old was he to be in such an old book?

She flipped the page to look at the family tree, surprised it existed. She hadn't thought vampires were capable of having children. Evidently, purebloods could. She wondered if that was what separated their blood as "pure."

What shocked her was seeing so many alleged immortals with dates listed for the deaths. In particular, a cluster seemed to have died between 1930 and 1945. Sarai cringed a little at that. She knew that World War II had been horrific for not only humans, but witches and vampires as well, and didn't want to think about the potential role some members of her father's side of the family may have played in that.

Four names were listed as surviving: the head of

the family, Lugh the Samildanach mac Ethliu, born in Ulster, dates unknown; Setanta CuChulainn mac Lugh, born in Ulster, dates unknown; Giovanna Aïdōneús of Rome, born in Venice, Italy, 1638, who seemed to have married into the family; and Artemisia ní Lugh, born in Tir na Fola, New Ulster, 1969.

So, the little girl was older than she looked at thirty years of age, yet younger than expected considering her immortal status.

"*Run*," whispered Liora in her ear, and Sarai froze. Not again. She began gathering up her books, wondering if she was overreacting. After all, the dream she'd had before the Vasi captured her could have been her subconscious mind reacting to the sounds of intruders she wasn't fully aware of. But seeing as she was in vampire territory, it was better safe than sorry.

"*Leave the books. Run.*"

The books were the only reason she was in the library, she wasn't going to just leave them. Her pile put together she was almost ready to leave.

A knock on the door startled her, and Sarai jerked her head up from the book as it opened. She hoped to see Rosaline, or perhaps Marcelle or Bear. Instead, the one person she most wanted to avoid stood there, blocking the entrance.

"I thought I recognized that scent," Nicolas said, and slammed the door behind him. "Better without the onions, but it's lingering a little. Like reading, do you?"

There was something hungry in his eyes, but also veiled anger. If there was any vampire at all that Sarai knew she shouldn't be alone with, it was him.

"Yes, and you're bothering me, so you can leave," she told him, attempting a show of confidence. If it failed, she had Marcelle's ring; the knight commander had reigned Nicolas in before, perhaps the threat of her vengeance would be enough to make him behave.

"You know what it feels like, for a vampire to wear silver shackles?" he said, ignoring her and fixing her with a glare. "It's not like you witches. It feels like fire. Like white hot metal pressed up against your skin. You ever smell burning flesh? It's disgusting."

"I'm trying to read. If you don't stop bothering me, I'll let Marcelle know you were misbehaving."

"Reading boring shit," he muttered, and pushed a stack of books to the floor. Sarai flinched at the sound. "Histories and biographies… I've got a good one for you. Bluebeard. The fellow it's based on is legendary. Ever read that one? This fair maiden decides to marry the scary man in a castle out of pity or whatnot, and he tells her he'll give her everything so long as she doesn't open one door. Of course, she opens it. Finds all the bodies of his previous wives stored there. Always loved that concept, a room full of bloody little ladies."

Sarai's heart was pounding. He was just trying to scare her; he couldn't do anything. Marcelle would punish him for it.

"If you're not going to leave me alone, then I'm leaving," she told him, and clutched a book to her chest to put some small thing between them. She could leave the ones on the floor or come back for them later. She didn't want anything to slow her escape.

"Sit," he hissed, and she froze.

Sarai raised a trembling left hand, the gold ring on her finger obvious. "I'm Marcelle's ward," she told him. "That's what she said. That anyone who messes with me deals with her. Didn't she put you in silver last time you tried to mess with me? Step aside."

"Marcelle's an uptight bitch who needs to remember how to loosen up. I'd be thrilled to get her in a good fight. And you… you got me silvered," Nicolas said, then darted forward and pushed Sarai back into the chair. An icy finger pressed against the pulsating vein in her neck, the sharp nail far too close as he lowered his face, inhaling. "There's that scent I love. That lovely adrenaline. Fight or flight instincts all screaming at you. But what happens when you can do neither?"

He was right, Sarai realized in horror. If he didn't mind getting into a fight with Marcelle, then that was all the protection she had. If only she hadn't been forced to keep her collar on, she could have at least a chance against him.

His lips stopped less than an inch from her neck and sighed. "Pity biting your neck risks burning myself." Nicolas pulled back a little, a cruel grin on his face as his eyes turned red and fangs grew in his mouth. "Lucky for me, there are other choice options."

Sarai shrunk back against the chair as far as possible, but she couldn't escape his traveling touch. The cold finger skipped over her collar and down between her breasts, then further just below her belly button. Then he gripped her inner thigh, hard. She winced; it would leave a bruise.

"Let go–"

"There's a divine artery right… here…" He rubbed his hand against her, just leaving space between his touch and her privates. "Makes my fangs ache just thinking about it." With that, he pinched the fabric of her shirt between his fingernails and sliced through as easily as a pair of scissors, revealing her bra.

She wanted to tell him to stop, but her voice was stuck. She wanted to tell him to go fuck himself but was too afraid to even move. She'd been naked in front of others before during two ill-fated one-night stands. They had been temporarily fun, and the men involved were allowed to take her clothes off because she'd decided so. They just saw her as a good time, and that was how she'd seen them.

Nicolas saw her as a consumable, something sexual or something to be eaten. Sarai made the mistake of looking down, just in time to see him cup her breast. It did something different to her; it infuriated her. She didn't want to be touched, yet he was touching her. She wanted to hurt him for it. He needed to suffer.

"Beautiful," he breathed. "You know what I love about human women? Your exotic imperfection. Vampires are perfect. Sexual in every way to lure in our prey. It gets dull. But you... those witches with the Vasi... you have such scents. Even just your pores, it's so special." He grinned at her with his fangs. "Are you a virgin?"

Anger turned to fear. She needed to get out. Before she had consciously made the decision to act, Sarai turned and jumped over the chair to get to the door.

"No, I don't think so." An arm looped around her waist and plucked her out of midair, then slammed her against the wall, the force reverberating like thunder in her skull. She would have screamed if the air hadn't been knocked out of her. "You're going to pay for the time I spent in silver. I asked if you're a virgin, witch." He pressed his body against her, his weight and strength keeping her prisoner.

Sarai tried to tell him it was none of his business,

but part of her was more afraid of what might happen if he didn't like the answer. What if he wanted a virgin, would he punish her if he found out she wasn't? She just stared at him, paralyzed and afraid.

The door burst from its hinges. The surge of hope and relief flooded Sarai's heart at the sight of Marcelle standing there, looking like an incarnation of absolute fury.

"How dare you," she snarled, eyes red and fangs extending.

Nicolas stopped, then smiled. "Marcelle, how nice of you to come. I was wondering if you were watching her, or if that ring was just for show."

"Let her go, and I'll consider not killing you."

"Yeah?" He flicked his fingernail across the top of Sarai's breast, and she gasped from the sudden pain. "Give it your best shot."

What followed next was a blur, leaving Sarai free to move, and she scampered into the back of the room, as far away from the fight as she could get. Then the room shook as Marcelle crashed against the wall, Nicolas with his fangs in her neck. Blood drenched down her front, and she shouted in pain, struggling to push him off. There was a dagger in her hand, pinned to the wall with Nicolas's grip on her wrist, useless.

"Don't hurt her!" Sarai screamed, her fear for Marcelle's safety taking her by surprise. If she could just do something... She clenched her gloved fist, wishing her magic weren't cut off by the collar. Was he going to kill Marcelle? No human could survive a bite like his, so very different from the neat pinprick bite that Bear had given Rosaline. And if he did kill her, then he'd have to kill any witnesses.

Nicolas pulled his teeth free from his victim and stumbled back as Marcelle slumped to the floor, her hand grasping at her neck to try and slow the bleeding. In her shoulder, Sarai saw that Nicolas had thrust something small that burned her skin. Silver.

"You taste like heaven," he muttered, transfixed by the sight. "All these centuries, you never thought I was good enough for you. But I finally got to taste you. I'm so sick of being denied." He bent over and picked up the dagger, pressing the flat edge against Marcelle's face. It hissed, turning her skin black, and she cried out. More silver.

"You'll have more than a day imprisoned for this," she snarled.

"If I stick around. No, I'm sick of this place. But I'm getting what I want before I go."

Sarai glared at him. Marcelle had rejected him, held him at bay for centuries, and he had the gall to do this? She felt more than fear and self-preservation instincts. She wanted to defend Marcelle as a woman. But she didn't even have a weapon.

No, she did. Her hand flew to the collar. It suppressed her magic, but it would hurt him. She didn't have to take it off to use it against him.

Sarai threw herself at Nicolas from behind, pressing her collared neck against the bare skin of his neck and locking her arms around him.

His scream pierced the air, and he tried to throw her off. She could hear and smell the sizzling of his flesh against the silver, but she had to ignore it and hold on. Unfortunately for him, as long as she kept the silver there, he was only as strong as a human, robbed of any supernatural abilities a vampire would have.

Unfortunately for her, he was still strong enough to slam back hard against the wall several times. That cracking noise followed by pain in her chest felt like a broken rib. It didn't matter. If she let him win, she was dead. She had to win.

The next slam stunned her, and he pulled her off, throwing her into Marcelle on the floor.

"Bitch," he spat. "This is all your fault, *Commander*. Should have just let me drain her at the raid. She's just some useless witch. We get to finish them off, that's how that works. Witches with the Vasi die, and we get our fun. You owed me her. Now I get both of you."

Sarai was shaking, her fingertips feeling numb. There was warmth spreading in her chest, and pain, and she was now certain something had broken. He wouldn't give her another chance to defend herself, and now he was going to drain her.

Marcelle's hand shot up and pressed against the collar. But her hand wasn't empty; Sarai heard a click and realized that her protector had the key. The silver fell to the floor, though the burn from contact lingered on Marcelle's palm.

"What the–"

Sarai stood, the pain in her chest edging away into nothing. Nicolas glared at her, cautious. He still had his strength and speed, sure, but now she could defend herself, and he had no clue what her power was. Of course, she still had to lay her hands on him for her power to work.

That was decidedly not a concern in the next moment when he rushed at her. All she had time to do was put her hands up and focus on her dark gift, feeling anger and power surge through her hands when they made contact with his collarbone. The power stopped him less than an inch from her neck. She could feel his cold breath on her skin, and adrenaline forced her power forward even further.

Nicolas gasped, unable to form a scream. Black and blue death expanded like a spider web across his skin as it traced through his veins, his eyes wide with shock until they glazed over. A trickle of black liquid oozed like a coagulated trickle from his nose as her control reached his brain. He was close enough that she could see every detail of what she'd done, smell what became of him. Bile rose in her throat, and she covered her mouth, slipping out from under him and moving away.

"Just... just sit in the corner," she ordered him hoarsely. He moved without protest and sat down in the corner, his glazed red eyes staring at the wall without seeing it.

"That's... unnerving," Marcelle said, having taken the silver out of her shoulder and held her throat closed as it healed. "What happens to him now?"

"I, I don't know. I've never done it to a vampire before. When they're human and I release them, they drop dead. Real dead."

"Are you hurt?"

"Healed myself."

As the shock wore off, her eyes drifted up to the remaining, triumphant vampire.

"What about you? Are you hurt?"

Marcelle lowered her hand to reveal that the wounds had completely closed just as Sarai's would if she were wounded and using her healing powers. It was strange to see happening to someone else. Unnatural. "A little low, but I'm fine."

"You fought him, for me," Sarai realized, and played with the ring on her finger. It felt heavier than it had before, now that she knew how serious Marcelle was.

"Of course. I'm a woman of my word." She smiled a little, then glared at the corpse sitting in the corner of the room. "He'd never gone this far before, not to challenge me like this. Not to challenge the law right under the palace roof. I need to tell our sire about this."

Sarai frowned. "'Our'? You mean…"

"We were both turned by the same person," Marcelle confirmed. "I was looking for you, so he could talk to you, but now with all of this…" She shook her head. "Maybe you should stay in your room for a little while. Recover."

"I'm okay, really." She had just destroyed a man after he threatened to rape her and had groped her, but she was okay. Maybe. She looked down at her healed breast, where his hand had been moments earlier. No, she wasn't okay. "He wanted to hurt me," she whispered.

"I'm sorry. I truly am," Marcelle said, taking Sarai's hands. "Let's get you out of this room. Here." She stripped off her long-sleeved, black shirt and handed it over, revealing a tight, spaghetti-strap undershirt beneath it. "Put this on."

Sarai pulled the shirt over her head to cover up. As she straightened out the shirt, she looked up to see that Marcelle was staring down at the collar on the floor, her lips pursed.

"You want me to wear it again, don't you?" Sarai

said, anger rising again.

"That might be best. Seeing what you can do..." She glanced at Nicolas's corpse. "I won't let you see my sire without silver." Marcelle tore a piece of her shirt and used the rag to pick up the silver collar. "Are you going to fight me on this?"

"Get up," Sarai said. Nicolas stood, staring wordlessly at the pair.

Marcelle lowered the collar.

"Really, Sarai?"

"You can't make me. And if I don't have a connection to my magic, I have no idea what'll happen to him. He might get loose again."

Marcelle sighed. "I need to report this now, so no one smells the death and goes on a witch hunt under the wrong impressions. You can keep it off if you stay in your room."

The thought hadn't crossed her mind until Marcelle said it. Someone might find a dead vampire and assume the new dangerous witch was responsible. She might be able to take on Marcelle with Nicolas under her control, but she'd never be able to take on the many more vampires hunting for her on their home turf.

Maybe she should wear the collar. Glaring at Marcelle, Sarai reached out and yanked the collar out of her hand. The moment the silver touched her skin, she felt the connection to her magic break. Nicolas crumpled to the floor in a heap and turned to dust.

"I suppose that answers that question," Marcelle said.

"If someone might come looking for a witch, I'd rather have you as back-up," she snapped. She locked it back in place around her neck, and handed the key back over to Marcelle, her savior and jailor in one. "I'm staying with you. You said your sire wanted to see me anyway, right?"

"Of course," the vampire said. "But first... I can't take you there looking like that. We need some fresh clothes; let's get you cleaned up."

Chapter Eight: Marcelle's Sire

"Is it all right if I carry you? It'll be faster that way," Marcelle asked, smoothing out her top. Sarai nodded and was scooped up in Marcelle's arms like a child, a hand at the back of her head to brace her against whiplash. Knowing what came next, she closed her eyes and curled against Marcelle's chest, her head resting on the soft breasts as the world spun around her, just like it had when they'd left the hunters' compound together.

When they stopped, Sarai found herself back in her room, placed on her bed. She clutched her head. How did vampires move so fast all the time and not fall over constantly?

"Here," Marcelle offered a new, clean shirt that Sarai changed into while the vampire woman went to the bathroom. The water ran and Marcelle returned with a wet washcloth. She sat next to Sarai, who found herself sliding toward her from the new weight indenting the bed and pressed the cloth to Sarai's skin.

Sarai bit her lip, not sure where to direct her gaze as the washcloth cleaned vampire dust and blood from her neck, face, and arms. It felt soothing, and she found herself watching Marcelle's alabaster arms. They were so slender, so fluid in their movements. Sarai sat on her hands, making sure she didn't reach out and touch them.

The moment of being almost tenderly cared for made her think back to the day before. She'd been so terrified of this vampire, but then she'd released her from her bonds, gave her the clothes off her back, gave her blood to heal.

"Are you sure you want to come with me? You'd be safe here," Marcelle said.

"I can handle it," she said. "Who is your sire?"

"He's, well, not a normal vampire. He's a pureblood," Marcelle revealed.

"A pureblood..." She thought back to the book she'd been reading. The two youngest were women, so it had to be either Lugh or Setanta. The latter was the younger, like the intense man who'd looked at her was younger than the more gray-haired vampire. The younger one had been the one to nod to Marcelle, so there had to be a connection there. "Setanta, right?"

"Yes," Marcelle with surprise. "How did you know?"

"Was reading a book about it," she replied. "*The Complete* Hifffftory *of the Kingdom of New Ulster.*" She placed extra emphasis on the "f" and couldn't help but laugh at herself a little.

"Gifted and smart," the vampire remarked.

"Is he nice to humans?" Sarai asked.

"Yes. Nothing like Nicolas at all. He's one of the ones responsible for a lot of our laws protecting humans."

Sarai nodded. Next on her reading list needed to be a book on vampire law. Soon enough, she was cradled in Marcelle's hold again. Without thinking much on it, she rested her hand against Marcelle's upper arm and closed her eyes. She felt safe.

Then they were flying again, and when they came to a stop, before them was a set of double doors, ornately carved, large, heavy, and wooden with images of trees and animals carved into them. They were themselves pieces of art, and Sarai found herself wondering about the artist who'd made them as Marcelle pushed them open. Did vampires have their own society of artists? Was there a vampire version of Michelangelo?

The room was a study, a grand one. There was a fireplace on one side, tapestries on the walls, and a large, oak desk with several chairs in front of it. Behind the desk sat a vampire, illuminated by the glow of a computer–a strange modernity compared to everything else in the room, including the vampire himself. His eyes were bright red, as was his hair. So, this was Setanta. His portrait didn't do him even a little justice. She gulped. Now that she was closer, she could get a better look.

There was an air around him, a force to him that drew attention and respect, like gravity to bring the world into orbit around him. His hair was neat, every strand in place as it was pulled back by a black ribbon. He had a face as smooth as marble, as only something not natural to the world could be. He wore all black, a stark contrast to his pale skin, and an open-ended bulky golden torque necklace with wolf heads shaped out of the gold on the ends that rested against his collarbone.

"Sire," Marcelle said. The vampire looked up and the glow of his computer dimmed as it powered down, leaving just the natural light of the large windows behind him to illuminate the room and cast him into a silhouette. He stood and walked in front of the desk, holding out his hand expectantly. As Sarai watched with some surprise, Marcelle knelt before him and took his hand, kissing it with her head bowed. The image looked like a knight before royalty. Which, apparently, it was.

"Rise, Marcelle," he said. The woman did and stepped back to allow the vampire's gaze to fixate on Sarai. He nodded his head in acknowledgement of her presence.

"Sire, this is Sarai Reinhart, the witch. Sarai, this is my sire, Crown Prince Setanta."

"Sarai Reinhart," Setanta repeated. She bristled a little, hating the sound of her last name. "It's good to meet you. Please, have a seat." He pulled out one of the two chairs at his desk for her. The beginnings of blue tattoos just peeked out from under his long-sleeved shirt where his wrists and neck were revealed.

"Thank you," she said, then added as an afterthought as she sat down, "Sir."

He pushed the seat in under her, just like a gentleman in an old movie would do for a lady. "It's been some time since I've conversed with a witch. You've stirred up the household quite effectively." He looked at Marcelle, whom he had not offered a seat. "I take it you're not just bringing her here to introduce us like I requested, but also to explain why you smell of my progeny's blood and dust?"

"I wasn't trying to hide it," Marcelle said, her arms open as if trying to prove that there was nothing for her to hide.

"He was disciplined recently, yes?"

She nodded. "I had him silvered for his behavior toward Sarai. And disrespect to his commander. I know you smell more than just his blood. You know it's mine too."

He held up a hand and she fell silent, as if spelled.

"Sarai, tell me what happened." His voice was gentle, but it was still a firm command.

She hesitated, and felt a comforting hand on her shoulder, yet it was light like the brush of a ghost. Imaginary Liora had her back.

"*You did nothing wrong. Tell him,*" the imaginary woman encouraged.

Sarai nodded and met his gaze with confidence. "Sir, neither of us did anything wrong. He attacked me in the library when I was reading to get revenge for the silver. Marcelle said I was her ward, so when she got there, she defended me the best she could."

Setanta sighed and rubbed his temples. "That stupid boy. I'd hoped when he returned to us he had changed his ways." He leaned against the edge of the desk, deep in thought, and Sarai breathed a sigh of relief. There was no anger, no retribution. She knew that Nicolas was in the wrong, and it helped to have Liora back her up even if no one else could see her, but how vampires worked was still a mystery to her. Nicolas was a pig, but he was one of them, and she was just a witch. An easy scapegoat.

"Sire," Marcelle said. "He earned his death. He would have killed us both. He almost had me, if it hadn't been for Sarai–"

"What do you mean by that?"

Sarai took a deep breath. "I killed him, sir."

Setanta frowned and looked down at her neck, at the collar there. "An impressive feat. Not just any witch can kill a vampire of his strength. How did you manage that?"

"He hurt Marcelle with silver, and she couldn't take him. So, she gave me the key to my collar. I... you know what I can do?"

"Yes." Setanta looked down at Sarai, his blood-colored gaze piercing through her, and she tensed. "You used your abilities to kill one of my people. You were freed, and now you're wearing the collar again. Did Marcelle force you?"

"I don't want to wear it, if that's what you mean. Am I in trouble?"

"Not at all. Had Nicolas survived his encounter with you, he would have been severely punished," Setanta said. He looked down. "That's a pretty trinket."

Sarai looked down at herself to see the ring he was staring at and was startled when he reached out and took her hand in his. Her brown eyes watched with a sense of trepidation. The light glinted off the ring's surface, but she wasn't fixated on the ring. Rather, she could only think of the way his skin felt. Marcelle was cold whenever Sarai felt her touch, like a corpse. This man was different. He didn't feel warm like a human, but there was a sort of lukewarm sensation to his skin.

"I'd like to assure you that you are in no further danger here. From me, my family, or my subjects. Marcelle is my blood and you are her ward. That connects us in a way. I'd like our relationship to be a positive one, despite this rough start. I'd like you to trust me."

She wasn't sure that she liked the idea of any sort of connection between them. It sounded too strange coming from someone like him. Someone so different and so respected and so beyond her. She bit her tongue a little as she thought about what he said. He wanted her to trust him.

"It's hard to trust someone who's keeping me prisoner, sir."

The room was still as the two vampires stared at her. She could feel their inhuman gaze, even as she looked down at his hand grasping hers. It tightened, and she held her breath in anticipation. He could easily hurt her; it would be simple for him to squeeze just a little harder and shatter her bones.

"It's an interesting gift you have," he said after a moment, letting go of her hand. "Do you use it often?"

"Only to protect myself against rapists, sir."

He let out a short breath of air that might have been a laugh. "Fair enough."

Setanta held out his hand to Marcelle and she handed him the key. Then he leaned forward and reached for her neck, careful not to touch the silver with his hands. Her heart pounded in her ears, leaping with joy as she felt and heard the 'click' of release.

"I will ensure everyone here knows that you are not to be harmed on pain of death. If anyone accosts you, I will deal with them myself."

She lifted her hands up to her neck and pulled the collar off, the heavy weight of the magical restraint like the world had been lifted off her shoulders, then looked up at him with wide, surprised eyes. It wasn't the same as before, when Marcelle had freed her. There had been so much anger, pain, and panic in that moment, and Marcelle had only done it because it was necessary. Setanta could have easily just kept her locked up. But he didn't.

"I'm not a prisoner?" she asked softly, looking

down at the collar in her lap.

"I'd prefer you think of yourself as our guest for the time being. But Sarai." Setanta's odd, lukewarm hand tilted Sarai's head up with a single fingertip. How was it possible to feel so much strength in merely a finger? "Do not use your power against us."

She gulped. Marcelle was terrifying in her own way, but that was in part because Sarai had seen her kill. Setanta held that power and terror without even trying.

"I-I don't use it much, really," she stammered. "Really. My father's family is still out there wanting to drag me back because of it, and it makes other witches despise me. It got me caught by the Vasi because I slipped up. I use my mother's last name because any association with my father's side, with those powers, it disgusts people. It's disgusting."

Setanta's eyes softened and he shook his head. "Don't talk about yourself that way. Gifts are not a curse. I knew a woman with your talents once before."

The news was a splash of cold water. "Sorry, what?"

"She was a powerful, strong woman," he continued. "A good woman, achieving good things for her people and helping others through healing, traditional witchcraft arts, and being a protector wielding her hands as weapons, turning enemies against each other. The nature of your ability does not define whether it is a curse or not: what you do with it does. It just takes discipline. At least, that's how we view our own abilities."

She nodded. It was nice to hear, but still shocking. Not only was it strange for someone to call her darker ability protective rather than offensive or evil, but he knew a witch. She couldn't picture any scenario in which a vampire crown prince would ever come to know a witch in a positive way.

"Was she... your enemy?" Sarai asked in confusion.

He smiled. "She was never my enemy. Marcelle?"

The woman straightened. "Yes, sire?"

"The sources are taking a trip to town soon, yes?"

"I believe so, sire."

"I'd like you to chaperone; escort our Miss Sarai to make sure she has everything she needs to be comfortable while she's our guest here."

"Yes, sire."

He turned his attention back to Sarai. "I look forward to learning more about you," Setanta said. "It was a pleasure to meet you, Miss Sarai."

It was a dismissal; she knew from his tone. Marcelle rested a hand on her shoulder. "Come," she said, and they started to go, leaving the collar on the prince's desk.

"Marcelle," Setanta said, and the vampire woman froze, looking back at her master with a sort of desperate admiration. "Don't punish yourself too harshly over this. I know he deserved his fate, despite how he used to be. Neither of us could have saved him."

"Yes... of course." She cleared her throat. "With me, Sarai."

As they left, it was easy to breathe a sigh of relief. Setanta was fascinating, but the experience was intense. While she was able to leave feeling more comfortable and secure, new questions about the vampires in the palace plagued her mind.

Who was the witch Setanta had known so well?

Chapter Nine: 1429-1454

As they neared the guest room, Sarai realized something. Her attention had been so focused on Setanta through the conversation that she hadn't noticed the expression on Marcelle's face. The man seemed to be her superior, monarch, and perhaps father all at once. It had to be stressful to come to him with the news that they'd killed his other progeny, even if it was someone as awful as Nicolas.

"Are you, um, okay?" she asked Marcelle. "Telling him about what happened…"

The vampire raised a perfectly arched eyebrow. "You're kind. I'll be fine, don't worry. I'm more concerned about you; I know he can be intimidating."

"That's… that's a word for it." Sarai wrapped her arms around herself, wanting some sort of comfort. Too much had happened in just one day, and it crashed in on her at that moment. Tears formed in her eyes despite trying to blink them back. She didn't want Marcelle to think she was weak.

"You're all right." Marcelle stepped closer and wrapped her arms around the witch. Sarai leaned against her, hiding her face against the vampire's shoulder as silent tears collected on Marcelle's shirt. It felt nice to have someone hold her.

"Sorry," she whispered.

"Don't be sorry." Marcelle's soft, cool lips pressed

against her forehead. A pleasant tingling sensation rang down from the back of Sarai's neck all the way down her spine like electricity. It almost made her think of how magic felt. But, of course, that was impossible.

"Sorry," she repeated, and smiled a little.

Marcelle laughed and pushed a strand of loose hair behind the witch's ear. Her heart pounded in reaction to the light touch. She had to get it under control, or every vampire in the mansion would hear it. "Come, you silly witch. Let's get you back to your room."

"Okay, just no more running with me. I can walk."

Marcelle nodded. "Of course."

As they made their way back, the silence felt too uncomfortable, and her mind kept seeing Nicolas's smile. She needed something else to think about. That was how she always handled horrors in her life, by thinking about something else. Not that it helped with nightmares, but she could fight to control her thoughts while she was awake.

"So, how did you meet someone like that?" she asked, determined to find a distraction.

"Well, he turned me back in France," Marcelle said. "Curious about us? I don't mind if you want to hear more. I'm old; we like talking about ourselves."

"If you don't mind, yeah. When did you meet him? How old are you? If it's not rude to ask, I mean."

"I don't consider it rude; it's not like I'm worried about vanity. I haven't done the arithmetic recently, but I was born in the year 1429."

Sarai did the quick sums in her head. "Five-hundred-seventy years old?" It was astounding to think of anyone living that long, but she had no idea what was a normal age for a vampire. "Is that... is that common, being that old?"

"Not terribly. The higher in the ranks you go, the more you find those of us that might be considered living, well, undead antiques. I'm not the oldest here, but I'm one of them."

"And, you're from France?"

"Paris, to be specific," Marcelle said. "Originally from a small farm, but my father sold me to a brothel in Paris when I was fourteen, so that's where I met Setanta."

There was so much in that sentence for Sarai to process. If she'd been drinking water, she would have done a classic spit take. Instead, she just stared. "You were, you mean, you were a—"

"A whore, yes."

Sarai winced at the word. She'd been called it before, without having ever even resorted to using her body in that way for money, and it always hurt. Any woman being sold into prostitution, no, sexual slavery by her father was beyond a horrible situation. Though Sarai's own father wanted to arrange a match for her, to continue his legacy of power, it wasn't the same. It wasn't a different man every night like the life of a prostitute, but it would have been forced, and it was the reason why she'd finally motivated herself to run, with the help of her half-sister Alma who had warned her of the impending match. Sarai had been only eighteen when it had been decided for her; old enough to escape and able to find her own way in the world. If it had happened when she had been fourteen, she would have been trapped, and she knew it.

"That... I'm sorry." She looked down at her shoes as she walked.

"Oh, I don't mind now. And you don't need to apologize if it's not something you're at fault for. Really, stop apologizing."

"I guess. I just... I guess it's hard to think of you like that."

The vampire rolled her eyes. "As part of the world's oldest profession?"

"As a human trafficking victim."

For a moment, something in Marcelle's face slipped, like a mask being tilted askew.

"Good thing I'm not human anymore then." The mask returned, a pleasant expression painted on her lips that didn't extend to her eyes. "So, you wanted to know about how I met Setanta?"

"Yes, um. So, Setanta, he went to you when you were, uh, like that?"

"He didn't want me for his bed," she said. "Vampires used to go to prostitutes a lot, for blood. No one's going to believe it if a whore goes screaming about a vampire. A few of the other girls there with me thought he was a red-headed devil, come for our damned souls. I was the only one brave or desperate enough to accept him as a client. He paid me double to just be on his arm, talk with him. Taught me how to play chess in his home. I think he was lonely. We'd play, and he always won, then he'd take me drinking. I may have been an alcoholic, always took any chance I could to get blacked out on someone else's *livre*. I'd wake up back in my bed with a sore neck and feeling lightheaded, but otherwise untouched." She rolled her eyes. "I thought he was a gentleman for not touching me, but he *was* using me for blood. In retrospect, the neck pain makes a lot more sense than it did then."

Sarai smiled a little. "I bet. Is he like a father to you then?"

Marcelle exploded into laughter. "Oh, goodness, no! There is a very big difference between a father and a sire. You can't fuck your father."

Her eyes widened, and she blushed at the frank statement. "Oh. Just, you said, he didn't want you like that." Somehow, knowing that the two were involved made her heart sink. She didn't know why. It wasn't as if she wanted either of them. She didn't want to want either of them. It was for the best that they were together, unavailable. The unbidden image of the two vampires together popped into her mind. Marcelle in Setanta's arms, his powerful hands touching her cold skin, teeth in her neck.

No. She didn't want to think about it.

"We've been together since he turned me," Marcelle explained. "He doesn't pay for sex on principle. Just blood. When he stopped paying me, sex was back on the table. And bed. Or floor."

"That's… a long time."

"It is a little unusual, I suppose."

"I'll take your word for it." The topic needed to shift back away from sex. Learning about vampires' habits seemed a good choice, so Sarai focused on that. "So, vampires pay prostitutes for blood. That's one way to do it."

"Well, purebloods usually don't," Marcelle amended.

"Don't go to prostitutes?"

"No, drink human blood. They just do it for enjoyment sometimes, for the warmth."

"They don't need blood?" Sarai asked. That was

information she needed, information that could be useful and went against what she assumed she knew about vampires.

"They don't need *human* blood," Marcelle corrected. "Do you know anything about purebloods? Why they make vampires?"

"Just that they're vampires. I guess, company?"

"Not quite. They need our blood. They can survive off of human blood in a pinch, but the amount they'd need would lead to a lot of dead humans. They're more powerful versions of us, born the way they are, and drink the blood of vampires to survive. They can even compel us into servitude if they want, force us to obey any commands. But this kingdom is less draconian about that particular practice, so we mostly have free will, and there are plenty of us who are glad to give our blood to the pureblood family."

"Then, that's what he wanted from you. Someone to drink from."

"It got more complex eventually." She held up her hand to show off a gold ring. It looked like a miniature version of Setanta's heavy necklace. Like a wedding ring.

"Are you... married?"

"No. No, purebloods can't marry non-purebloods. But I do get the title of his official mistress and a fancy room next to his. This ring is similar to what I gave you. Except, unlike our situation which is just a one-way arrangement where I protect you and you haven't agreed to anything else, with him it's a two-way relationship. His devotion, his companionship, in exchange for my blood."

Sarai thought back to the aloof man she'd just met.

"He didn't seem that, well, you two didn't seem very close just now."

"We were being professional. I do still work for him, for the kingdom. Did you expect us to start making out?" Marcelle teased.

"I didn't mean that!" Sarai blushed, trying once again to push the image out of her head.

"Relax, little witch," she said as they arrived in front of the guest room. "Setanta said to take you with the other humans tomorrow, but if you'd prefer, we can go on our own, just you and me. We can make it a date." She winked playfully, and Sarai rolled her eyes. Now that she knew Marcelle was taken, all the flirting seemed harmless.

"Wouldn't want to make Setanta jealous," she retorted.

Marcelle smirked. "Don't worry, he and I have an understanding. Eternity would be boring otherwise."

Sarai's heart rate doubled. Was Marcelle being serious? It gave the witch a frightening spark of hope.

"I, I met Rosaline today. She's nice," she said, deciding she wasn't ready to take the chance if the vampire wasn't joking.

"We can go with her and the rest, if you like." Marcelle closed her eyes for a moment. "Sorry. If you're all right, I'm going to have to leave you for now."

"What's wrong?"

"Lost a little too much blood. I need to find a source."

"Oh." No matter what sort of human experiences Marcelle had that Sarai felt sympathy toward or related to, there was the proof that she was still a vampire. Still a blood drinker. "Okay. I should shower anyway."

"Then, I'll see you tomorrow."

Sarai nodded. "Thanks." For a moment, she felt the urge to lean forward and hug the vampire again. Instead, she hurried into her room and shut the door, the thought of how Marcelle's lips against her forehead felt lingering in her mind.

****

That night after a friendly dinner with Rosaline and returning to her guest room for bed, Sarai had nothing but nightmares. Liora's Hebrew lullaby ran through her mind, hopping back over one line over and over like a broken record player trapped on a loop in her dreams.

"Aba halach le'avoda,

Halach, halach, halach, halach, halach."

They'll leave me, she thought. Everyone will leave me, they're not coming back. If I don't go to sleep, I'll have to be awake, all alone...

Sarai tried to get up and found herself unable to move. The sun was too hot, like a spotlight as it scorched her, burned the sand underneath her. The desert was empty, her throat dry, her body sizzling. She needed to find shelter.

An oasis loomed on the horizon, and she forced herself to surge forward as the sand threatened to swallow her. There were tents there, water. People.

Yet, the people didn't help her. They watched her in silent judgment and turned away from her. As they looked away, human shaped figures with desert scorpion claws wearing lab coats scuttled around her, rising from the depths of the sand like monsters.

One figure that stood out as fully human without

claws was a pale girl just a few years older than Sarai. She had stick-straight blonde hair and sparkling heterochromatic eyes, one bright amber and one forest green; both worried. It was Alma Reinhart, Sarai's half-sister.

"Cut me a piece of breast meat," echoed Nicolas's voice, his face coming into view above her, eyes blood red with sadism. "I'm hungry."

"You need to get out of here," Alma shouted, but her voice was distant, as if she were far away. "They're going to eat you. You need to run; why can't you just run?!"

The monsters crowded around her, but she couldn't scream. Her voice was stuck, and all she could hear was the snipping of her flesh in their claws, the sound of the lullaby over and over-

"*Halach, halach, halach.*"

Sarai shrieked, jolting out of bed, covered in sweat.

"No!" she shouted, her eyes landing on Liora. "Stop it! Stop singing! Just leave me alone already!" She threw a pillow, only for it to hit the wall, with the imagined woman nowhere to be seen. Of course, Sarai thought. She wasn't real. Just a figment of her own broken mind.

Sarai threw a bathrobe over her night clothes and slipped on her focus, feeling a little soothed by the feel of the red glove over her hand. Now that she had her magic again, she could magic up a solution.

The mansion was busier at night. Passing vampires stared at her in confusion as she kept her eyes down, wandering the halls. She found one that looked a little familiar wearing gloves like Marcelle's usual pair and mumbled a question about directions to the kitchen.

"I'll escort you. Is everything all right?" the dark-skinned vampire asked.

"Just great." She glanced up, and realized where she'd seen this vampire before; in the car on her way to the palace. She'd been the one to take her glove back from Nicolas and return it. The silence felt too awkward, and their footsteps too loud, so she decided to try to talk to the hopefully friendly vampire. "Um, my name's Sarai."

"I know. Lilly."

"So... you work for Marcelle?"

"Not directly. I'm the king's spymaster, so we often work together. Marcelle is more... an apt comparison would be something between secret service and military."

"Oh. Okay then. If you're the spymaster, should you be telling me that?"

Lilly just smiled. "Here's the kitchen. I assume whatever spell ingredients you're gathering are nothing I should be concerned about?"

Sarai gulped a little. "Could be getting a snack. How did you know?"

"I didn't."

"It's just to help me sleep better. Promise."

Lilly nodded, and held the door open, following Sarai into the kitchen. Trying not to feel nervous, she set her concentration to the contents of the kitchen.

Kitchens were the perfect places for quick spell ingredients. She went directly to the teas, then to the spice selection. Potions worked better if she could grow the herbs herself, but it was an emergency, so whatever was available would do. Chamomile tea: perfect. She set a pot to boil with water, then rummaged through the spices available. Bay leaves, thyme, anise. Those would do. Not the best tastes to mix with chamomile, but she needed all the help she could get. Once the water was ready, she dumped all her dried leaves and herbs into the water and sat with a cup.

"*Shomer chalomi*," she murmured, letting the magic channel through her focus to spell the potion, empowering the magical properties of the plants in her water, and amplified by the water itself. She repeated the words, concentrating on her intent until the potion glowed a light green, and she smiled. It felt good to use her magic again. To use proper magic that required knowledge and skill in the craft rather than just mindless gifts.

After the spell, she glanced at the food around her, and looked at the vampire. "Can I take some with me, is that all right?"

"Take what you will."

Sarai snagged a few rolls of bread and fruits to save for later, then wrapped up some spare herbs in a napkin to repeat the spell if needed and put the pot away.

Her supplies gathered, Lilly escorted her back to her room and bid her goodnight before disappearing into the shadows like a proper movie vampire.

Sarai curled her legs up to her chest once she was in bed and sipping the warm potion. She felt safe. Her conversation with Lilly was so contrary to her experience with Nicolas that it almost made her feel welcomed, that she could look forward to further interactions.

Adding to her comfort as she prepared for bed,

Liora remained absent and silent.

Good.

When the liquid was gone, she pulled out a glowing bay leaf and put it under her pillow to ensure her dreams wouldn't trouble her anymore. Sleep took hold, and Sarai had peace at last.

Chapter Ten: The Mall

Marcelle slept as she always did that night, dreamless and motionless. It was a perk of being dead. She had to sleep, but she could be certain that she wouldn't be plagued with nightmares of Nicolas's teeth in her neck.

To escort the humans, she chose an outfit for comfort. Wedge heels, the only type of heel to ever exist that she found remotely comfortable; an open back, dark red halter top made from the softest material she could find while also being sturdy; and black, form-fit pants. Since she was on duty, she pulled on her uniform's soft, black, leather gloves, the golden embroidered hound symbolizing her sire on the cuff. Realizing she'd put them on before doing make-up, she yanked them off and applied a touch of white pigment added to rosewater based on an old-fashioned recipe to her face. Next, she put on some light eyeshadow and mascara for her eyes, and a bold deep red shade of lipstick to match her shirt, before putting her gloves back on.

Gloves were a good way to accessorize, as well as being a safety precaution against accidental contact with silver. Her fingernails had been trimmed short at the time she'd been turned, a necessity for anyone dabbling in certain aspects of her old profession to ensure the comfort of others, so painting them was something that more often looked ridiculous than elegant. Gloves made her look elegant.

The thing she hated the most about her outfit was the lack of pockets. Back when dresses had more material and room underneath, she used to stitch pockets into them if they didn't already have pockets. But since those had long gone out of fashion and been replaced with suffocating tight clothes that wouldn't pass for undergarments in centuries past, Marcelle was cursed to carry a purse. The positive side was that it was easy to hide a handgun in one.

Her hair was one thing she wished more than any other had remained fashionable. Long ago, she'd been able to stun the highest classes of society with all the elaborate styles she could twirl it into. In the current era, it was an obvious anachronism. What modern woman wore her hair five feet long? But it could never be shortened; every attempt to cut her thick black hair resulted in the removed hair turning to dust and the hair on her head re-growing to its original length moments later. She was frozen in time.

Still… she could have a little fun with it. She spun it up on the back of her head and chose from a vast collection of decorated hair accessories with pearls and gems to add something special. She was in the mood for one of her favorites: a Victorian hair comb carved from a turtle shell with gold filigree around the edge. It was far from her finest piece, but it had been a present from Setanta, so she was partial to it.

And it had once been so *in*. Marcelle sighed. Once she'd tried so hard to keep up with changing styles. She'd loved every elaborate hat, every new dress. Now everything was so streamlined, so manufactured, so…

impersonal. She liked the freedom to wear pants but missed ornate *style*.

And too often she found herself being a stereotypical vampire missing the good old days. Shaking her head, she picked up her custom designer purse, made of the best leather possible so that she wouldn't have to constantly replace it as the years went on, and made her way to where she knew the humans would be waiting.

Watching the group of humans outside through a cracked open door, was Sarai in a set of borrowed sweatpants and long sleeve shirt. Chuckling to herself, Marcelle darted behind the girl.

"They don't bite, you know," she said.

Sarai jumped, the sound of her heart rate elevating.

"Don't sneak up on a girl like that!" she gasped, holding her hand over her chest. She stared, blatantly taking in the vampire's put-together appearance.

"I didn't mean to scare you," Marcelle said, and raised an eyebrow. "Everything all right?"

"Yeah. I'm fine. Just, you're all dressed up."

"I don't always wear work clothes, you know," Marcelle teased. "I like to look good."

"You do. I mean, you, you're very…" The witch bit her lip and blushed in a most human way. "You look pretty."

Marcelle smiled. "Thank you. But let's not spend the day gawking at me when we have an excursion to attend. What's keeping you here?"

Sarai shifted a little. "Just haven't spent a lot of time with people. Had dinner with Rosaline last night, and that was great, but I haven't met the rest of them."

"Come, we'll go together." Marcelle pushed one of

the large entrance doors open and led the girl through. She squinted in the light. While vampires didn't burn like legend suggested, bright lights still hurt her sensitive eyes. Since she too often got stuck with daytime work, she made sure to carry a pair of rhinestone-studded sunglasses.

Rosaline was the first to notice the pair, and her face lit up with excitement. "Guys, that's Sarai!" she exclaimed, and rushed over to grab the witch's hand and pulled her over, introducing her to the group.

It was cute, but not any of Marcelle's business. Keeping an ear on their conversation in case Sarai said anything of interest, she slid into the passenger's side seat of a van next to the vampire driver, a lower ranked knight named Paul she had never interacted with much. He looked bored, and perhaps sleep deprived, his eyes hidden by his "secret service" style glasses. She'd be tired too if she were on simple guard duty. It was dull, one of the less intensive jobs available.

Babysitting humans wasn't part of her usual responsibilities, though she understood why her sire had ordered it in this unique case. Building the witch's trust and comfort around a familiar face made her easier to control. Marcelle loved the game, the manipulation. A smile here, a light touch there; she could manipulate kings. And with the way Sarai's heart fluttered around her, she would be far easier to manipulate than a king.

The job was certainly better than sitting in a cold interrogation room with a Vasi scientist or hunter, trying to pull truths from their pathetic tongues. Bear could do that and give her a report. Sarai was an intriguing novelty. If there was one thing an older vampire couldn't resist, it was novelty. But more than that, Marcelle felt compelled to learn about the girl. Her attitude was fun and drew her in. And there was that taste… It almost made her feel alive for a moment when she'd tasted Sarai's blood.

The humans clambered into the vehicle, their inane chatter following as they did, and the group was off.

"There's this great little pizza place you gotta try," Rosaline said to Sarai. "Oh, and junk food. Candy and fast food and all that. They don't let us eat a lot of junk food, so gotta stock up while we can, right?"

"Junk food isn't good for you," Marcelle said. She wouldn't stop them from indulging on their day out, but it was preferable to have sources in the peak of health.

"It's totally good for our taste buds," said one of the boys.

"We wouldn't know," Paul muttered.

The human's town and the mall wasn't too far, at most a half hour drive. At some point, the mortals started singing some of their favorite pop songs off-key, but Sarai's smile was too precious for Marcelle to complain. She could pick out the girl's voice from the group, and it was pleasant. Not trained at all, and nothing that would ever perform in an opera house, but sweet. Marcelle was almost upset when they arrived, and the singing stopped.

The humans divided themselves into two groups: one wanted video games first, and the other wanted food first. Sarai decided they would go with the food group, so Marcelle tagged along. Once, the smells might have been appetizing, but as a vampire, they weren't any more mouthwatering than perfume. Sarai at least was enjoying herself, and the kindness and attention from the other mortals.

Shopping was much more interesting to Marcelle, once the humans were done with their food. She enjoyed going through racks of clothing, looking for things that would flatter Sarai. The other girls with them seemed just as happy to make the shy girl try on clothes.

At first, Sarai tried to insist that she didn't need so much. But after the first well-fitted outfit, and the awe at which the girl looked at her body in the mirror, Sarai grew more comfortable. Her confidence bloomed, until she was the one picking outfits and being more vocal about her own style. It was a beautiful transformation to behold, and the beauty had nothing to do with Sarai's clothes. It was all her smile.

There was one falter when she realized the prices on her items and went into sticker shock, but Marcelle took her hands.

"I wouldn't have taken you here if I expected you to worry about price," she assured her.

"I-I can't pay you back for this. It's so much, I can't let you get this. I have some cash back at my old place, but someone's probably stolen it by now and nothing else there is worth anything so I can't–"

"Hush your worrying, little witch," Marcelle said, caressing the back of Sarai's hands with her thumbs as she held them. "You don't have to pay me back, now or ever, in any way. This is on me. It's a gift."

Rosaline came running up, holding a casual but flowing green dress in her arms as she stopped short, and giggled at the sight of the two holding hands.

"You know, if you two want to be alone, you could just say so," she teased, and wiggled her eyebrows suggestively.

Sarai's eyes widened, and the vampire could feel every muscle in the girl's body going rigid at the implication.

"N-no, that's not what–!"

"Don't worry, I won't tell." Rosaline winked, and Sarai seemed too surprised to pull her hands away. Marcelle decided to play along.

"Darling, we are discovered. But why should it be so secret?" she said, and theatrically pulled the girl by her waist, then lowered her into a romantic dip. Sarai squealed, and Rosaline cackled like a hyena. "Surely there are worse things they could think of us, my sweet little witch?"

Sarai blushed, her body reacting in just the way Marcelle wanted, but then she froze, the sharp scent of fear punctuating the air. Rosaline gasped and put herself between the pair and anyone who might have walked by.

"Um, ma'am, your eyes…"

Marcelle looked up and caught her reflection in the mirror outside the changing room to be stunned by what she saw. Her eyes had turned red.

She quickly pulled Sarai upright and gave her a little push in Rosaline's direction as she flicked her sunglasses down over her eyes.

"Go try on your dress," she ordered.

Sarai didn't need to be told twice, and the two disappeared into the fitting room, leaving Marcelle to wonder about her role. She was meant to be manipulating and controlling the witch. Yet, there she was, her eyes turning red as if she were a new vampire with no self-control. She could even feel her fangs aching in her mouth, despite the fact she'd fed just the day before. It had nothing to do with the need for blood, she realized.

There were a handful of reasons for a vampire's irises to change, for their fangs to grow. Hunger, anger, even pain. But they also changed for a different reason.

Lust.

Some part of her wanted Sarai.

Chapter Eleven: The Midnight Boutique

By the end of the shopping spree, Marcelle and the mortals with her had helped Sarai create a new wardrobe as well as get a handful of necessary toiletries. The vampire had gotten her eyes to return to their human blue, though kept her sunglasses on her head to make sure she would be able to cover them in case of another slip up. Despite how inconvenient it would be, she found herself envying Setanta and other purebloods, whose eyes never changed, never betrayed their emotions.

"Rosaline, why don't you and the others take Sarai's things to the van for her? I need to go by one more stop before we leave, and I'd like her to come with me," Marcelle said.

"Sure thing," the girl said, and gave Sarai a hug. "We'll see you soon."

"Where are we going?" she asked over Rosaline's shoulder.

"It's a surprise," Marcelle said with a secretive smile.

Sarai sighed and followed her into the more expensive section of the mall. Their destination was a privately owned establishment named the Midnight Boutique; small store compared to all the chain and brand names around them and not someplace Marcelle imagined Sarai would have expected to ever visit, given the look of confusion on the girl's face.

A bell rang somewhere in the shop as the door opened. Inside were mannequins dressed in fine formal wear, many of them heavily embellished. Some looked like typical prom dresses, but the further back one looked in the shop, the more obvious it was that they were all handcrafted works of art, each more elaborate than the last.

A small, middle-aged woman looked up from a book at the counter and broke into a wide smile. "Marcelle! *C'est bon de te voir!*"

"It's a delight to see you too," Marcelle said in English. The two leaned over the countertop and kissed each other's cheeks twice. "Sophie, this is my new ward, Sarai. Sarai, this is Sophie."

Sophie's eyes flashed with a tinge of red, indicating to Marcelle that she'd caught a hint of the sweet witch blood in Sarai's veins.

"You are ze witch girl, *oui?*" Word had travelled fast, as it usually did. Vampires loved their gossip. "It is a pleasure to meet you." She smiled, looking much more like a plump mother than a vampire, and her thick French accent was nostalgic to Marcelle. She stepped out from behind the counter and pulled Sarai in for a kiss on each cheek. "You are a beautiful young girl, aren't you?" she said, stepping back an arm's length to look at her.

"Oh," Sarai said, glancing at her protector. "Uh, nice to meet you. Thank you?"

"Marcelle, if you are 'ere about your dress, I still have ze 'em to finish." Sophie's voice trailed off as the other vampire shook her head. "You cannot mean... for 'er?"

Marcelle smiled, feeling a little excited for this special treat she had planned for Sarai.

"I have something for you," she said. She pulled from her purse a parchment letter written in red ink and sealed with a wax stamp and handed it to the girl. "I hope it's not too much? He wants to make up for the way you've been treated so far."

Sarai ran her fingers over the wax seal, as if it were something she'd never seen before, and opened the letter. Marcelle found herself reading upside down along with her, having not had the chance to read the exact wording before, despite knowing what the approximate contents were.

Dear Miss Sarai,

I am writing this letter on behalf of my family to inform you that as a show of good faith, you are invited to attend the upcoming Midnight Festival. It is a special gathering held once every five years; a weeklong ball celebrating our history and our future. This year it holds a unique significance, as my father plans to step down so that I may be crowned king. It would greatly please me to see you attend, should you choose to accept, and so I request your presence as my honored guest at the coronation.

I would also like to invite you to speak with me at some point this week, so that we may discuss your situation in greater detail.

Please address Knight Commander Marcelle with any concerns or questions you may have.

Most Sincerely,

Crown Prince Setanta mac Lugh of New Ulster

"If that letter says what I was told it says," Marcelle said with a smile, "Then we're in just the right place. Of course, you can decline, but I figured since we were already out and about, we could stop by here and take your measurements so that you have the option."

But who would refuse such an honor? Marcelle knew that most women, let alone a poor witch on the run, never had the chance to attend such a fine affair and every little girl fantasized about it at some point, she was certain. At least, she had.

"Marcelle…" Sarai stared at the letter, her eyes traveling to the top again as she reread it. "What the… is this some kind of mistake?"

"Are you implying I make mistakes? How offensive," Marcelle teased.

"No, just, well, maybe. I mean, a coronation? Me? I chop onions for a living."

"I can tell the chefs to add a few onions if it would make you feel more at home."

"I think I'm good, thanks," Sarai said with an eye roll. "This is for real then? Not some practical joke?"

"Trust me, this is real. The prince doesn't hand-write letters for practical jokes. Not his style."

"*He* sent it personally?" Sophie interrupted. "But she is mortal, and a witch! Zere 'as never been precedent."

"Please calm yourself. You know he wants to change the way things are done now that he's going to be in charge," Marcelle said, then turned back to Sarai. "I know it might not mean as much, but I'd very much like to see you attend. I'm certain you will be the belle of the ball."

"I don't know about that," Sarai laughed, and reread the letter again. "I guess, if you want me there…

It's just so ridiculous. Me, at a coronation?"

"There's the spirit," Marcelle said, but Sophie was still in shock.

"But she is mortal."

"Sophie, be a dear and mind your elders," Marcelle taunted the technically younger vampire, despite the fact that it looked as if Sophie were the older one. "Now take Sarai's measurements."

As the seamstress went off to get her measuring tape, Marcelle asked, "Is there any particular era you're fond of? Any style? Traditionally we wear things from the eras we've lived through, but it's not like it's going to be a secret you weren't around in the sixteen hundreds. We'll do one custom dress for the opening night's coronation and get a few simpler things off the rack for the rest of the event. The first night is the truly formal one, so we can probably get away with some of the nicer clothes we just got you for the others."

"I'm going to go to a coronation," Sarai said, "Don't ask me about style, I'm still trying to wrap my head around this. She's really going to make *me* a custom dress?"

"She can make anything. She's the most talented seamstress I've ever known. Isn't that right, Sophie?"

The seamstress reappeared with a roll of measuring tape that she let unfurl down to the ground. "*Oui, mademoiselle,*" she said with a slight bow. She took Sarai's hand and led her up to a stand so that she could start wrapping the measuring tape around different points on her body, jotting down scribbles on a paper left on her countertop. "Red is a good color. Show off, be startling."

"A few decades," Sarai repeated with a laugh. "I'm

not sure I'm the showoff type. Never had the opportunity, I guess. It does sound fun to wear something nice for a change."

"Trust me, you'll have a grand time," Marcelle reassured her. Of course, there would be political maneuvers and relationships. Setanta wouldn't have invited the witch out of the goodness of his heart; he wanted to make a show, a gesture that would resonate to the rest of the witches as well as the vampire world. It was a power play, sharing that power and opportunity with a new pawn in the social game. But there was no need to worry the girl with that just yet.

"I'm going to look ridiculous," Sarai murmured.

"No one I dress looks ridiculous," Sophie said, as if the very notion was offensive. "*Cherie*, tink. Every little girl dreams of beautiful dresses, *oui*? So tell me, what beautiful dresses did you dream of wearing as a little girl? I will put you in your dream."

"I'm… not sure. I never thought about it," she said. "I guess I've always liked Cinderella stories because of the happy ending. I think I like the big dress too. But with more color so it's not so wedding-ish. I like blue though, instead of red. Not navy or pastel, just a bright blue. Bright colors make me happy."

"*Oui, oui.* I can make a nice gown in royal blue for the guest of ze royals."

"Actually," Marcelle interjected, "Plenty of us wear blue. What's the one color no vampire would wear?"

Sophie frowned in thought, then her eyes widened. "Zat would be daring indeed!"

"What, am I missing something?" Sarai asked. "What color are you talking about?"

"Silver, of course. Wear a silver colored, shining gown."

Sarai grinned. "I can see how that would be daring. Fake silver, not real, right?"

"Obviously. Do you like it?"

"Hell yes. Silver. But put some blue in there. I really don't want to look like a bride." The witch giggled. "This is so weird. I don't even think I've ever seen a ballgown in person before today. Well, not that I remember. Maybe I have."

"Wouldn't you remember that?" Marcelle asked.

"I don't have any memories before I turned six, so..." Sarai shrugged, and Marcelle made a mental note. That would go into her reports to Setanta. Sarai sighed. "I don't know what I want. I'd feel like an imposter in any of these. You've got all these evening dresses everywhere with beads and lace and–"

"Oh, silly girl," Sophie laughed. "Zese are ze dresses I sell 'umans. Zese are my preferred style, but 'ave not'ing to do with my services for ze crown. Do you see men's clothes here? Of course not, because men in zese times wear dull identical suits. I make my men clothes from every time period and style and culture. I can make you somet'ing you feel right wearing, be assured. If you don't like beads and lace, we will 'ave no beads and lace. What do you think of scale mail?"

"Uh, like armor?" Sarai laughed. "I mean, cool, but I don't think this is something to wear armor to, right? Not exactly delicate."

Sophie pulled back the measuring tape and tapped her chin as she thought. Then she turned away sharply, found a sketch pad from behind her counter, and began scribbling on it, her hand moving faster than a human's would for such fine work. "Anyt'ing can be delicate if done well. Do you like zis?" she asked and turned it around.

The skirt was large like a classic ballgown, but more elaborate with pleated layers draping about the shape. The top covered one shoulder and left the other exposed in a modern slant, with geometrical patches of what was marked with notes to be chainmail decorating it. It looked fun. Yet, Sarai's expression was one of contemplation, even a hint of embarrassment as her cheeks flushed.

"It's gorgeous. Really. But, um… Maybe just one thing." She gestured to the collar of her shirt and hooked it with a finger, pulling it down to expose a hint of cleavage. Marcelle's fangs nearly extended in response, but she managed to keep them in check.

Sophie laughed. "But of course, of course." She took back the sketch and made alterations. "You like, or too much?"

Sarai's eyes almost popped out of her skull; the top of the dress had been changed so that the neckline plunged down almost to the waist, and the decorative mail now rested on the shoulders.

Marcelle wanted to shake her head. There was no chance this little witch who leaned toward wearing baggy clothes when left to her own devices would wear something so daring. "You're just trying to mess with her now," she said, keeping her lips still as possible and speaking in a tone too low for a mortal's dull hearing to pick up. "Please take this seriously. I'm sure she's just thinking of a sweetheart neckline."

"I always take dresses seriously," Sophie replied in

the same manner as Sarai studied the sketch, oblivious to the conversation. "Ze witch may surprise you."

"Fuck it," Sarai proclaimed. "Yeah. Yes, let's do it."

Well, well. The little witch had indeed surprised her.

The two vampires spoke briefly together in French before a farewell. On their way out, Sarai turned to her protector, parchment letter in hand, and asked, "What does he mean, about my situation? What does he want to talk with me about?"

So, it hadn't been lost on her.

"Well…." Marcelle wasn't sure how much she should say. It was technically pureblood business. She worked for them, and she loved one, but that didn't mean it was up to her to tell Sarai everything. "You are staying with us. We've never had a witch as a guest before. I believe that he feels this could be an opportunity. Vasi are dangerous, like I told you. Witches under attack, vampires under attack. But we don't have diplomatic relations of any kind between us. Through you, we could perhaps change that."

Sarai stopped and spun toward Marcelle, anger in her eyes.

"You want me to talk to witches for you," she said. "This is political. He's trying to butter me up with this." She waved the invitation.

Marcelle sighed; she should have kept her mouth closed. The girl was smart.

"I'm sorry, I shouldn't have speculated. It's not my business. This is something to discuss with Setanta when you see him again. Regardless, you can decline or accept however you please. No one is forcing you one way or the other. You are a guest." It was best to give the illusion of choice, in Marcelle's experience.

"You and him, you just want to snatch up the first witch that's not contracted to the Vasi and use me for politics!" Sarai shouted, getting the attention of several people passing by.

Marcelle snatched her hand and jerked her into a nearby bathroom. After a quick listen for anyone else and ensuring they were alone, she turned on the girl.

"For someone so smart, you can be a daft little thing, can't you?" she said.

"Excuse me?"

"Do you really think it's smart to be shouting the name of a secret cult bent on hunting you down and enslaving you? No wonder they captured you, you're as subtle as a hammer to a skull."

Sarai's mouth snapped shut, and she looked down sheepishly.

"Listen to me. We're not asking you to swear fealty to the kingdom, just to show up. And, frankly, it's fun to attend a ball. Take the opportunity, Sarai," she said. The poor girl; all she knew was being used. She had a right to be angry. Marcelle knew what it was like, yet here she was, another person using the witch. She wanted to stop it. To show this girl that life could be good. Her grip on Sarai's hand loosened. "I know that there's been difficulty in your life, but I promise, I'll do what I can to make sure you enjoy your experience."

"Marcelle…" Sarai whispered, her eyes widening. "Why do they do that?"

"Do what?"

"Your eyes… they're red again."

Marcelle looked down at their hands. Somehow, she'd entwined their fingers together. That hadn't been the cause, had it? She looked up into the bathroom mirror to see red vampiric irises staring back at her.

"Oh."

"That's all you have to say?" Sarai said, her hands trembling in Marcelle's grip. "The last time I saw you like that, you were fighting Nicolas. And before then, when you killed the Vasi. Why now, why today?"

"I won't hurt you. I promise."

Sarai didn't look convinced. "It's my blood," she accused. "You said it was sweet, better than most. You took that first taste and now you're like a shark, and I'm a bleeding fish. Well, I'm not giving you any so you can forget about it."

"No, it's not that."

"Then what *is* it?"

Marcelle reached up to the witch's face and caressed her. She was so warm. Her pulse had quickened, the heat flushing about under her skin. Sarai's eyes widened with realization.

"Oh."

Marcelle smiled a little. "That's all you have to say?" she parroted. She moved forward, feeling the heat of Sarai's body closer, inviting her. She could read the reactions; Sarai's heart rate, her dilated pupils, her flushed cheeks. The witch wanted her. In any other circumstances, Marcelle would have taken advantage of the situation, played the mortal in question to fall for her, to give what she wanted. Maybe steal a kiss.

She leaned in closer, and Sarai didn't pull away. They were so close, their lips inches apart. Desire was hot in the limited air between them, and Marcelle breathed it in like an opiate.

But, there was a bitter scent of fear in the air. It wasn't just any mortal with a poorly concealed crush; it was a witch. That added a level of complication Marcelle wasn't sure how to deal with just yet.

She stopped and took a step back, hands dropping to her sides. "Apologies. It's just a reaction. It means nothing. Let's get back to the sources, they'll be waiting for us."

Chapter Twelve: Beneath the Palace

Marcelle kicked herself mentally all the way back to the palace, grateful for the way the humans swarmed Sarai and asked for details about the invitation. They were attending too, after all, though less as guests and more as entrees. It was unheard of for a mortal to attend and not be working as a source, so they were excited at the development.

Once they arrived, Marcelle left Sarai with the humans. Maybe she should have had someone else escort the witch and build a relationship, and she could have been the one interrogating Vasi bastards. She decided to go check on the progress and made her way down to the dungeon.

They had a fair-sized dungeon, on the floor under the basement. It was separated into several sections. There were the interrogation rooms, punishment rooms, and the holding cells. The cells had bars coated in silver and silver chains for the prisoners, so they could hold either vampires or humans. Even witches, if the occasion warranted.

Marcelle passed by several occupied cells, not making eye contact with any of the inhabitants. They weren't important enough for her attention at that moment, but she did notice that one was missing. The captured scientist.

"Commander," said one of the two vampire guards,

giving her a salute.

"At ease. Is Bear or Lilly in there?"

"Bear. Just started on this guy."

Marcelle nodded. Since he'd just started, she didn't feel too bad about interrupting. She was his boss, after all, and he hadn't had the time to work on this fellow much yet.

"Thank you." She pushed open the door to reveal a small room. In the middle was a metal fixture in the floor to which the chains binding the scientist were attached. Other than that, the room was bare and cold, with only a folding chair for Bear. While many assumed vampires would torture their prisoners, they had long ago realized it didn't work. Their natural ability to read humans was much more reliable.

Bear looked up at her. "Commander," he said, with a nod of respect. "I'm just getting to know our guest. This is Dr. Stearne."

"A doctor?" Marcelle mused. "What sort?"

"B-biology, ma'am," the doctor volunteered. "I got my doctorate in biology from Duke University, class of 1992."

"How impressive," she purred.

"I didn't get into this to hurt people. I've been telling your... your friend here. Didn't mean anything by it, nothing personal. Just wanted to study. I'm not even religious like the rest of them. I couldn't pass up the opportunity to learn about you, you know?"

"The good doctor here has been very helpful and informative," Bear said.

"So, so you won't kill me, right?" Dr. Stearne begged, leaning forward and causing his chains to clink against stone and metal.

"I have no intentions of killing you," Marcelle lied with a practiced, convincing smile. He relaxed.

"I, that's good! Good! And, might I say, I appreciate you guys not, you know, doing the... well, using that room next to us."

Marcelle chuckled. That particular room was for punishment alone, not for extracting information. There was nothing anyone who went into that room could say to make their sentence stop.

"I'm sure there's no need for that with someone as smart as you, Doctor," she said. "You're just curious about us, aren't you?"

"No need, no need. And yes, exactly. I don't have anything against you. Or witches. I just wanted to learn all about it. All of it. I could work for you! I graduated summa cum laude, I'm good. And I... I always loved studying vampires most. That girl, she was so fascinating. I learned so much. I could share!"

"Bringing up that you and your ilk performed experiments on our princess might not be the best course of action right this moment," Marcelle said.

His face paled. "R-right, of course. Yes. No. You're right."

Marcelle smiled at him. This one was too easy. She sat down next to him on the floor, not oblivious to the way he glanced at her curves. "Dr. Stearne," she said. "You seem eager to help us out."

"Absolutely."

"Were his colleagues this forthcoming?" Marcelle asked Bear.

"Not remotely. Very offended at the notion of talking to unholy creatures and all that nonsense."

"Shame. But you're different, aren't you, Doctor?

You don't see us as unholy creatures, do you? You're smarter than that." She smiled again and put a hand on his knee. "Tell me, why did the Vasi decide to target poor Artemisia?"

"We want to know how you work, that's all. We were making other vampires, from her blood and some of the weaker witches we had. Fascinating process to study. We didn't give them much of a shelf life for safety reasons, and never more than one or two at a time. We let her finish them off for us. But what we learned from them... so much, it was so exciting."

"And what does Sarai have to do with that? Or is she an unrelated side project of yours?"

"A lucky accident, but we were looking for someone like her," he said. "We wanted a necromancer just in case it got out of hand, and that was the best we could find. Not even a real necromancer. But..." He shook his head. "I didn't have much time with her, but I realized... something magnificent. I mixed blood in petri dishes, out of curiosity. Do you, well, do you know what I found? What that witch girl is?"

Marcelle kept her emotions hidden and portrayed childlike interest. "Do tell me, Doctor."

"Well, obviously, your blood is different from humans, under a microscope. It looks the same, but it dies faster, isn't that weird? My hypothesis was that it would have been the other way around, but that's not the point. The witch is like... an anti-vampire. The problem with vampire blood is the way it changes human or witch blood it comes in contact with, right? And yeah, when you put her blood in direct contact with a pureblood's blood, it changes the way it's supposed to since purebloods are like vampires on steroids, but... If you mix her blood with a vampire's, it's like, like it can slow it down. Maybe even reverse it under the right circumstances."

The mask slipped from Marcelle's face.

"You mean to tell me that the Vasi were experimenting with..."

"Curing vampirism, yes," he said with a wide smile. "See, they'd thought of it as this supernatural curse for so long, but with someone with a high enough IQ, we can move away from the superstitious dogma and nonsense. With her blood injected or ingested to medically counter–"

Marcelle stood abruptly and he stopped.

"Lock him back up," she snapped at Bear.

"Wait, but this could be good! You have the witch girl, right? If you let me continue my research, I can *help* you."

Her eyes turned red with anger. "We don't need your help, Dr. Stearne. I have lived for over five centuries. What on earth makes you think I have any interest in a cure that could destroy the foundations of my society?"

"But, but you could eat food again," he said, his heart racing like a captured rabbit in the jaws of a fox.

"I enjoy the taste of blood, Dr. Stearne."

The doctor looked up frantically at Bear. "And, and you? Wouldn't it be nice to be able to be part of a real, civilized society, not hiding in shadows?"

"A real, civilized society?" Bear repeated and stood tall, all six feet and eight inches of him. Dr. Stearne fell back on his behind as the smell of his fear permeated the room. "The last time men came to tell me how to be part of real, civilized society, they killed ninety percent of my world. If you'd have offered me the cure a thousand years ago, I would have taken it. Now, this is my world. The world I have left. I would never let you destroy it."

The prisoner clearly realized his mistake. "I, I didn't mean to word it like that. Just, okay, what about the people who are turned now? The ones who don't want it, like you back then? Shouldn't they have the option to go back?"

Marcelle frowned and exchanged glances with Bear. She hated that the man made a point; there were some vampires that despised their condition or had been turned unwillingly. It would provide a nicer way to die than what was available to vampires. The only ways for a vampire to die were murder, tragic accident, or suicide. Being able to become human and live out life until old age was preferable to many.

It was a decision too important for either of them to make.

"I'll speak to His Highness about what to do with him," Marcelle said. "I'll expect a full report when you're done here. I want details about everything."

Bear nodded, and sat back down, staring icily at their prisoner as Marcelle left the room. She barely acknowledged the guard but did look at the two other Vasi prisoners on her way out. They were both glaring at her. She put on a fake, malicious smile for them, which dropped off her face when she was out of their sight.

A dark thought struck her; Sarai was a threat by existing. While he was a reasonable man who did not condone the deaths of innocents, Setanta's primary duty was to protect the kingdom, to protect his vampire citizens. There was every chance that if he deemed it necessary for the safety of his subjects, the pureblood would kill Sarai.

And Marcelle didn't want to let her die.

Chapter Thirteen: Life

Sarai spent her day with Rosaline and the other humans, glad but upset not to see Marcelle again after their trip to the mall. It had been so confusing. To help her get to sleep, she read more books about vampire history in North America as well as New Ulster laws. The old English was dull, and lulled her to bed, leaving her well-rested in the morning to return to studying over breakfast.

She picked up on an explanation of compulsion: that a magical order from a pureblood vampire could not be disobeyed by a made vampire, and such methods had historically been used by purebloods to control their kingdoms. She was halfway through a chapter about the hierarchy magically imposed by birth order on which compulsions were the final authorities when someone knocked on her door. Half expecting Rosaline or one of the other humans, it was a surprise to see the tall, red-haired vampire prince in front of her, Marcelle at his side.

"Uh, hi," she said. Both their expressions were too stern, and her fight or flight instincts triggered. She took a step back. "Can I help you?"

"I'd like to talk to you," Setanta said, and gestured for Marcelle to step ahead of him.

"Is this about the letter, or... Am I–"

"You're not in trouble," Marcelle reassured. "We

just need to talk to you. Come, sit with me?" She gestured to the bed.

Sarai sat down cross-legged, pulling her feet in close. It felt awkward to try and make eye contact with Marcelle considering the red-eyed incident from the last time they'd spoken, but Setanta was overwhelming in his own way. She ended up staring at their noses rather than their eyes. His was a very straight nose. Marcelle's was smaller, cuter. His might have cut something.

"What's up?"

"Well, we've been interrogating the Vasi we captured," Marcelle started as she pulled two chairs close to the bed, and she and Setanta sat down. Images of medieval torture devices filled her mind, and Marcelle must have noticed the look on her face because she followed up with, "Just talking, asking questions. Nothing else. The scientist we captured told us about the blood samples he was taking from you."

"I remember that." She crossed her arms over her chest, hugging herself. She spent most of her time trying not to think about it and was struck with a sudden longing for a sleep potion. "Why are you bringing this up?"

"Because we'd like to verify something that was told to us," Marcelle said. "I… I'm not sure how to ask this."

"I need you to let Marcelle drink your blood," Setanta stated.

Sarai stared at him in disbelief, followed by indignant anger. "Excuse me?" She turned on Marcelle. "I told you, I'm not letting you have my blood. I'm not one of your sources!"

"This has nothing to do with whether I want your

blood or not. I can find someone else, if you'd rather a different vampire do this. The Vasi think that your blood can be used to 'cure' vampires," Marcelle said. "So, we need to see how potent that risk is. I know it's not anything instant since I already tried a little, but we need to know how we'd react to more than a few drops."

"That's ridiculous," Sarai laughed. "Vampires are dead. I can heal and I can animate a few corpses, but I can't bring anyone back from the dead, not for real."

"Nonetheless," Setanta said, leaning forward. "I need you to indulge us."

"Or what?"

Setanta's eyes narrowed, and fear gripped her chest. He hadn't even moved, yet she could feel the predator in the room's presence become more prominent, more threatening.

"Sarai, you are our guest, but only by my good graces. You don't want that to change."

Of course. He might have taken off her collar, but her fate was still in his hands. It was something she'd known in some way but felt uncomfortable to have it brought to light. He was still a vampire, after all.

"Fine. Just a little blood and you're out of here," she said, clutching her hair and hesitating to pull it away from her neck, to make herself vulnerable.

Marcelle shifted onto the bed, her eyes turning red and her fangs extending. "I'll try to make it hurt as little as possible," she said, taking Sarai's hand in her cold grasp. Sarai tensed and tried to pull away.

"Does it hurt a lot?" she asked. "I... is there a different way to do this?"

"Would you prefer needles?" Marcelle asked. "I

can have someone go find a syringe."

The thought made her flinch; the Vasi had used needles. Somehow the idea of vampire fangs was less terrifying.

"No, not that," she blurted. "I, I've never been bitten by a vampire before, you know. Just nervous about what to expect." She looked at the fangs in Marcelle's mouth and took a deep breath to try and calm herself. They looked sharp, so it wasn't as if she was consenting to be bitten by something blunter like rounded fangs. They had definite points that could pierce straight through flesh. "Don't hurt me too much?"

"I'll be as gentle as I can."

Sarai could feel Setanta's eyes on her and glared a little. "Is this a thing that gets voyeurs?" she snapped, though not sure if having the bite be a private affair would make the situation better or worse.

"Sometimes, but that's not why I'm here."

"Why *are* you here?"

"If you tried to fight, I would subdue you," he said. "And to observe the effect on Marcelle, counter your blood with mine if needed."

How could he subdue her? Sure, physically he was more powerful, but how would he counter her magical ability? He was strong and fast, but she could kill him with a touch. At least, she assumed she could. Sarai looked at his waist to see if he had any silver weapons he could use against her and didn't see anything, not even her old collar. It made her feel both uneasy and a little confident.

"If you say so."

"You don't believe I could win, if we put our

abilities to the test against each other," he said, reading her tone and expression correctly. "Rest assured, I have not survived this long without knowing how to subdue a witch, regardless of their power."

Sarai shrugged as if it didn't bother her. "Whatever. Let's get this over with."

The vampire woman raised a hand to caress Sarai's face, now blushing from the touch.

"You're shaking," Marcelle said. The feel of her chilled, dead skin didn't help Sarai's nerves at all.

"Just do it already. I don't want to think about it." If she had to think about it much longer, she'd end up fighting back, and wasn't sure she wanted to test Setanta's ability to control her. She pulled her hair to the side and held her breath, as if she were about to drown.

"Do you want your neck? I can do that, or your wrist," Marcelle said.

"I... I don't know," she mumbled, her hand gripping her own hair. "Movies always have neck bites, right? Is that not how it's done?" Her own memories answered the question, when she remembered Rosaline offering her wrist to her client.

"Here." Marcelle's strong, porcelain arms made Sarai's heart pound faster as they wrapped around her and guided her to lay on her back, then carefully took her hand, raising the witch's wrist to her lips. "I'm sorry about this. It isn't what I wanted."

"Just fucking do it."

Marcelle nodded. "Look at the wall," she instructed. "It might be easier to not watch."

Sarai thought about it but didn't look away. She couldn't. Both because she was afraid and curious to observe the process, and because she wanted Marcelle to see the anger in her eyes at being forced into the situation. Marcelle waited, then realized Sarai wouldn't look away and accepted it with a nod. Her lips parted to expose her elongated pearl-white fangs as if in slow motion, even though it all happened fast. She struck, the twin needles piercing into Sarai's flesh.

The witch gasped a little, eyes locked with Marcelle's as they widened from the sudden pain and whimpered. The movement of the vampire's throat as she gulped the freed blood was hypnotic. The pain wasn't as bad as she expected. It was precise, clean. There was a light tingling against the wounds that dulled it just enough that the pain was manageable. She was grateful Marcelle had her lay down first. The slow blood loss and adrenaline rush had her head swimming.

Sarai tried to focus on something other than the dull pain, and found her mind captured by Marcelle's red lips, her wet mouth. It was almost like a perverse kiss. Even the tingling around the wound almost felt nice; Rosaline never mentioned that aspect of the bite. Then there was the sensation of her tongue, slow and cool against the wound…

Marcelle pulled her fangs free, and two trickles of blood oozed down Sarai's arm, though it stopped as the wound healed.

"You taste so… rich," Marcelle murmured.

Setanta stood, taking Marcelle's face in his hands, as if performing some sort of doctor's check-up examination. "How do you feel?"

"Like I drank raw sunlight. It's almost like you."

He frowned. "Like my blood?"

"Well, not as powerful," she said. "But there's a

similarity. She's bitter and sweet at the same time, and so strong… It was a trial to stop, more than it was when I just took a taste from her. Though that probably had something to do with her smelling like onions last time. A younger vampire might not have been able to stop."

That made Sarai a little uncomfortable. There had to be other vampires who were younger with less control around the palace. "So, no problems, right? Not feeling human?"

"No, I—" Marcelle stopped, her eyes wide, and she looked up at her sire as she gripped her chest, inhaling sharply.

Setanta's frown deepened, and he put a hand against her chest. "It stopped."

"What stopped?" Sarai asked, propping herself up on her elbows.

"Her heart."

"Is that… that sounds bad?" Common wisdom told her that hearts stopping was bad, but what about for someone who was an undead corpse?

Setanta didn't answer her though, instead pressing two fingers to Marcelle's neck to check for a pulse. "Vampires don't have pulses. Your blood started her heart for a moment."

The implications made Sarai dizzy, or maybe it was the blood loss. "Are you saying that I really can change vampires back to human?"

"I think… it would take more blood than you have to change a vampire to human," Setanta said, still examining his progeny. He touched a finger to the corner of her red lips and found a drop of blood, bringing it to his lips. It felt like a violation; she hadn't said he could taste her blood, yet he did it anyway.

"Perhaps with the right ritual, the right magic to amplify what you have. But not on your own. It's unrefined."

"Then, are we good?" Sarai asked.

"For now," he said. "Do not explore this road. I would forgive you for causing my citizens to decompose sooner than I'd forgive you for making them human."

"Isn't it a good thing though? If someone wants to be human again…" Her voice trailed away when he glared at her. The weight of a predator in the room returned, and the message was clear.

"No," Setanta snapped. "Hunters would use the possibility to destroy us. For that reason, I think you should keep this potential to yourself. The ones who were experimenting with it are nearly all dead, so the news won't have spread far. You will be a target if you let anyone know."

A target of the hunters, she knew, but did he mean he would target her too? She didn't want to find out. "I get it," Sarai said.

"Good. I'm glad we have an understanding."

Marcelle got up from the bed. "Are you feeling all right, Sarai? Do you need a few drops from me, or is your healing gift enough?"

"Just a little dizzy," she said. "It tingled when you bit me. Is that normal?"

"There's a numbing effect from our saliva," Marcelle said. "Not much, but it helps pacify less willing victims a little, makes it easier for willing sources. Here, for the dizziness." She sliced her finger on her fang and offered it. Sarai hesitated.

"It… blood's not kosher." But she longed for that

sweet sensation she'd experienced only once. Marcelle raised an eyebrow. "I, I don't know if I'm supposed to drink blood?" Sarai stalled.

"Let me scratch you and press the blood against you that way. Blood transfusions are accepted, right?"

"Yeah, I think that's okay. Let's do that." She extended her arm again, and Marcelle gave it the lightest cut with the tip of her fang, like a paper cut, then pressed her own wound into it. It wasn't the same as drinking the blood, but it felt... amazing. Sarai closed her eyes, drifting in the sensation of bliss like an orgasm. Lost in the experience, she barely realized that both vampires were watching her. She wasn't sure how to feel about that, and pulled away when the cut healed, embarrassed at how eager she was.

"Thanks," she muttered, heat burning in her cheeks.

"I appreciate you permitting this trial," Setanta said with a nod of his head. He and Marcelle turned to leave, and a strange instinct gripped Sarai. She wanted to know if she could best him. She was powerful, and so many feared her throughout her life, yet he was so certain he could beat her if it came to whose powers were stronger. He was confident, no, cocky enough to even let her wander his home without a silver collar. She had to know more.

Sarai reached out and touched his wrist, letting a small spark of her power touch his skin and leaving a spot of death.

The reaction was immediate. Before she had time to process what had hit her, there was a hand at her throat and her body was slammed against the floor. Setanta's red eyes pierced through her soul like daggers, and her heart froze in fear as she looked up and saw his lips parted just enough to bare his fangs.

"I-I'm sorry!" she gasped. "I wasn't going to try anything for real, I promise."

"Do not test me, Sarai," Setanta said, his tone calm despite the fact he had a hand on her throat. She could feel her pulse fluttering against his hand and felt like a butterfly under a pin against a board. Glancing down, she was shocked to see that there wasn't even the slightest blemish on his skin. Had he healed that fast, or had her power not even affected him in the first place? Either way, she wasn't going to try again.

Setanta let her go, but Sarai stayed on the floor, trembling.

"Tomorrow, you are invited to take lunch with me," he told her, his fangs retracting. "We have much to discuss, you and I."

It was an order, not an invitation, she knew that from the tone of his voice.

"Yes, sir," she whispered.

"Marcelle, with me. Leave the witch to her own devices."

Marcelle nodded, and looked at Sarai with pity, before the pair left her alone in her room, overwhelmed by the entire experience and wondering what on earth had just happened.

Chapter Fourteen: Henriette

It felt safer to be in the human quarters after Sarai's harrowing experience. Considering they were designed as servant quarters, and still were in a way, the rooms were rather nice. There was a full kitchen, a living room, dining room, and personal rooms like one might find in college dorms. The best part by far was the game room, where air hockey and video games were popular. Sarai found herself enjoying quieter games like chess or checkers. It helped her relax, and Rosaline was kind enough to indulge.

"You tried to… sorry, but what were you thinking?" Rosaline said as she took a pawn with her bishop.

Sarai analyzed the board, plotting out several moves ahead in her mind. If Rosaline stayed distracted, she could checkmate her opponent in three moves. "I wasn't thinking, I guess. Never met anyone who could match me without silver. Just reached out to give him a little jolt, see what would happen. I wasn't actually trying to hurt him."

"Girl, he's a pureblood. You don't mess with purebloods, or they'll mess with you. You don't want that. Seriously."

"I don't think he was too mad. I mean, he didn't like it, but it didn't even hurt him. And then he invited me to lunch tomorrow." Sarai moved her knight.

"Check."

"So... like a date?" Sarai snorted in response and Rosaline giggled. "Yeah, okay, I don't think he does dating. Don't think any vampire does, they just jump into bed. Or arrange marriages if they're purebloods. If he's asking you to lunch, he just wants to talk." She moved her king out of harm's way.

"Good to know. Probably not going to, you know, sleep around with any vampires. I'm a witch, remember? We don't do vampires. Check."

"Damn." Rosaline analyzed the board, trying to find a way out of the trap Sarai had laid for her. "Well, just don't try to attack him again, and I'm sure it'll be fine." She moved a pawn to take the remaining knight. Perfect.

"I'll behave next time," she sighed. She moved her bishop to take a pawn. "Checkmate."

Rosaline groaned when she saw the trap spring shut.

"Good game. You know, not a pureblood, but vampires can be good stress relief, witch or not. You're here. Just go up to one of the guards you think is pretty and say 'take me, I'm yours'. Bear's a good time if you like guys. Or you could go for Marcelle." She winked.

"We're not involved!" Sarai blushed, and flicked over Rosaline's king for her, watching it roll like a lopped-off head on the ground.

"Her eyes were going red for you. You know what that means, right?"

"I smell like a medium-rare sirloin?" Her face burned as she thought back to the way Marcelle had reached out to touch her face at the mall, the unspoken words between them. She kept her head down, focused on resetting the chess pieces.

"Well, that too. But it means she likes you. Like, *likes* you."

"Oh, she like *likes* me." Sarai laughed, trying to play it off. "Are we children?"

"Whatever. Go ask her about it." She paused. "Actually, scratch that. Wait to ask her about it when I'm around. I would love to see Miss Perfect French Couture in her designer sunglasses squirm for a change."

Marcelle had already said it meant nothing. Sarai had to believe it. Yet, when she'd been close to her in the mall, almost close enough to kiss, it hadn't felt like nothing. She wanted to melt from just the thought of Marcelle's rosewater scent, the intensity in her eyes… Sarai shook her head.

"Look, I told her I didn't want her to bite me. I told her I wasn't giving out my blood, and then she comes in with his seriousness and gets him to demand I let her drink from me. That wasn't okay."

"Did they have a legit reason for it?" Rosaline asked. "They never take without permission. Ever. At least, I can't think of any of us that it's happened to."

Sarai slumped in the chair. She didn't want to talk about how the Vasi wanted her to be a weapon against vampires, and the vampires didn't like it. About how even her harmless healing power now held danger to others. "I guess. Just… I don't like it."

"So, tell her that," Rosaline said, rolling her eyes. "And tell her she can make it up to you with a fancy dinner. She got a meal out of you, you get a meal out of her. Sounds fair to me."

Tired with the discussion, Sarai guided the

conversation to who Rosaline liked (another source boy who was too shy to make the first move) and stayed with the humans for dinner before returning to her own room.

It took a little while of tossing and turning, her mind flashing back to how it felt to have Marcelle's fangs in her wrist and Setanta's hand on her throat, but she did manage to fall asleep once she realized her bay leaf had fallen on the floor and she put it under her pillow where it belonged.

The peaceful darkness of sleep was shattered with a loud bang. Sarai shot up out of bed, fear coursing through her as she stared at the doorway. The door itself had been thrown off of its hinges, and an angry Marcelle in a black silk robe stood there, her hair wild as if she'd just come from bed.

"You," she snarled, fangs bared. The vampire darted forward before Sarai even had the chance to scream, and cold hands like shackles gripped her wrists, and the weight on top of her kept her trapped against the bed. "What did you do to me?"

"Get off!" Those fangs... they were so much more threatening than before.

"What did you do to me? A curse, a spell? Answer!"

"Nothing!" she gasped. "But if you don't let me go, I'll use my power, I swear!"

There was a low growl from the monster above her, and the grip on her wrists tightened.

"I didn't do anything," Sarai gasped, trying to pull free. Marcelle had been so nice; she didn't want to kill her. "You're hurting me!"

That seemed to snap the woman out of her rage.

Marcelle eased her grip, and Sarai scampered back up as far as she could, back hitting against the wooden headboard, her legs tangled in the bedsheets.

"What the hell is this about?" Sarai demanded. "I was sleeping. I like sleeping, you know. I didn't do anything to you."

"I… had a nightmare."

"Okay, and? How is your nightmare my fault?"

"I haven't had a nightmare or any dream in over five hundred years. Vampires are dead. When we sleep, we don't dream. We're corpses. You didn't curse me?"

"Oh." It didn't take long to put together the pieces. "My blood. It made your heart beat for a second, right? Why couldn't it make you dream a little?"

"Yes," Marcelle said, easing off to sit on the side of the bed. "Yes, that makes sense."

"Why would you think I would curse you?"

"Retaliation. I thought maybe you cursed me for biting you when you didn't want it. I wouldn't blame you, just in shock. I'm sorry, I'm not usually so out of control." She smiled weakly. "You do something to me."

Sarai hugged her pillow and said nothing.

"I'm sorry about this. I'll let you go back to sleep."

Marcelle started to get up, but before she could dart away, Sarai interjected, "Wait!" The vampire turned her head back. "Do you… want to tell me? About the nightmare? I didn't have much of a childhood, but I did have what I guess you could call a nanny I would talk to whenever I had nightmares." Six-year-old Sarai hadn't known better than to trust her psychopathic stepmother before her half-sister got around to warning her it could be used against her, but it had provided some small comfort at the time.

"You want me to tell you about my nightmare?" Marcelle mused. "After I've taken your blood and attacked you, you're trying to make me feel better about a bad dream?"

Sarai looked away. "I get why you took my blood. I'm not happy about it, but I get it. Rosaline says you owe me dinner for it."

Marcelle chuckled. "All right. I can do that for you. Dinner and we'll call it even."

"As for attacking me, you shouldn't do that, yeah. I guess, I'd attack if I thought someone cursed me." She shrugged. "Must have been a very bad dream."

"An understatement." Marcelle sighed and sat back down. "It's funny. I can think back about so many things in my life and laugh when I'm awake. But when I'm asleep it felt…"

"It feels real again."

Sarai played with the hem of her bed sheet as she stared down at her lap. She could relate to that. If she had a quarter for every bad dream she had, she would have had enough to buy herself a nice house. At least she had her spell.

"It was like I was there again. And I couldn't stop…" Marcelle shut her eyes. "I shouldn't be talking to you about this."

"I have dreams that are too real sometimes," she said. "I dream about being locked up. About my dad beating me. People I've hurt that I didn't want to." And about scorpions performing vivisections on her, but that was too strange to talk about.

"Mine beat me too. But that's not my nightmare."

Marcelle pulled her robe tight around her body, as if trying to keep out the cold that was innate to her very skin. "People I've hurt…"

"Look… if this is because of my blood… I didn't mean to hurt you. I think I can help," she said. "There's a spell I use to sleep better. Gets rid of dreams. But I need to know what kind of bad dreams I'm banishing." She pulled the bay leaf from under her pillow and twirled it between her fingers. "If you tell me your dream, I can help you sleep." She reached over to her nightstand where she had a small stash of herbs and tea stolen from the kitchen, pulled out the proper mix, put it into a cup, and then pulled on her red glove focus. "I'll make one for you."

Marcelle looked at the spell ingredients longingly, then nodded.

"I dreamed about my daughter," she said. In response to the question halfway out of Sarai's mouth, she added, "I had a daughter when I was alive. She's dead now. Actually dead, not undead."

The worst possible scenario she could think of penetrated Sarai's thoughts. Marcelle must have killed her own daughter, in some sort of blood lust fueled horror show. That's what vampires were famous for. Even witches knew that nothing was more frightening and uncontrolled than a newborn vampire.

"Sorry." She fidgeted a little. To prod for more, she asked, "So, did she have a good life?"

"If she had, I would have had kinder dreams." Marcelle looked up from the soft embroidery on her black robe. "You don't really want to hear me reminisce. I've done enough to you."

"I can't do the spell if I don't know what I'm

blocking out," Sarai reminded her.

"If you insist. But it's not a story that will bring *you* good dreams."

"I can handle it." She waved the leaf in the air.

The vampire nodded. "All right. Well, I told you I was a whore because I was sold to a brothel and about how Setanta saved me from dying, but there's a lot more to my life as a human and what I did after I turned. I was fourteen when I was sold and, well, given the nature of my new profession and my own naïveté of avoidance methods, I was pregnant soon after. I don't know who the father was. It's impossible to say. There were so many; I had to earn my rent, money for food. It just happened. Her name was Henriette, and she was the only good thing that happened to me there. A small spark of light. I couldn't send her back to my old home while my father was still there, obviously, but I didn't want her growing up to inherit my work. That's what happened back then. The daughters of whores became whores. I wanted to give her everything, but I had nothing. By the time she was six, she started understanding what was happening. What her mother did every night, what society thought of me. Of us. She started mimicking me. I'd gotten her a cheap doll for her birthday, and I found her... I found her practicing sucking on its little straw crotch so that she could do a good job like her maman."

Sarai's stomach turned. The idea of a little girl practicing on her dolls something so profane made her own childhood seem innocent. She used to wonder what it would be like to have a child of her own one day, what kind of mother she would be. Being impoverished or her father's prisoner most of her life left the possibility limited, as she always feared what sort of life she could have provided and what her father would do. She couldn't imagine being in Marcelle's position as a prostitute, raising a daughter to take over that role one day. Raising a daughter to be subjected to the same abuse she knew. Children needed to be protected from the horrors their mothers knew whether it was Marcelle's child in medieval France or some theoretical child Sarai never had to save them from her father.

"Is that what you were dreaming of? That's horrible."

Marcelle laughed, but it was a hollow sound, devoid of any joy, full of bitterness.

"No. I could stand that. If it was just that. I went back to my parents' home."

"Oh no," Sarai couldn't help but mutter.

"Indeed. My mother had died, and my father was bedridden with disease. I was certain he would follow soon, leaving my three older brothers and their wives. I begged them to keep my Henriette, to pretend she was an orphaned cousin. They agreed and I thought I'd saved her. I left her there with them. Playing in a meadow with my nieces and nephews."

The vampire stopped, staring off at the wallpaper. Sarai uncovered her legs from the bed sheets and moved a little closer to slide her hand into Marcelle's. Their entwined fingers felt nice, and she hoped it would comfort the commander.

"That's how I want to remember her," Marcelle whispered. "Little flaxen-haired girl, running around like a child should." She smiled. "Must have gotten her hair from her father. She had my nose though. And my eyes."

"Must have been beautiful."

"She was. She was the most beautiful little girl I've ever met, and I gave her away. I thought it would help her to have a good life, a normal life. Maybe even marry some nice farmer boy someday. I sent my family money when I could. Every spare coin. But once I got sick, I was kicked out of the brothel. The madame didn't want the other girls catching what I had. Then you know Setanta found me. After the initial shock and joy and confusion, all I could think about was my daughter. Setanta promised we could go get her, that we could raise her as a young woman of the noble class. Maybe turn her if she wanted it later in life or find her a husband of good standing and let her have a life she would enjoy. One where she would never go hungry. We could be a family. But when I went to get her, she was gone."

Marcelle let go of Sarai's hand and got up, pacing at the foot of the bed. Her hands clenched into fists, nails digging into skin and drawing blood that dripped down in a black silhouette created by the light from the hallway.

"My father had recovered. So miraculously," she spat the word. "The neighbors were all gossiping. Everyone knew the girl they'd taken in was a whore's bastard because he would get drunk and complain. My family didn't want to be associated with a whore's bastard. So when I stopped sending them money after a few years…" Marcelle paused, anger flashing red in her eyes. "They sold her. They did to her what they did to me."

"That's horrible," Sarai whispered. "Did you find

her?"

Marcelle shook her head. "I didn't get there in time. All the speed and strength in the world, and it didn't matter because at that point it was too late for her. There's always some human monster with a taste for young flesh. One of them strangled her, left her in an alley. No idea who, and no one cared because she was just a... My baby girl died a whore, alone and afraid in the dark without her mother to hold her."

There was no sound in the room at all. The word whore, it felt like a stab to the gut. It was an insult, but to think of it literally, to think of a poor little girl being subjected to some evil monster and dying at his hands, she couldn't imagine. And to have that little girl be her daughter...

"Marcelle, I'm so sorry," Sarai whispered. She got up and went to take her hands. The blood that smeared against her palms was cold. "You dreamed about that?"

"I'm not done with the story. My dream." She shook her head. "While Setanta slept, I snuck away and returned home." Marcelle closed her eyes. "I slaughtered them, Sarai. I slaughtered them all. I only meant to kill my father, my brothers; the ones responsible. But I was new, and my control wasn't very good. My emotions were erratic, and my bloodlust... One of my sisters-in-law tried to protect them and I killed her first. Then my father. I lost my mind. When I came to, I'd killed my father, my three brothers, their wives... Each of those brothers my parents had deemed more worthy of life and dignity than me and my little girl. As if it was her fault how she was born, my fault what they'd sold me to do. All because my father didn't want a useless daughter eating their food and needing a dowry, taking money away from his alcohol habit." Marcelle opened her eyes as tears streamed from them. "I dreamed of my family's screams, Sarai. The family I killed."

Sarai let go of Marcelle's hands, trying to process what she'd heard.

"And now you're afraid of me. Of what I'm capable of doing," Marcelle said. She laid down on the bed and stared up at the canopy.

"Do you... regret it?"

"Maybe. I didn't then. When they were all dead and I realized what I'd done, I didn't regret it. I felt numb. As if my family were a disease and I'd scrubbed the earth clean of the infection. But they weren't truly the guilty ones, not like my father. Their shredded and drained bodies are my eternal nightmare."

Sarai sat on the edge of the bed. "That's a lot to process." She should hate Marcelle for it. She really should. It was exactly how witches always described vampires, as monstrous bloodsuckers. "I see why you were so freaked out at least. But... I mean, sorry for saying it, but isn't that what new vampires are like? You guys aren't famous for your control."

"That doesn't make the pain stop. Five hundred years later and one silly nightmare about their faces is enough to send me off like some irresponsible idiot, throwing around accusations, assaulting more innocents. Hurting you."

Sarai took a deep breath and shook her head. If Marcelle was a monster, she wasn't much better herself. "I'm not innocent."

Marcelle rolled her eyes, wiping them clear of her tears. "Obviously you are. You didn't curse me. This is self-inflicted."

"I mean, generally speaking, I'm not an innocent person. My dad taught me to hurt people. He wanted me to be like him, have his ideals, so he tried to raise me like him. I know what my powers can do because he made me practice. I've killed people too, people who didn't deserve it. I'd kill them and my dad would praise me. If I didn't, he wouldn't love me. It took me years to stop associating murder with praise." She kicked at the bed half-heartedly, and immediately regretted the action, feeling a sharp pain in her heel where she made contact. "So there. You weren't in control, being a new vampire. I just murdered because I wanted dessert and a pat on the head from my father."

Sarai picked up her spell components and tried to concentrate. After a little while, she summoned the proper magic through the channel, through Hebrew murmurings, and a bay leaf glowed green.

"Put that under your pillow," she instructed as Marcelle accepted the gift. "You won't dream about your past. Or mine. Sorry, was hard to keep focused just on your story."

"I guess we've both done some horrible things."

"Yeah."

Oddly, Marcelle chose that moment to burst into laughter. "I'm supposed to make you like my company, not rant about murdering my family or burst into your bedroom in the middle of the night to punish you for something you didn't even do. I'm terrible at my job lately. And here I am, telling you you're horrible, and so am I."

"Supposed to make me like you, huh?" Sarai said and forced a little smile. "Yeah, you could be sucking up to me a bit more. Bonding over killing people's not going to cut it. I'd like more pampering, maybe a massage."

The vampire lifted an eyebrow. "A massage?"

"I, well, not that I've ever had one, just something people say they like, right?" she said, tugging on a curl of her hair awkwardly. "A-anyway, you seem like you're under more stress right now, you should probably go get one of your human servants to give you one."

"Just might. Does wonders for the rigor mortis."

Sarai turned to look at her as she lay motionless in her bed. "Do you actually get rigor mortis?"

Marcelle sat up in an all too stiff manner, like a zombie corpse rising up off a mortician's slab, then smiled. "Just joshing with you, I don't." She glanced at the door. "I guess I need to get someone to fix that for you. I can find someplace else for you to sleep."

"Got a spare coffin lying around?"

"Oh, aren't you the sassy little thing. No, but you can have my bed if you like. I'll sleep on the couch. Or, try to. Too stressed from all this to think of sleep." Stress. Rosaline had talked about a way to release stress. Sarai's heart rate spiked at the thought.

"Are you all right?" Marcelle asked.

She's reading me, Sarai realized. *She can hear my heart.*

"Can't hide things from you, can I?" she joked.

"Not at all."

She took a few more deep breaths, while the vampire waited patiently. "Can I... I just want to see." Sarai slid closer and grasped Marcelle's cold hand.

"You're trembling, little witch."

"I know."

"Are you afraid?"

"Yes." There was no point in lying.

"Why?"

"I, I was talking with Rosaline earlier. She had some ideas about your eyes turning red. It's not nothing, I know it's not. I know you were lying to me." She took a deep breath. "I think I'd like to try something but I'm afraid."

"Don't be afraid."

It sounded like an invitation, and the look in Marcelle's eyes was expectant. As Sarai watched, the irises shifted in hue, turning red. It was like watching a deep sunset consume a blue sky, desire wiping away the calm. The vampire knew.

Sarai leaned forward and pressed her lips tentatively to Marcelle's. A shock pulsed through her body and made her skin tingle from her head to her toes. Marcelle's lips were so soft, like petals. The men that Sarai had kissed in the past had lips that were coarser, and they'd never smelled good. Like beer and sweat. Marcelle had that now familiar scent of gentle rosewater, and her touch as a cool hand caressed Sarai's cheek was just as delicate.

Then, too soon, Marcelle pulled away. Sarai leaned forward, hungry for the kiss to continue, but was stopped by a finger over her lips, which trailed down to her chin, making her look up. The vampire's ruby lips parted, revealing a pair of sharp points.

"Are you sure you still want to kiss me?" she said, exposed fangs visible as she spoke. "Even like this?"

The red eyes were one thing. Sarai was able to overlook that. But the fangs had tips like needles.

Witches didn't have relationships with vampires because it was taboo. Then again, Sarai's existence was already taboo. What was one more rule broken? If someone as beautiful as Marcelle was interested... She'd already said that she 'played' with others, despite her long-term relationship with Setanta. A little play time could be fun, for both of them.

Still, vampirism aside, she'd never been with another woman before. Not that she hadn't had the thought that some were beautiful and attractive, but her limited experience was only with men. Neither of her sexual encounters had ended well. Both men had lied to her, used her. The first had robbed her, the second had been married without telling her, and neither cared about her. Sarai already knew that the vampires were interested in using her for political purposes, which felt like just another set up to be used. Everyone wanted to use her. Marcelle admitted she was supposed to make friends with her. But maybe Sarai didn't need to trust her. She could use her right back and it could be fun if Sarai could get over the fangs.

"You said it's just a reaction before," she said. "A reaction to my blood?"

"It means you're a very attractive woman, Sarai." Marcelle smirked. "In crude terms, think of it like a vampire erection."

Sarai blushed. "So, you do like me then."

"Was the kiss not proof enough for you?"

She couldn't help but smile at that. Still, the fangs were imposing. She already knew from experience how sharp they could be but kissing with them was different from submitting to a bite. Sarai touched her hand to Marcelle's cheek.

"Let me see them?" she asked softly. Marcelle's lips parted, exposing her fangs. Sarai stared at them. There was security in knowing that this vampire wouldn't hurt her, that she could look at the teeth without fear. She hesitated, then touched her fingertip to one of the teeth. It was smooth, cold. Her fingertip slid down, to carefully touch the end.

"Oh." It pricked her skin without even the slightest pressure, and she pulled her hand back, but Marcelle caught it in one hand, pinching the fingertip so that a single drop of blood swelled there.

"May I?" Marcelle asked.

Without a word, Sarai nodded, then watched as Marcelle wrapped her voluptuous lips around her finger and sucked at the wound. The now familiar tingling graced the pinprick. Sarai barely suppressed an aroused whimper. Her body was aching for more, and Marcelle had to know, with her advanced senses. She gave the small wound a sensual, slow lick before letting go.

"Is this romance for vampires then?" Sarai asked, trying to keep from hyperventilating.

"Sometimes. Do you like it?"

"I'm still figuring that out, I think." The answer was leaning toward yes. "Just... promise me one thing?"

"What is it?"

"Don't bite me or drink my blood without my permission again, okay?"

"I promise. As long as Setanta doesn't order otherwise, I won't bite you again." Her red lips curled into a grin. "Unless you ask nicely."

Sarai blushed. Well, that was the best answer she was going to get. "Y-you think I'll ask you for it?"

"I know you will." Marcelle's strong arms slid around Sarai's waist and pulled her close. She smelled sweet as roses, her closeness was so enticing. "Would you like to come to my room?"

There was only one answer Sarai could give.

Chapter Fifteen: La Petite Mort

Sarai found herself scooped up into her vampire's arms, her head hidden against Marcelle's beautiful soft chest to shield her eyes from the wind as they darted through the palace to the new room. Sarai expected to find herself in the same hall that Bear lived on, but they went a floor above. It was quiet there, and each door was in a different style. Some were plain, some looked medieval, and some looked exquisite. The one they stopped in front of was a pair of white double doors with ornate gold designs in the wood. Very elegant, very baroque.

"It's a little ostentatious, I know, but it makes me think of Versailles," Marcelle explained as she opened the doors to reveal an apartment that matched the doors. The colors were blue, gold, and white, and the elegant furniture included a boudoir, sitting area, a record player, and a four-poster canopy bed.

"Wow." Sarai was star struck. "You, uh, you've got a nice place here." It felt like she'd walked into a room for royalty from centuries past. The sitting room was lavish, with textiled sofas sporting lion's paws for feet. Drapes covered tall windows that matched the sofas, and the wallpaper looked custom printed to match the renaissance feel of the room. There was a fireplace as well, framed with marble. Above the mantle was an old painting of two figures sitting in stiff, beautiful French clothes. The faces were recognizable, even under the powder and costumes: it was Marcelle and Setanta.

Sarai stopped and stared at the portrait. "That's... cool." Seeing the two together like that knowing what she knew about their relationship gave her an uncomfortable feeling. It didn't matter for now though; she was here to enjoy herself.

"It's a little outdated," Marcelle said with a sigh as she looked at the painting. "Sentimental, I suppose."

"It's nice."

"Ignore it." Marcelle stepped behind Sarai, and the mortal's heart raced as a hand trailed from the small of her back to stop at the waistline of her pants, dancing against the thin line of exposed skin in a way that made it difficult for Sarai to remember how to breathe. "First, tell me what you want."

"Uh... like, kissing?"

"Obviously more kissing." Marcelle moved in closer and whispered in her ear. "What else?"

"Is-is fun an acceptable answer?"

"Fun is always an acceptable answer to a vampire. Have you been with others before," Marcelle said, her hands sliding a little lower to rest on Sarai's hips. "For fun, or otherwise?"

"I've had a few one-night stands." Her hands were making concentration difficult. "Never went well, but I like fun while it lasts. I might regret the people afterwards, but I never regret the experience."

"Men or women?"

"Men. You," Sarai cleared her throat awkwardly. "You would be my first woman."

"I'm honored." She found herself with her back

slammed against a wall, Marcelle pressed against her, lips inches away. "Then, if it's what you want, let's have fun."

Sarai squeaked against a new kiss as Marcelle picked her up by her thighs, so that her legs were wrapped around the vampire. She was drunk on the sensations, happily allowing Marcelle to take control. Her hands explored the woman's sides, lingering on the curves, clinging to her shoulders, sinking into soft hair.

Suddenly, they were moving, and Sarai found herself gasping on her back, a soft comforter of a bed under her. Her entire body tensed. This was what she wanted, and it was happening. Despite fear, her leg rose up to wrap around the vampire, to keep them locked together.

"Tell me if you want me to stop," Marcelle said as she looked down at her, eyes red. Sarai felt a cool hand slide under her shirt against the smooth skin of her waist.

"I want more," Sarai demanded as firmly as she could considering how nervous she felt.

"Your wish is my command," Marcelle said. "The moment it's too much, say the word. I won't bite." She laughed a little. "Would you like to see me?" Her hand left Sarai's waist and gripped the tie on her own robe.

Sarai's eyes scanned up and down the beautiful being with need, her private, feminine places clenching with excitement, and nodded.

Marcelle stepped back away from the bed and slowly untied the robe. The sleeves slipped down her shoulders but before it could uncover anything, she turned around and removed it, dropping it to the floor.

Sarai was hyper self-conscious of her breathing,

her racing heart, knowing that the vampire could hear it all, but she didn't have control of her response. The hourglass shape of Marcelle's body before her, exposed and yet teasing in the way she hid herself by turning around, looked like art.

Marcelle turned around, her hand gracefully covering her chest. Sarai looked up and was captivated by the look of confidence and the promise of sexuality in the vampire's red eyes. She lowered her arms, revealing pale, smooth breasts, pink nipples pointed with arousal.

"Oh my god."

"No gods here, little witch," Marcelle said with a smirk. "Only me."

She slid off her underwear, leaning over as she did to show off the swell of her curves, then stood up naked, with surprisingly no hair between her legs. As Sarai's heart pounded and her mind panicked about if she should be embarrassed about her own lack of grooming in that area, Marcelle slinked back onto the bed and lay out exposed, her curves accentuated to perfection by her pose.

"You're beautiful," Sarai whispered. She reached out to touch but stopped as if she were in a museum and there should be some glass between her hand and something so perfect. "I don't know what to do. Before, the guy would kind of just do what he wanted. And I don't know how to have sex without, well, you know."

"A cock involved?" Marcelle teased. Sarai blushed but nodded. "Have these men not pleasured you well? Fingers, tongues? That's part of sex."

"Fingers, yes. Mostly by myself. Tongues—" Sarai cleared her throat. "No. Well, one sort of tried. More like he was checking off steps on a list. Wasn't very good. They were more focused on themselves and their, uh, cocks."

Marcelle rolled her eyes. "How typical." She sat up and Sarai found herself on her back, looking up at the naked woman and hyper aware of the way Marcelle's body pressed against her. "I promise, you will not leave this room unsatisfied."

Sarai's hand found a pale breast. It was cold as the rest of the woman, but soft. She'd felt her own plenty before, but it was different to feel the firm yet giving body of someone else.

"You're soft," she said.

"Women tend to be softer than men."

Her fingers found Marcelle's rosy nipple, and the resulting moan made her body clench with need. She leaned in for another kiss. Her hands moved as if they had a mind of their own, in a blissful daze and half drunk on her own desire between the kiss and the caresses.

"You need to take off your night shift," Marcelle ordered. "Or I am going to rip the clothes from your body."

Sarai wanted nothing more. She grinned mischievously. "Yeah?"

"Oh, you like that thought, do you?" Marcelle's hand slid under the loose shirt the witch wore. "Do you want me to strip you?" The hand moved lower and gripped the hem of Sarai's pants, and her heart skipped a beat.

"Wait, I…"

Marcelle stopped, frozen as she waited for the rest of the sentence.

"I, I'm not like you."

"Undead? I assumed."

"No, I don't shave. Down there."

Marcelle laughed. "Little witch, I don't care one way or the other."

"But you…"

"I'd rather not discuss the grooming habits of medieval prostitutes, Sarai. It kills the mood completely. Now, sit up," she said. Sarai complied, and Marcelle leaned forward to whisper a single word. "Good."

Clothing tore like tissue paper in the vampire's hands, and a blend of cool air and arousal rushed over Sarai's body. She gripped the bed under her to keep from trying to cover her breasts, reminding herself that Marcelle had already seen everything. Yet, in the new context, she felt so flawed.

"Do you like them?" she asked, worried that someone as physically perfect as a vampire might find a human's body substandard.

"Oh yes. Beautiful," Marcelle breathed, and Sarai found herself laying on her back again, the naked temptress's mouth covering one of her nipples. *Beautiful.* Marcelle called her beautiful. It relaxed her, and Sarai closed her eyes, focusing on the sensation of an expert tongue swirling against her, cool hands roaming across her skin. She needed to hold onto this moment. Put it into a bottle to save forever, to experience again and again.

Intoxicated by touch, Sarai's hands struggled for more, searching for any unexplored skin they could find. Cold fingertips found her pants and they were shredded in moments as the fingers slipped further down. Pleasure sparked with the lightest application of pressure, and Sarai moaned. She remembered that sensation when her previous partners had pawed at her. But there was something far more attentive and skilled in Marcelle's movements. Her fingertips moved in small circles, and Sarai's hips buckled upward, the cold heightened the sensation.

"Spread your legs."

Sarai didn't need to be told twice. The commanding tone of her new lover's voice thrilled all on its own. Marcelle's fingers continued to play as kisses trailed down from her lips and neck to her chest. She was attentive in the best ways. Her tongue flicked pleasure through Sarai's nipples and her lips caressed the sensitive underside of her breasts. A sharp fang rested against Sarai's nipple, but before she could fear what might happen, it pulled away and was replaced with the cool attention of Marcelle's tongue. The spark of fright heightened her senses just as much as the cold, and her body jolted as if a bolt of magic had shot through her every nerve, electrifying her skin. She wanted to beg for more, but all Sarai could do was whimper.

The vampire curled like a serpent, sliding down her body, adorning it with light kisses down to her inner thigh. Heart racing, Sarai thrust her fingers into Marcelle's black hair and tried to push that perfect, porcelain face with its ruby lips against her sex.

As soon as Marcelle's tongue touched her, Sarai knew the difference between a lover who cared about their partner's pleasure and one who didn't. Her former lover had tentatively poked at her, as if a few almost clinical licks were significant at all. He'd just wanted to do the deed and get on with his own pleasure. Marcelle wanted to taste it all. She was eager and enthusiastic, French kissing Sarai, her tongue exploring every part of her without any hesitation at all.

"That feels amazing," Sarai gasped.

"I know just how your body works, Sarai. I can read your responses, know what you want. I know how to make you feel paradise like you've never dreamed of before."

She believed it.

"Don't you dare stop."

Marcelle grinned, her fangs and lips glistening, and two fingers spread apart Sarai's lips. Her tongue began again, smooth and slow. It found its way up, then began to lick that one, perfect spot. Sarai clenched her fists, moaning. Her toes curled and muscles tensed to keep from kicking out uncontrollably.

"*Ton corps est à moi, ma chérie. Ma petite sorcière.*" The foreign words washed over Sarai in a seductive wave. Then the finger slipped inside her. "There's a lovely spot inside you," Marcelle whispered. "Just… here." The finger curled and stroked a spot she had never reached on her own. "It gives such sensations when touched just right, doesn't it?"

Sarai's breath quickened and her fists held the bed cover in an iron grip as she stared up at the textiled bed canopy and drapes, at the engraved oak wood, at the gold trim with tassels. The tassels swayed back and forth with the slightest, most minute movement, rocked by the motions on the bed. How did such a small movement of something that wasn't even related to sex look so sensual?

A second finger pushed inside, and she arched off

the bed. Her moans raised in volume with every new spike of bliss, and her legs trembled when the perfection that was Marcelle's mouth covered her clitoris.

The fingers moved in and out of Sarai, slow at first, as slickness dripped against her skin and rubbed against her thighs, then faster. Again and again, they drove inside, precise and determined, all while Marcelle's mouth worked wonders against the throbbing button just above her opening. Sarai's eyes rolled in pleasure and her mouth opened, but the sound was caught somewhere between her vocal cords and her lips. There was tension in her muscles, in her legs, and deep inside her body. It squeezed against the intrusion, feeling stretched in a way that almost hurt from how good it felt. The pleasure built in her body, like pressure behind a dam.

"Marcelle," she managed to gasp. Tears formed in her eyes, and she burst, shouting in shock. It was a convulsion that tore through her, left her gasping for air and withering on the bed.

Then it didn't stop. She looked down wide-eyed at Marcelle, fear tingling in her limbs. She couldn't handle more, but the vampire wasn't letting up. If anything, her fingers moved faster. Just a little faster than humanly possible, her tongue almost vibrating with speed.

"Nonono, wait, I can't–" The wave hit Sarai again as another explosion erupted within her, and she screamed, throwing her head back as her body thrashed. Her hand reached down to grab at Marcelle's head. She couldn't tell if she was trying to push her down or pull her away, only clenched her fingers in her hair.

Slowly, Marcelle's attentions and the clenching

ended, and Sarai laid there panting. There was a pure, blank numbness in her, and it felt wonderful. She moaned as the fingers pulled out from her, and after a minute of recovery, looked down to see Marcelle's smirking, red-eyed face half wet with feminine nectar.

"You taste amazing," Marcelle said. She held up her fingers, covered in smokey liquid. Sarai's heart skipped a beat as she watched Marcelle lick them clean.

"Never had two at a time like that before," she managed to say. "Always just stopped after the first one by myself. Is that normal?"

"It is when I'm your partner," Marcelle smirked. "Have you ever tasted yourself?"

Sarai stared. "Uh…"

Marcelle brushed her fingers against Sarai's wet sex and slid herself up her body, their lips inches apart. The vampire was already the embodiment of sex itself, but the sight of her crawling up her body threatened to cause a third wave of pleasure all over again. Fingers touched Sarai's lips.

"Try it."

Sarai's mouth opened, her eyes never leaving Marcelle's. She allowed the finger to slip halfway in before closing her lips around it and licked. It was a new flavor, and an oddly pleasant one. She closed her eyes and swirled her tongue around Marcelle's finger.

In the darkness, she could focus on the taste, and the feel of Marcelle's movements. The finger slipped away, to be replaced with a needful pair of lips that tasted like sex. Sarai moaned into Marcelle's mouth. Tasting sex made her want more, and her tongue pushed against those lips, against the vampire's tongue, even daring to slide against her lover's pointed teeth. She wanted everything. The taste, the kiss, tongue, maybe even fangs. She wanted to taste Marcelle in the deepest way possible.

"I want a turn," Sarai said when she had a moment to breathe.

"I'd like that," Marcelle replied, and gave her a sensual kiss that lingered. "Though don't be disappointed if I don't react quite as quickly as you did. I'm not as easy to satisfy."

The warning scared Sarai a little, but also provided her new determination. She gave Marcelle one more slow kiss, then pushed her onto her back and laid on top. She could feel Marcelle resist, then move as if guided rather than pushed. As she fell to the vampire's breasts, she remembered what Marcelle had done earlier, when she kissed hers and put them in her mouth. If it had felt so good for her, it had to be pleasurable. She looked up nervously before she opened her mouth to lick and nibble at the gorgeous curves. Her tongue played around the nipple, then she closed her lips around the hard bud and licked with passion.

A hand rested against the back of Sarai's head. "You're a fast learner," Marcelle said. "And so eager."

Sarai continued to suck with enthusiasm. Her hand grabbed at the other breast and squeezed. After a few seconds, she smiled up at her new lover. "I want to be good for you." Her mouth returned to the nipple, but her eyes remained on Marcelle's.

"You are. You're making me wet." She winked.

Sarai's smile returned. She unlatched and sat back, looking down at Marcelle's spread legs, getting her first good look at the glistening beauty between them. "Oh," she whispered, and just stared. What if she wasn't good? What if she tried to give Marcelle pleasure, and failed?

"Don't be afraid," Marcelle coaxed, obviously reading Sarai's emotions. "Touch me."

Trying to stay calm, she touched her finger against the hairless, pink lips, and pressed in deep. As Marcelle sighed in pleasure, Sarai leaned forward and pressed her tongue to the swollen nub. She hadn't expected to enjoy the taste so much and found herself licking in an almost ravenous fashion to drink those drops of nectar.

"There you go, your body knows what to do," Marcelle purred, and her insides twitched against Sarai's fingers, giving her a spark of delight. "You feel... you feel so warm."

It did take longer for Marcelle to reach a climax than it had for Sarai. Her fingertips started to feel a little like raisins, but she didn't mind. She could feel the tension inside Marcelle, feel it mounting. Finally, the vampire's body froze, then buckled. She gasped and her eyes rolled back as the spasms struck, and Sarai felt almost as if their power might crush her fingers. As it died down, the vampire looked down with a smile, then pulled her up for a kiss. "Not bad," she said, and licked a stream of feminine liquid from Sarai's chin, who blushed with the heat of the sun in response. "You got very into that."

Sarai giggled, and kissed back, wanting to ravage those lips. She could taste both of their sexes at the same time and loved it. Then, something sharped grazed her lip, and the taste changed. They both froze as the thin line of blood swelled, then healed thanks to Sarai's power. Marcelle pulled back. The skin tingled as she tried to make sense of what had happened.

"I didn't mean to do that," Marcelle said. "I'm sorry."

Sarai nodded. It hadn't hurt that much, and that was food for thought. An idea struck her, and a smirk formed. She pushed forward, her mouth meeting Marcelle's neck to kiss her, then clamped her teeth down.

Marcelle gasped and arched forward, but it quickly turned into a moan. The vampire's arms tightened around her, and Sarai felt nails in her back. The sharp pain felt... good. Exhilarating. There was a new level introduced to the intimacy, and Sarai wanted it.

"Little vixen," Marcelle purred, and pushed Sarai back, sitting over her with a pale thigh on each side of her face. The scent of sex was her wine, and Sarai was drunk. "Ready to go again?"

"Definitely."

Chapter Sixteen: Separate Showers

"Go to the bathroom," Marcelle said as the two women lay in bed, the witch's heavy breathing and racing heart the only significant noise in the room. An hour of moaning made the near silence very loud in its own way. And there had been plenty of moaning: Sarai showed that she was capable of easy, quick orgasms, almost the exact opposite of Marcelle who historically would sometimes take between half an hour to a full hour with just manual stimulation from a mere mortal.

"Mm?"

"Human women need to use the restroom after sex," she explained. "Otherwise, you risk getting an infection."

"But I can't move. You made my legs turn to jelly."

Marcelle smirked a little to herself. "Well, when you can, get up and go to the restroom."

Sarai hadn't been the best sex she'd ever had, not by far, but it was hard to compare to vampires' performance in bed, so it was foolish to juxtapose the two experiences. The mortal's technique was clumsy and imprecise, yet so lovely in its fumbling naïveté. Marcelle adored it, adored how passionate she was. It was such a nice change of pace.

Sarai groaned as she sat up, then slowly got to her feet. "I'm going to be so sore tomorrow if I'm already feeling it like this," she said happily.

"Likely. Now go to the bathroom before I worry about you."

She nodded, and hobbled in the right direction, disappearing as she closed the door behind her.

Marcelle sat up, leaning back against the headboard. This hadn't been according to plan. If the witch's blood hadn't been so sweet and tempting, she could have suppressed her desire and kept Sarai from ever noticing any giveaways like her red eyes. It wasn't as if she hadn't torn a few witches apart and drank their blood in a fight, so she wasn't unfamiliar with the unique and desirable sensation of witch blood, but Sarai was in a class all her own. Marcelle wanted her.

It was all so unprofessional of her. She supposed getting Sarai in bed could help the girl trust them and be more willing to work with vampires toward the purebloods' goals. Marcelle had used sex to manipulate people and get what she wanted in the past, but for the first time in a very long time, she felt ashamed for thinking it. Sarai was different from some lecherous politician or horny, uncooperative prisoner. She was vulnerable in a way that made Marcelle want to protect her.

There was the sound of a flushing toilet, rushing water from the sink, then Sarai came back, still smiling. She was exquisite in her newfound naked confidence. Marcelle needed her.

Sarai plopped back onto the bed, and curled up against Marcelle, while also pulling a blanket over them. Marcelle wrapped an arm around her, holding her close. The warmth was the most beautiful part of being with a mortal. The cold of her own body was something she hardly noticed most of the time, but whenever she felt warmth, it radiated through her, made her feel amazing. She stretched her body out, pressing against Sarai.

"Am I too cold for you?" Marcelle asked.

"A little. The blanket kinda balances it out. I feel so good," Sarai said, and a kiss landed on Marcelle's neck. She closed her eyes. Those lips had such heat to them. She craved their touch. "Thank you, for this. It's been a while since I've felt like I could have fun."

"It's good to have fun."

"Just, just for fun."

Marcelle hesitated, analyzing the tone of Sarai's voice, the way her heart and breath changed.

"You want more than just fun?" Marcelle asked, trying to keep her voice casual.

Sarai said nothing for a very pregnant minute of silence.

"I... don't know. You're a vampire. Even just for fun, I'm not supposed to be doing this."

"Do you care?"

"I don't know if I've decided yet."

The silence returned.

"I'll be blunt," Marcelle said. "I don't mind keeping this as only sexual entertainment. I've done that before. I have no qualms about it. But I do like the idea of getting to know you better. Would you allow me to court you?"

"Court me?"

"Take you on a date. I believe I owe you dinner? My pussy doesn't count as eating out."

Sarai laughed, her voice vibrating against Marcelle's skin. "All right. Yeah, you owe me dinner.

We'll just have to see how that goes." She yawned. "Think I'm passing out right now."

Marcelle could feel the unique exhaustion of the undead tingling in her own limbs, calling her to sleep to let the living blood she'd consumed rest. "Sleep sounds like a good idea," she agreed.

The pair were soon curled together in unconsciousness, after a quick dash from Marcelle to get both their spelled bay leaves and place them under the pillows to ensure a good night's sleep. When they woke up, Marcelle found Sarai's big, brown eyes staring at her.

"Good morning, beautiful," Marcelle said. "See something you like?"

"I wanted to see what color your eyes are when you wake up."

"What color are they?"

"Blue. They're pretty that way."

"And when they're red?"

"Well…" Sarai's eyes widened as she watched the eye color change. "Scary."

"But," Marcelle said as she listened to Sarai's body respond, watched her pupils dilate. "That excites you?" The witch didn't have to respond for Marcelle to know the answer.

"Do you… need blood in the morning?" Sarai almost whispered.

"I'm still set from yesterday. But I will never say no to a chance to taste you."

Sarai pursed her lips. "Not now. Maybe after you buy me dinner."

Marcelle laughed, and kissed those adorable, pursed lips, lingering to enjoy their heat. "That is fair, my little witch, *ma petite sorcière*." Sarai returned the kiss with need, but Marcelle put up a hand to stop her.

"Is something wrong?"

"I have duties to tend to, unfortunately. Why don't you take a nice cold shower?"

"Do you have to go?"

"Trust me, I would much rather lose myself here with you."

Sarai sighed but complied. "See you soon, I hope." She disappeared into the bathroom, and the water began to run.

Marcelle threw on some comfortable clothes, combed her hair, then left.

As she did, she realized she should have showered. Every vampire she'd come in contact with would know she'd slept with someone from the scent and be able to tell from that alone precisely who her partner had been. She couldn't go back into her room to shower with Sarai there. If they showered together, Marcelle would never leave.

Instead, she made her way to her sire's chambers, next door to her own for convenience due to her position as his official mistress. Other rooms in the royal wing included the reigning king and queen's separate chambers, their daughter Artemisia's room, Setanta's, and multiple empty rooms that had once belonged to various deceased members of the pureblood family. A walk in the royal wing was like a walk through a memorial.

Once inside, she was relieved to see that he wasn't home. That saved her from the awkward conversation, and she could slip into the luxurious shower. Her own shower was lovely, of course, but the pureblood's shower was something else. It had excellent water pressure, excellent space, and water that ran not just from a large shower head at the top, but also from the sides of the shower, creating an immersive experience. She turned up the water so it was nice and hot, and suppressed a moan as the sensation seeped into her skin and down to her bones, chasing away the perpetual cold of undeath.

Over the rush of the water, she just heard the faint sound of the front door opening and sighed. Now she had to explain herself.

"Normally I wouldn't question a beautiful naked woman in my shower," said an amused voice. "But I have to wonder what's wrong with your own?"

Marcelle smiled a little and wiped the fog from the glass of the shower door, resting her body against it, and looking over the pureblood prince smirking at her as he leaned against the sink counter.

"Maybe I just felt like breaking into your room?"

"I could punish you for that."

She grinned. "You could."

Setanta chuckled and approached, his finger running down the fogged glass as if caressing the shape of her body. "The problem with punishing you is that you enjoy it too much."

"That's a problem?" She winked at him, then began to rinse out her hair as he watched. She liked this better than formal meetings in his office. When they were alone, they could almost pretend they were equals, rather than royal and servant. She liked that. Almost as much as she liked him taking command and dripping hot wax down her cold body before he whipped it from her skin. Her consent to the submission, sex, and pain gave her ultimate control, even as he dominated her.

"So why are you in my shower, Marcelle?"

"I needed to shower and there's someone using the one in my room."

"Sarai?"

She glanced at him. She'd expected much more disapproval in his tone. "Yes."

"Are you doing it to manipulate her?"

"No." She might have been insulted if she hadn't used that exact tactic in the past. "She... is an enchanting little thing. I don't know that I've ever been around someone whose scent draws me in so completely." She almost added, no wonder Nicolas snapped and tried to take her, but decided it was best not to mention the late monster.

"Don't break the poor girl's heart. I'd like her to be at least a little emotionally stable," Setanta said. He pulled a towel from a bar on the wall and offered it as Marcelle stepped out. She nodded in thanks, and acknowledgement of his words.

"Do you think she'll help us? Her father's side has a reputation, and other witches aren't too fond of her skill set."

"We don't need her to be a true ambassador and trusted by all witches," Setanta said. "We need her to get our foot in the door. Literally. I can handle the diplomacy after that."

Marcelle tucked the towel around her waist and paused, looking down at the water dripping from her hair. A pit formed in her stomach at the mention of diplomacy. "Have you... given other diplomatic problems anymore thought?"

"You mean, have I chosen a queen?"

Marcelle said nothing. She nodded and went to the vanity, where she kept a brush. A few strands were pulled out as she worked through knots and turned to dust that collected in the bristles, replaced by new hair that grew to the same exact length.

"I've narrowed it down to either Xian MeiXiang or Meritaten of Kemet. The Xian Empire is one we could use a formal alliance with considering their growing global influence, but I've had a strong friendship with Meritaten's grandmother since I visited the Nile centuries ago. Marrying her would cement that bond between our families. I sent messages to both countries to enter final negotiation stages, and of course an invitation so I can meet both women at the Midnight Festival."

"Meeting someone before getting married is a good idea."

"Marcelle," he said softly, stepping closer and taking her brush from her hand, locking eyes with her through the mirror. "You know I'd pick you if I could."

She looked at him longingly. It wasn't that she was bothered by the idea of sharing Setanta with another woman. She had shared him plenty of times in the past, with men and women alike. Relationships, sex, love; all were free to be given to whomever either of them liked. And with a political arrangement, his future wife could bring her own vampire lover or lovers to live with her, just as Setanta's step-mother had when she'd married the reigning king, Lugh. No, what bothered Marcelle was that their relationship could never be more because she was undead. Because her body couldn't change, and so she couldn't give him the heirs vital to the continued existence of the vampire kingdom. With how few purebloods of his line were left after World War II—only his father, new half-sister, and himself–heirs were needed, or neighboring kingdoms would think them easy targets.

She just had to fall in love with one of the only vampires she could never marry.

"I know."

Setanta began brushing his fingers through her hair, and she closed her eyes to enjoy the gentle way he cared for her long tresses.

"I should get downstairs," she sighed.

"You don't need to continue with the interrogations. With the information we have, I know enough. There's more to worry about than the Vasi are aware of, and with Sarai out of their hands and their laboratory destroyed, the threat from them is subdued for now. Let Artemisia execute the two who are less forthcoming. They're hers for what they did. Did you speak to Sarai about the one that belongs to her?"

"I mentioned it. A lot has happened though, she may have forgotten."

Setanta nodded. "Bring her as planned to the terrace at noon today."

"As you wish, Sire."

Chapter Seventeen: Lunch with a Pureblood

Sarai fidgeted with the end of a frizzy braid, then brushed it behind her ear to try and keep composed at the prospect of meeting Setanta again. She knew he wanted to talk to her about some political nonsense she had no interest participating in, yet part of her was afraid. She'd slept with his mistress. She knew Marcelle said they had an arrangement, but maybe there had been some miscommunication, and now the prince was angry at her? He had to know. His knight commander wouldn't keep anything from him, after all.

If he was mad, he didn't seem to show it. The place Marcelle had brought her to was beautiful: a terrace with a view overlooking the palace gardens. There was a table set for a meal and chairs for two people to sit. She could smell the food all the way from the door; grilled vegetables, stew with a mouthwatering aroma, a basket of what had to be fresh baked bread, and a pitcher of water awaited her. Oddly, there were two sets of plates and utensils.

The pureblood himself stood against the balcony rail, the sun illuminating his crimson hair, so it looked as if it were aglow in the form of a fiery halo. He gave her a slight, closed-lipped smile.

"Sarai, it's good to see you again. Apologies for our last encounter, I know it wasn't to your liking. I hope we can mend this. Please, make yourself comfortable." He went to the table and pulled out a chair for her. Marcelle gave her a gentle nudge forward, and Sarai sat as he pushed the chair in under her.

"Thanks. For the invitation," Sarai said. She felt the urge to sit up straight, to pretend she was fancy in some way to measure up to the people and setting around her. She glanced at the utensils laid out before her. They looked so proper. If her host hadn't been a vampire, she would have guessed they were silver. The plates had what looked like real gold along the antique edges. She wondered how much they'd get in a pawn shop.

He sat across from her and gestured to the food. "I hope you'll enjoy the stew. It's one of my favorite dishes, but if you're not partial to it I can have something else brought up from the kitchens," he said.

She looked at it cautiously. It smelled good, but a little unusual, and she wasn't sure what sort of meat was in it. "Is it pork?" she asked.

"Venison."

"Oh." She frowned, trying to remember if deer was on the list of kosher animals. She'd never encountered it before, so hadn't a clue.

"Is something wrong?"

"No, just, can't remember if it's kosher."

He nodded. "You're Jewish?"

"Sorta? I do the bare minimum. No pig, no shellfish. Makes me feel close to my mom." Deciding ignorance was bliss, she ladled a bowl full of the delicious smelling stew for herself and grabbed a roll. It was so fresh it was still warm.

"I won't pretend to be an expert, but I believe venison can be kosher. Though this wasn't slaughtered according to any religious rules."

"Works for me then."

"I don't believe I've heard of a Jewish Reinhart witch before," he said.

"Yeah, not their favorite. They were after my mom's power. Her being Jewish just meant it was more okay to keep her locked up like livestock." She shrugged and took a bite of the bread.

Setanta filled a bowl for himself. She stared, half chewed bread sitting in her mouth, as he took a spoonful. Then he ate it.

She looked at her bowl skeptically. It could be some sort of trick, to get her to eat vampire blood. No, it was unlikely. She couldn't think of a reason for it to be. As she pushed around the contents with her own spoon, all she saw was meat, potatoes, carrots, celery, onions–all standard stew materials. There was a flash of something maybe red, but upon inspection it was a piece of a tomato. The strongest scents were of thyme and, ironically enough, garlic.

How odd.

Sarai took a taste, and her mouth was delighted by the flavors. It wasn't spicy or overwhelming, but the flavor was strong and hearty.

Satisfied that the stew was indeed a stew, she asked the obvious question, "You can eat?"

"I'm a special kind of vampire," he said without elaboration, and took a sip of water. "I assume you received your invitation from Marcelle?"

She nodded. "I'm even getting a dress made."

"I'm sure you'll be lovely. Sophie mentioned to me she was excited about the prospect of dressing someone such as yourself."

"A witch?" Sarai mused. "We have the same body parts to dress, as far as I know."

"Someone historic. Sophie does love the spotlight for her work."

That made her shift a little in her seat, as if the discomfort was something physical she could fix.

"I'm not sure I should be in the spotlight, sir." She put down her spoon and looked up at him. Dancing around issues wasn't her style. "Is the food and the dress and everything supposed to be bribery, to get me to work with you?"

Setanta smiled. "Is it working?"

Sarai snorted. "No stew is that good. Especially after you had Marcelle make a meal of me. You'll have to do better." She pushed her bowl away a little to emphasize the point.

"I can do that." He picked up a book she hadn't noticed leaning against the table leg and held it out for her across the table.

The moment she laid eyes on the leather-bound book, she could feel the magic. It was old, older than any magical object she'd ever seen. She reached out with her gloved hand, using her focus.

"*Lirot ha'emet*," she said, channelling her magic and intent to cast the spell. Her eyes widened as the knowledge flooded her. It was a grimoire, as old as the first books ever written, protected from decay with proper witch enchantments far beyond her capabilities, and overflowing with magic. Grimoires were prized possessions in families, passed down through generations, containing knowledge specific to their line, and spells and potions developed by ancestors. They were rare considering how many witches throughout history had lost family and homes. The older, the rarer.

"How can you have something like this?" she whispered, her hand hovering over the book, almost afraid to touch it. "Is this what I think it is?"

"It is a grimoire," he confirmed. "It originally belonged to the woman I told you of, whose powers mirrored yours."

"Then…" It would be full of knowledge about her powers, how to utilize them best, how to incorporate them into other aspects of her craft. If Sarai were a cartoon, she might have licked her lips with greed; there was no possible better bribe than what was in front of her.

"You can look, you know," he said. "No strings attached just yet."

Sarai hesitated, then took it from his hands and opened the front cover. Her hopes were dashed when she saw a strange script that looked like a variety of grouped vertical and diagonal lines drawn across rows of horizontal lines. Of course. If it was as old as it felt, there was no way for it to be in any form of modern English.

"I can have it translated from the Ogham," Setanta said.

Any witch worth their magic would have cut off a limb for the opportunity. But there was going to be a catch. She flipped the cover shut and met his red gaze. "And all I have to do is…?"

"I was hoping you would be willing to help us contact other witches," Setanta said.

"Look, I'm not a diplomat or anything. Other witches don't even like me. I tried to go to my mother's people, and they wouldn't let me in because of what I can do," she explained, ignoring the pang of pain in her chest as she recalled the rejection. "Their land is literally warded to expel someone like me. Good witches don't raise dead bodies."

"Gray witches do." He nodded toward the grimoire still in her hands, and she clenched the sides. Gray witches... She'd never heard that term before, but wanted everything to do with it.

"Can't you just go ask to talk to them on your own?" she asked a little desperately.

"That's neither safe nor possible. You are familiar with the myth that vampires cannot enter a building without an invitation?"

Sarai knew exactly what he was talking about. There were spells that kept out specific types of people or creatures. Such spells would ward against things like disease, rival covens, specific bloodlines, and the undead. None could enter without an invitation.

"I know it's not fiction," she told him. "Undead can't enter any coven with decent protection enchantments."

"Yes. Which means I can't send my knights or nobility in my place to establish contact. A pureblood like myself would need to be directly involved in any negotiations and have some way to ensure I wouldn't be attacked on sight," he said.

"If you're trying to ask me to get you through a spell like that, I can't counter an anti-undead protective spell cast by any decent coven, no matter what bribes you offer. I don't have that kind of spell power or knowledge."

"I know. That's not what I'm asking. All I want is for you to stand next to me when I go to Ellis Island."

She'd never been herself, but the Ellis Coven was both famous and infamous among witches. Sarai had considered trying to reach them once, before she'd settled a life of quietly hiding among humans. Located in a pocket dimension accessible through magic on Ellis Island, they were known for welcoming outcasts, advocating against the sort of power-based arranged marriages, and forced pregnancies her father's coven adored. That made them famous. What made them infamous was being open to accepting witches with more taboo gifts. If any decent coven would be willing to listen to a vampire, it would be them. At least, based on their reputation.

"I... don't think you'd be able to get in anyway though, right?" she said. "I mean, big covens have defenses in place that keep out anyone but witches, so humans don't wander in. Not that you're human, but you're not a witch. I don't even know if you'd be able to set foot on the human's side of Ellis Island since any coven like that would protect themselves against vampires. Forget about getting to the witch side."

Setanta smiled. "Why do you think I have a witch's grimoire?"

Sarai stared at him. No, that couldn't be right. Sure, grimoires were passed down through generations of the same family, but vampires weren't witches. She looked back at Marcelle, standing professionally by the door like the guard she was. No, she wasn't a witch. That was obvious. Marcelle was a risen dead body, with her soul and mind intact. But Setanta was alive. His skin was lukewarm and he ate human food.

"Stolen, or a gift at best. You can't be a witch," she managed to say. "Vampires aren't witches. I mean, I guess you could turn a witch, but…" Sarai frowned as she tried to figure it out. "Are you what happens when a witch gets turned into a vampire?"

"No, but that's a good guess. I was born this way." He smiled a little. "When people fight, they demonize each other and neglect knowledge of how they're connected. After hundreds of years, it's forgotten. There are more similarities between us than you've been taught."

"Similarities? But you are a vampire, aren't you?"

"According to the last few centuries. It's a relatively new term. You have more than one ability, don't you?" Setanta asked.

"I can heal and… raise…" Sarai stared at him in disbelief.

"Witches around the world for all of time have crafted their families using magic and arranged marriages to create powerful offspring," he said. "The term 'vampire' is more appropriate for Marcelle, or any of those who are undead. Purebloods are different. We are the result of witches playing with selective breeding and blood rituals. My father was the result of such techniques, the first pureblood of our bloodline. Simplified, all pureblood vampires are witches who have more than one ability, in a specific configuration."

Sarai stood up and held out her hand clad in her magical focus.

"*Lirot ha'emet.*" See the truth.

She reached out with her power, funneled through the focus, to analyze him as he sat calmly, and her eyes widened. While he was warded against spells, what he wore was less protected. The gold torque necklace around his neck was enchanted, she could feel it. Not only that, but she could feel that he had been the one to enchant it. How had she not noticed something like that earlier? That had to be why she hadn't been able to cause any harm to him with her power the day before. He was a witch, with magical protections.

"You're telling the truth," she whispered. "You can cast spells?"

"Yes, and no. Spells aren't your strongest point as far as magic goes, am I right?"

"Yes… because I have two powers, most of my magic energy gets put into that."

"It's the same with purebloods. We *can* cast spells, but our ability to do so is significantly limited in comparison to other more typical witches. It's also why silver burns my skin, and the skin of made vampires, instead of just nullifying my abilities. There's more raw power for it to react to."

It made sense. She sat down hard, staring at the grimoire. How much else of what she thought she knew was wrong? Had she been lied to, or did everyone just forget over time? It seemed like a very important thing to remember.

"So, you wanting to ally with witches isn't a case of vampires wanting to use witches or trick me into helping you get past protection spells," Sarai said. "You want to reconnect with your people."

"Perhaps in part, though my primary goal is uniting against the Vasi. I won't pretend to you otherwise."

Defeating the Vasi was fine by her. And if anyone knew how it stung to be rejected by the people who should embrace her, Sarai did. So many witches wanted nothing to do with anything that might be related to dark magic, out of fear and ignorance, without even considering that the people born with those dark gifts had no choice in the matter. Setanta was someone who could understand that better than anyone.

Sarai looked up at him, and handed back the grimoire, fingertips lingering on the ancient cover. "I'll help you." She smiled a little. "But I still want a translation of that, I'm not completely altruistic."

Setanta smiled back. "It's a deal."

She turned back to the meal, feeling a little more at ease knowing that these vampires did seem genuinely interested in peaceful relationships with witches. That was good for her. The ease disappeared with Setanta's next words.

"There is one more thing I need to speak with you on," he said seriously. "We need to discuss Dr. Stearne, the Vasi doctor in our dungeon."

Chapter Eighteen: Dr. Stearne

Seeing the Vasi again wasn't something Sarai had anticipated happening. It was strange to see him dirty and in a dungeon. It was strange to see the dungeon in the first place. Damp, stone, cold, and underground; it was the antithesis of the experience she'd been given, with her freedom and comforts. Bars and chains suited the Vasi.

With Marcelle beside her, she had the courage to look at the single Vasi still left. What had happened to the other two was apparent from the dried blood smear of a dragged body pulled into a room in the back. He was the scientist. Sarai could remember his cold eyes. He was more of a monster than Marcelle and Setanta and likely most of the vampires in the palace for what he and his people did to witches, that she was certain of. And it was so satisfying to see him curled in a corner on his cushion-less cot, huddled in a thin blanket.

"They've hurt so many witches," Sarai whispered, afraid to wake the unconscious man.

"You can take your satisfaction," Marcelle said, putting a hand on her shoulder. It should have comforted her, but somehow made her tense.

"I'm not sure what I think of your laws."

"You understand them, right?"

"He hurt too many people to be allowed to leave.

So, he needs to die. And I can kill him, because he hurt me, and on behalf of the witches who can't reach him. Payback. I get that. It's just, well, different from any kind of justice I'm used to. He didn't even do much to me personally, just took a little blood."

"Would you like to hear what he did to witches before you? Why we offer him to you?" Marcelle asked. Sarai hesitated as she mulled over the question before she gave a short nod. "He wanted to dissect magic. So, he dissected witches on his table to study them. Collected organ tissue, bone marrow, all while they were awake. He would have done it to you if we hadn't been there to stop him."

Anger filled her heart like poison threatening to choke her. "How... how do you know that?"

"He told us about his experiments. He is proud of them."

Sarai turned around to look at Marcelle. "The other two are dead, right? Who killed them?"

"Artemisia."

"How... how did she do it? Back there, in that room?" She pointed at the trail of dried blood.

"I wouldn't recommend that room if you have a delicate constitution."

"I'm just trying to figure out what's expected of me."

"Nothing. If you don't want his blood on your hands, then the honor goes to me."

"I've killed before. I'm not afraid of it." But her shaking hands told a different story. She'd killed before, but not someone who deserved it, and who also terrified her and haunted her nightmares to the point that she banished her dreams with magic. Would the cries of pain from someone who deserved the pain feel less horrific than the cries of the innocents her father made her kill? "They scream. When I kill them."

"Artemisia had them gagged before she would come near them. Said she didn't want to hear their talking, their voices. I can gag this one for you. Or if you'd rather not do this…"

"No. I don't want him gagged. I want to talk to him." Sarai took a deep breath. She'd never had such freedom in her ability to kill. Being able to talk to the victim. No. She was *his* victim. So were so many others. "Is he still sleeping?"

Marcelle looked at the slouched Vasi, then banged on the bars with the hilt of her dagger. He jolted up with a start, the chains on his ankles clanking.

"Dr. Stearne," Marcelle shouted. "Time to wake."

He smiled a little, a welcome expression on his face when he saw Marcelle.

"Miss, er, Commander. It's good to see you. I was thinking, about our last talk, and I'm worried I gave you a bad impression, so I wanted to say—"

"I'm not here to speak nor to listen. I'm afraid pleasantries are over. Dr. Stearne, as a member of the Vasi acting against the kingdom of New Ulster, the Crown Prince Setanta acting with the authority of King Lugh has sentenced you to death."

His face paled. "But, but you said! N-no, wait! I can be useful, I—"

"Do not beg *me* for mercy. As one of your most recent victims, your life is Sarai Reinhart's to take, should she claim it."

He met Sarai's eyes for the first time, and the borderline friendliness he'd feigned slipped away.

There he was, the man who had tortured witches.

"I... Miss... Sarai, was it? I didn't mean anything personal. We just wanted a way to cure a disease, that's all."

She stared, not replying. He was trying to bargain. How funny.

"You, I didn't want to hurt you, you see. That's what the rest of them want with witches, but I don't have anything against you, really. I don't mind witches." He smiled, his face twitching between terror and faked attempts at friendliness.

Sarai said nothing, and her silence unnerved him.

"Witches seem like fine people, I'm sure you're a fine woman yourself, we just wanted to cure vampires."

"What about the other witches?" Sarai demanded.

He shrugged like a nervous twitch. "They all helped the cause! Knowledge is important, you witches understand that, right? I know you do, with your books and–"

"Stop," Sarai said. "Just... just stop."

There was silence in the dungeon. All Sarai could think was how pathetic the man was. He was a torturer who wasn't worth the air he breathed.

"Marcelle, open it."

The vampire commander's keys jingled as they found the lock, as did the chains on the Vasi man's ankles as he scrambled to his feet and pressed back against the wall. The door squeaked as it swung open and the noise as it struck the stone wall was deafening.

Sarai stepped forward, then stopped. The idea of putting her hands on him, killing him, made her nauseous. She wanted him dead, but she'd never killed this way before. She had killed under threat or coercion. Kill someone or be locked in a closet. Practice her power or go without food. Kill or be tortured as punishment. Or, in the rare case with Nicolas, kill in defense.

"Is this too much?" Marcelle asked softly. "You don't need to do this. It's an offer to you as our guest to have a right to his life, not a duty you must fulfill. You can leave him here now, and when you go, I'll make sure he never harms anyone else again."

"He hurt witches," Sarai said. "He hurt me, but I…" She took a step closer, then stopped. "I don't think I want to kill him. I just… I don't want to be an executioner. That's my father. That's not me."

Dr. Stearne breathed a visible sigh of relief.

"That's fine, Sarai," she said, and Sarai breathed her own sigh of relief, the weight lifted from her shoulders. "I'll take care of this for you. Why don't you go wait outside, I'll make this quick."

"I… think I'll stay." She didn't want to kill him herself, but seeing him dead, knowing he would never hurt any witch again, could help her sleep easier.

Marcelle raised an eyebrow. "You want to stay for this?"

"Wait, she said she doesn't want me killed!" Dr. Stearne exclaimed. "She said!"

Sarai's eyes narrowed. "You still deserve to die. You think I want you alive? Fuck you. Marcelle, just, he's not worth it. Just do it quickly, please? I want to leave."

"Wait! I–"

He was dead before he could utter another word, Marcelle standing over him as he fell over onto the floor, eyes wide with shock, then glazed over in unseeing death.

Curious, Sarai tried to see a mark on his body as to what had just happened. His neck hadn't been broken, and there were no bites or wounds. Not even a drop of blood had spilled.

"How did you do that?" she murmured.

"I listened," Marcelle said. "There's a point between heartbeats. Hit a human in the chest at just the right moment, and their hearts stop."

Somehow that ability to kill so seamlessly sent a shudder up and down Sarai's spine despite the memories she already had of Marcelle ripping people to shreds while drenched in their blood.

"Come on. Dungeons aren't nice places, and you shouldn't be in one," the vampire said. "Let's get you back upstairs and away from this unpleasantness."

Sarai could only hope that the unpleasantness remained in the dungeon. At the very least, he was gone. One less Vasi was a good thing.

As she climbed the stairs back into the palace, Sarai's thoughts turned to Setanta's plans and the witches they were to visit. Perhaps, if they were successful, the Vasi would never hurt anyone ever again.

Chapter Nineteen: His Holiness, the Vampire Pope

Thanks to a refreshed bay leaf spell (the first became crumpled and fragmented from use), nightmares once more spared Sarai, but her mind was far too busy to sleep. She had an invitation to Marcelle's bed, but stayed up late in the library, thumbing through books on vampire law. While it had started as a way to better understand the events of the day, it turned into a way of distracting herself from her fears.

It was one thing to agree to help the vampires, and another to agree to see witches again after so long on her own. She'd avoided them after being denied entry to her mother's coven. After all, if her own kin could reject her, why would any other coven want her around? Except, of course, her father's coven, which no doubt had its agents across the country hunting for any sign or whisper of her whereabouts. She felt safe from them with the vampires since no witch could infiltrate them, and only an idiot would attack them, but the Ellis Coven was another matter. They could have spies in their midst and not even know.

Eventually, she became too tired to keep her eyes open without a struggle. She even saw shadows likely cast by bats through the windows and found herself imagining she saw the things much larger than they could be. Hallucinations brought on by exhaustion, no doubt. Giant bats didn't exist. Sarai ended up curled against and asleep in her protector's arms in the lavish French bedroom.

It was all too soon before the time came to get ready to leave. And somehow, as a result of her nerves, she found herself stressing over the simplest, most unimportant things.

"I think you should just go naked," Marcelle teased, and yanked the laces on her boots tight. "Then you won't have to worry about a thing."

Sarai rolled her eyes. As if. "You're lucky with the whole uniform thing," she said, staring between the various outfits she'd fetched from her room, most of which still had price tags on them. "Don't need to think about what to put on, just put on what you have to."

"I do look good in black," Marcelle said, and posed as she adjusted one of the army of pins holding her hair up in a strict bun. "Want help?"

"I don't even care. I'm too nervous to care. You pick something."

Marcelle closed her eyes and stuck her hand into the pile of clothes and pulled out a simple green shirt and a black skirt, then opened her eyes. "This works."

The clothing was made from comfortable material, didn't make her look homeless, and wasn't a waitressing uniform; a certain upgrade to most of what she owned prior to her stay with the vampires. As she put on day clothes, Marcelle put her weaponry in place. It was strange, watching her suit up with guns and sheathed silver weapons hidden in multiple places on her body. And unnerving.

"You don't think you're going to use that stuff, right?" she asked.

"I'd rather have it and not need it than need it and not have it," Marcelle said. "But I promise, if I use any of these, it'll be defensive use only. It's more a precaution against Vasi than against anyone from the Ellis Island Coven. We're not going there immediately."

"You can just call it the Ellis Coven, no one says 'Ellis Island Coven'," Sarai said, stuffing the rest of her clothes into a small suitcase. "Should I be taking all this?"

"Well, you need clothes for today, probably going to the witches by tomorrow. Not sure how long all the diplomacy will take, but I think you're fine with all that. If not, we'll buy you something new or you can borrow some of my clothes."

When both women were packed, Marcelle much more neatly than Sarai, they went together through the mansion out to a smaller building adjacent to the palace.

"This used to be stables," Marcelle said wistfully. "I don't miss the smell, but horses are so much more beautiful than cars."

"Been updated a little," Sarai noted.

"Just a little."

'Just a little' was an understatement. It was a modern looking garage, with a few luxury cars Sarai was afraid she might accidentally leave fingerprints on if she touched them and other assorted vehicles: corvettes, limousines, windowless black vans, and even full-blown eighteen-wheeler trucks.

A car door slammed shut, and two vampires looked up from one of the luxury cars. One was a youthful blonde woman with light blue eyes, her hair pulled back into a tight, long braid. The other, Sarai recognized, was Bear, the vampire with a teenager's taste in band posters.

"Hey, Sarai," he said with a smile. "Good to see you again."

She stared at him. He was wearing a T-shirt with a faded yet psychedelic peace sign, but the other woman and Marcelle both had black uniforms.

"You're... coming with us?" she asked.

"Yeah. Can't let his royal holiness the vampire pope prance off by himself. The king wouldn't have it," he said, resting his hands by his thumbs on a belt she now noticed had several weapons on it. Ironic, given the content of his shirt.

"He's not a pope," Marcelle said with an exasperated expression directed at Bear. "You'll confuse her like that. Sarai, these are my top subordinates, and allegedly respected knights of New Ulster. Angela takes her job seriously. Bear thinks it's a joke, apparently."

"That's Sir Bear to you," he said, puffing out his chest in a mock-pompous pose. "And if we all dress the same, we'll be boring." He sat on the hood of one of the cars Sarai would have been afraid to touch.

"Bear is short for Teddy Bear, by the way," Marcelle said with a smirk.

Sarai couldn't resist a giggle at that. He did have a bit of a big softy aura, so she wouldn't be surprised if it were true. Even if he did drink blood, but she pushed that memory of him out of her mind.

"So, where's the pope?"

"Prince," Angela grumbled.

"He's right here," said a familiar voice. Sarai spun

around to see that Setanta was standing behind them, the spymaster, Lilly, by his side with her hands clasped behind her back. She wore a plain button-down shirt tucked into dress pants, professional but not a uniform. "I thought I was just taking Marcelle and Lilly? We don't need an envoy. This is a small diplomatic mission, not a raid on Vasi. We'll be well protected by the knights in the New York haven."

"Your father insisted, my prince," Angela said formally, bowing her head. She had an accent that Sarai couldn't quite place, perhaps from a romance language?

"At ease, Angela." Setanta ran his hand along the top of a sharp looking sports car. "I suppose if my father insists. Bear, Angela, you'll follow behind. Six of us would be a tight fit in one vehicle."

"We could always put Bear in the trunk," Lilly murmured, earning snickers from Marcelle.

"So, we're taking a plane up to New York, right?" Bear asked, hopping off the car. "Looking forward to the flashbacks."

"Flashbacks?" Sarai asked.

"I used to live… well, a little further north, but in general New England was my stomping ground for a while," he said.

"You're from New England?"

Bear frowned, thinking for a moment. "I think, more Canada than New England. Didn't have maps back then, and landmarks change when concrete cities get plopped down, you know?"

"You're that old?" Sarai asked. Anthropologists would have a field day interviewing him, not to mention everyone else at the mansion.

"I wouldn't have the skills to be on Marcelle's

team if I wasn't," he said.

Sarai frowned, thinking. "Wait, when did Setanta and the purebloods come to the continent? I was reading history and they weren't here that far back."

"New Ulster started way after I was turned," Bear said, opening a car door and putting a cooler in the back. "His folks hadn't found us at the time."

"I didn't think, well... I mean, there are witches and magic all over, but I didn't realize North America had vampires too," Sarai said. How many different cultures managed to come up with the ritual to make pureblood vampires? Was it so common that every culture had their own version?

"Don't get him talking, he'll go on forever," Marcelle said with a sigh.

"Well, I'm interesting!" he said.

"He is interesting," Sarai agreed.

"See, she likes me. Anyway, we don't have as many vampires. Well, my specific people didn't. Anything that would have led to them was really frowned upon. *Some* folks in the world are decent people who think eating human beings is wrong," he said, grinning at Setanta. "Dunno what cannibalistic, vampiric debauchery you guys got up to back in the day, but we were more moral than that."

Setanta laughed. "Maybe. But we had more fun."

Sarai was suddenly very concerned what the vampire pureblood considered "fun", but it was strange to see him laugh. Until that moment, he seemed too important or serious to laugh.

"Sarai, come on," Marcelle said, gesturing to a black car. It looked like a nice car, but it wasn't flashy like the sports cars.

"Wait, so who turned you?" Sarai asked, hesitating at the open door.

"Some Viking bastard," Bear said. "Got back at him though. Killed him for it."

"Oh."

"Good times, right?" he said as if he weren't bothered even a little by it.

A loud blaring noise made them all jump. Angela had her hand on the horn. "We have a trip we're supposed to be on, yes?" she said. "Or are we going to stay here all day and talk about who killed who? It's tedious."

"Fiiiine," Bear sighed dramatically, and slid into one of the cars. "We can talk more on the plane if you want."

Sarai nodded. She got into the car with Marcelle in the driver's seat and was offered the front passenger seat, while Setanta and Lilly sat in the back, and together they were off to New York.

Chapter Twenty: The City

Sarai kept an eye on Lilly through the rearview mirror while they drove. Despite the playful banter and her relative comfort with the vampire, it didn't escape her attention that Setanta brought a self-identified spymaster.

"So, are you guys spying on the Ellis Coven?" she blurted.

"We have no witch spies, or mortal spies able to infiltrate a witch coven," the woman said. "Rest easy."

"Lilly is with me for advisory purposes," Setanta reassured.

While the motion of the car along with her general tired state had Sarai feeling a little groggy, she was awake enough when they arrived to marvel at the plane, putting her hand against the exterior of the door as she hesitated to step inside.

"Is everything all right?" Marcelle asked.

"Yeah. I've never been on a plane before."

"Really?"

Sarai shrugged. "There were a few teleporters with my father's people if we needed to go anywhere. I never did, they kept me in the coven. And when I got out, I walked, hitchhiked, bussed, and magicked myself wherever I needed to get to."

"Well, let's make sure you get a window seat."

Getting a window seat was easy, since it was a

private plane, and a comfortable one at that. Watching out the window as the plane took off was like magic. She'd been surrounded by real magic all her life, but this mundane human technology was so enchanting to her. It was stunning to think humans had made flying machines of that caliber while witches stayed on the ground. Sure, there was the odd magicked broom or carpet, but they'd fallen out of fashion along with too many careless riders plummeting to their deaths. A few still rode around in spelled cauldrons, but cars were far more practical and stood out less to humans.

While in the air, Lilly and Bear took the chance to socialize, while Angela put on a headset attached to a portable CD player and kept to herself. Marcelle loudly joined in with teasing Bear as the latter kept trying to answer Sarai's questions about his past.

After a while, she curled up in Marcelle's lap, and the hum of the engines had Sarai fast asleep. She was still half asleep when they arrived in New York City and followed the vampires through the airport like one of her raised corpses, half aware of the stares they got up until they climbed into a limousine that was waiting for them.

"I think I can get used to all this nice stuff," Sarai said, starting to wake up a little as she reached into the mini fridge there and pulled out a box of apple juice. "You should have woken me up for when we were coming down, I wanted to see the city."

"You'll see it soon enough, don't worry," Marcelle said.

Sarai had never been anywhere so big. All the skyscrapers were incredible, with the glass windows reaching up to the heavens, the busy streets, and the sheer amount of people around them. It was overwhelming, and she couldn't stop staring up at the buildings and lights. The vampires had a different reaction, which became more apparent as they got out in front of a skyscraper along the edge of Central Park.

"God, I forgot how much this city stinks," Marcelle said with a sigh, dabbing a touch of perfume under her nose, then offering it to Setanta. He accepted with a nod of thanks and did the same before passing it along to Angela, Bear, and Lilly.

"Has it gotten better or worse since the last time?" Setanta wondered.

"Worse," Angela said, her nose wrinkled in disgust. "Definitely worse."

"I thought it was bad enough when cities all smelled like the shit being dumped in the streets, now it's all gasoline and trash," Marcelle said.

"The shit was worse," Setanta murmured, and pulled on a pair of dark, oval sunglasses to hide his red eyes. Marcelle took back the perfume vial and stuffed it into her cleavage for storage.

While the vampires reminisced about the stench, Sarai's neck bent at a ninety-degree angle as she looked up at the buildings around them. Let the vampires be grumpy, she thought to herself. She was in love with New York.

"This is amazing." she whispered. "I mean, I've seen pictures. And I've been around tall buildings before. Just not so many in one space."

"Well then, I'm sure you'll love the view."

They went inside, where a man stood expectantly. He was an obvious vampire, but not because of fangs or red eyes; he had a very old-fashioned hairstyle. It was slicked back like something from 1900, and he had a mustache that looked like a comical villain's, ready for twirling. It screamed, "I can't cut my hair because it will grow back, please send help."

"Your Highness. It's an honor to have you in New York," the vampire said, bowing just enough that it wasn't too obvious to humans around them, but enough to show respect.

"Duke Matteo, it's good to be back," Setanta said, nodding his head. Matteo's eyes flickered toward the witch in the room. "This is Sarai. She'll be staying with us for a little while."

"Of course. It's a pleasure to meet you, Miss Sarai."

"Thanks. Uh, same."

It was an awkward meeting, to be sure. At least they quickly were allowed to escape up to their rooms. Or rather, to the penthouse that the royal family owned. It wasn't any more elaborate than the mansion but much more modern. It was nice to be able to walk into a room and not question whether the lights would be electric, gas, or candle, but artificial light wasn't even needed. There were so many windows, with light flooding in to illuminate the apartment from every angle. She was in awe.

"Nice place," Sarai remarked. "This is crazy. If you'd told me just a month ago I'd be in a penthouse, I would have asked what drugs you were taking." She stepped up to the window and could see over Central Park. "That's spectacular."

"It is pretty great," Marcelle agreed. "Want to go explore it?"

"The apartment?"

"No, silly, the city."

Sarai looked at her with a raised eyebrow. "We just got here. Don't we have diplomacy or something to prepare for?"

"We don't, that's the prince's business. We just show up. And we are in New York City. How could I not take the opportunity to ask you on a date?"

Sarai blushed and looked out at the city. "On a date, huh? Don't you mean courting?"

Marcelle slipped her arms around her from behind and laid a kiss on her cheek that sent erotic shivers through her body. "Maybe I do."

"Did the shopping count as a date?"

"Maybe half a date."

Sarai laughed. "All right. Let's go on a date then." She tried to push to the back of her mind the 'promise' she'd made, to let Marcelle bite her again after the vampire bought her dinner. She could always back out, and decided not to think about it, turning around to give her lover a peck on the lips. "Where are we going?"

"Well, I thought I would give you a few options, see what strikes your fancy? We can do the tourist route. The Statue of Liberty, Empire State Building, Central Park, Museum of Natural History, Metropolitan Museum of Art. Any of that sound interesting?"

"Um. All of it," she laughed. "Natural history, that sounds like a fun museum."

"I had a hunch you'd prefer that. Let me go change. Can't go into a museum with firearms. You get your things settled in, and then we'll go."

The experience was fantastic. While humans had a lot to learn when it came to the nature of things in a magical sense, they had learned so much on their own about history and animals and the earth. Seeing mammoths and dinosaurs in full size in front of her was something Sarai had never imagined. Standing under the massive blue whale hanging above them was terrifying and beautiful all at once. To think, such creatures really did exist. With so much to see, even something as necessary as lunch had been an unwelcome break to learning, and she made sure that Marcelle knew it didn't count as a proper meal for the dinner that was still owed.

As she was clearing her trash in the museum cafe and making her way to the garbage cans, Sarai found herself looking out at the crowd. There were a lot of families. Parents enjoying their time with their children, smiling and laughing. A thought popped into her head: what kind of parent had Marcelle been? Marcelle certainly didn't look like a typical parent. It was such an irrelevant thought, Sarai knew. It wasn't as if an undead person like Marcelle would ever have a chance to become a parent. Sarai wasn't looking for someone to have children with, let alone a vampire she barely knew. Yet, as she watched a mother wiping ketchup from her squirming child's mouth, she wondered what kind of parent she could be, if she ever had the chance.

"Something the matter?" Marcelle asked.

"Nothing, just staring out into space. Come on, I want to check out that T-Rex skull we saw coming into the cafe." The vampire could probably tell it was a lie, but Sarai didn't give her a chance to question it, dragging her out to see more bones.

The visit to the museum consumed the day faster than Sarai wanted, and she still felt she hadn't seen everything. On their way out through the gift shop,

Sarai was ready to walk past all the nonsense for sale. She'd never bought trinkets before, but Marcelle ended up staring at some of the jewelry. They did have beautiful stones, but Sarai would never think to even touch such things.

"Did you want anything? I might get myself a pair of earrings," Marcelle said. "Pity so many of these are silver. At least there are some gold options."

"You just walk in and buy whatever you like wherever you go?" Sarai asked, the concept foreign to her.

"I do get a very nice salary," Marcelle said, flashing a smile. "Might as well spend some of it on shiny things. Honestly, I'm always misplacing earrings and necklaces, so it's nice to restock once in a while. There's nothing that stands out to you?"

"Well, yeah, but I'm not... I don't think jewels and stuff are my style." And she wasn't going to let someone she was possibly just using for fun buy her anything too fancy. Though, it did cross her mind that perhaps if it all ended with her back in some studio apartment, it would be good for her to have some fancy things she could pawn.

Marcelle thought, then smiled. "How about amber?"

"Amber?"

She pulled her over to a selection of bracelets and held one up. "Not too expensive, not too shiny, but something special to remember today."

Sarai couldn't help but smile. It was perfect. She left with the smooth amber beads around her wrist and couldn't stop playing with them. They got dinner at a small pizza place, with Marcelle ordering nothing, as expected, to the odd glances by the waiter.

"This makes us even then," Sarai informed Marcelle as she stuffed her face. New York style pizza really was all it was talked up to be, a perfect greasy treat to end the day.

"At long last, my debt is repaid," the vampire said dramatically, with a flourish of her hand and a bow of her head, making Sarai giggle. Though, it was a little awkward to sit and eat while being watched, again. "You should have let me take you someplace a little nicer though."

"Next time maybe. I guess you can't like... lick it for taste or something?" Sarai asked, only half joking.

"Wouldn't taste like much to me," Marcelle said with a shrug. "It smells good, but not in an appetizing way. Like, when you smell flowers, they smell lovely, but you wouldn't bite into a bouquet."

"I dunno, roses are edible. Dandelions, marigolds. Back before I had a place, I used to go out and harvest dandelions from parks. Ate them all the time. They're good for you, you know."

"So, if I handed you a dozen red roses, you'd bite the blossoms off?"

"Might do it now, just to prove the point," Sarai said, and stuck out her tongue.

By the time Sarai finished her meal, completed with the most exquisite slice of cheesecake in the world, it was dark outside. The sleepy town she'd squatted in was never so noisy and busy. It made her want to jump out into the lights and streets to continue their perfect date, but with the blood rushing from her brain to her stomach, Sarai was too tired. They decided to head back to the penthouse.

It was sweet to walk together, hand in hand. It got stares from the humans, but Sarai didn't care. In fact, in response to a glare from one uptight brunette, Sarai slid an arm around Marcelle's waist and rested her head against her, smiling at the woman's offended reaction as she stormed away.

"You don't mind?" Marcelle asked.

"It's kind of funny," she said honestly. "I hadn't even thought about it at the palace. No one seems to mind there. They don't, do they?"

"We can see natural reactions, read bodies. Our society sees it as foolish to scorn or deny nature. Sapphic attraction and affection is no different than any other. I could marry another woman if I wanted to, according to our laws. Or several."

It made Sarai smile. For all its bloody faults, vampire culture had its perks. "Witches aren't like that. More like humans. Can't think of anywhere that allows that kind of marriage off the top of my head. If my father knew..." She shook her head. "I guess I'm getting more comfortable around vampires than other mortals."

As they passed by an older woman with a scowl on her face, Sarai caught a snippet of muttering under her breath, with emphasis on the words, "... *disgusting dykes*..."

All it did was make the witch laugh.

"It amuses you?" Marcelle asked, her eyebrow perfectly arched.

"Yeah. What's she going to do about it? She can die mad."

Marcelle laughed. "Very true." She turned to face Sarai and pressed her against the wall of the building behind them, smiling. "Kiss me."

And so, she did, whimpering in response, giving her lips and her breath away to the beauty before her. She didn't even care that they would get looks. In fact, it heightened the need. And as her tongue felt Marcelle's fangs elongate, a memory came to mind. Laying on the bed, Marcelle's fangs in her wrist. At the time, she hadn't wanted it, but… it hadn't been that bad. And she loved feeling her mouth against her skin that way.

"Are you… thirsty?" she managed to ask between kisses.

"Thirsty?" Marcelle pulled back. "Just a reaction, you know that. You excite me."

"Well, you got me dinner. Maybe I want you in my debt again."

Marcelle gave another slow kiss that sent heat like magma through Sarai's body. "My dear little witch, are you asking me to bite you? Out here, in public? How daring."

"You're not the only one who's turned on. When you scratched me in bed… I like that. Do it before I change my mind," she whispered, her body shaking with anticipation. This time, it would be her neck. She pushed her hair back a little and waited with bated breath.

Marcelle's kisses started at her jawline. For a moment, the images she'd created as a child, hearing stories of monsters, flashed through her mind, but they quickly evaporated. All she could think of was how close Marcelle was, how her lips and tongue felt, her hands, her skin. The anticipation wasn't unlike waiting for an orgasm to hit. She wanted it.

Hidden by her curly hair, twin points of pain pierced Sarai's skin, and a moan vibrated the fangs as Marcelle took her pleasure. Just like before, it hurt, but a cool tingling helped dull the pain. Sarai shuddered and closed her eyes. It did feel good. She felt vulnerable and that excited her, to submit to Marcelle of her own free will. The danger of people looking and maybe seeing more than they should thrilled her.

Marcelle didn't drink much, swallowing blood sparingly before pulling her fangs out. They caught with a slight hiccup of pain in Sarai's skin, but the pain disappeared as the wound healed.

"Did you like it?" she said, her voice low with need and lips scarlet with blood.

"I, I think I might," Sarai breathed.

"Let me show you what it does." Marcelle took Sarai's hand and placed it against her skin, just above her breast. She expected the skin to be cold as usual, but what she found was completely different.

"You're warm," Sarai realized. Not hot, and not at a comfortable 98.6 degrees Fahrenheit, but warmer than before.

"This is what it does to me, what you do for me," Marcelle explained. "That's life you feel, that's what I get from this, what all vampires crave. What you gave to me."

Sarai gazed curiously at the place where her hand was. She could swear even Marcelle's pallid skin had a little more color than usual. Her eyes flickered upward to lock with her lover's. It all made sense, it all clicked into place. She could understand vampires a little more.

She leaned in so she could kiss her lover once

more, but as the wind shifted around them, Marcelle slowly pulled away, her brow furrowed. Sarai leaned forward for more, but the look on the vampire's face made her pause.

"Is something wrong?"

"We're being watched," Marcelle said quietly.

"I thought that was half the fun?"

"By a witch."

Sarai tensed, her grip on Marcelle turning white-knuckled. "Vasi slave?"

"Maybe. No way to know. I just smell someone not human, and it's not us or another vampire."

Sarai nodded, and flexed her hand a little, letting power flow through her glove focus as she held onto Marcelle's shirt, channeling her power into it.

"*T'shmor la.*" Protect her.

She closed her eyes. Quick spells weren't her forte when she didn't have a comfortable environment to concentrate, but anything could give them an edge. She repeated the spell, changing the word 'her' to 'me' as she held onto her own shirt, which made her skin tingle as the magic took hold. Panting a little from the effort, she nodded at Marcelle.

"Thank you. That's… interesting," the vampire said, clearly uncomfortable.

"Just something quick, the magic won't hold forever. I'm not that good, so let's get back."

"No, I don't want them following us. If they want to confront us, let's give them the opportunity." Marcelle gave her a second quick kiss, then led her around the corner into a dark alley. Sarai had the distinct impression they were about to be mugged, and gripped Marcelle's hand as tight as she could, anticipation pounding in her chest.

Rubber soles landed hard on the pavement behind them, and the pair spun around to see a red-haired young man with glasses and a sparse goatee, glaring at them with dark blue eyes and aiming an arrow notched to a bow at Marcelle.

"Let her go."

"And you are?" she said, raising an eyebrow.

"Your executioner. Let her go, and I'll consider letting you leave with your unlife, leech."

Marcelle stared at him, then burst into laughter. "That's adorable. Really, you're adorable, boy. How old are you?"

"Old enough to kill you." He looked at Sarai. "I saw her hurt you. Are you okay?"

"It's not what you think," Sarai said, stepping in front of Marcelle protectively, realizing what this was about. This was no Vasi, just a normal witch thinking he was protecting his own. "You've got this wrong."

"Get the hell out of the way!"

"No."

His arrow tip burst into flames as he kept it trained on them. Sarai inhaled sharply. Surely someone like Marcelle could snatch an arrow out of the air before it became a problem. But if it was a magic arrow, that could pose a genuine threat. Her limited protection spell likely didn't have the strength to block a direct hit.

"A firestarter," Marcelle said, the calm in her voice reassuring Sarai a little. "Out here vampire hunting all by yourself? How brave. Are you contracted to the Vasi?"

He spit at the sound of the name, confirming Sarai's suspicions. "Fuck the Vasi. I don't need a contract to tell me to hunt leeches."

"Well, that makes things more complicated," Marcelle sighed.

"Why's that?"

"It means I can't kill you." She disappeared from behind Sarai and reappeared in front of the bowman. The arrow let fly, and Sarai narrowly avoided a grazing thanks to her protective spell. The flames erupted into a fireball behind her down the alley and flooded the space with heat. Marcelle knocked the bow from his hands in a swift move from one hand and stabbed a silver needle into his shoulder with the other. The fire still lingered in trash behind them, smelling something foul, but he wouldn't create any more fire.

He shouted in pain, and drew a switchblade, but Marcelle had his hands in her iron grip, twisting them behind his back and slamming him against the wall, forcing a grunt from him.

"You're out of your league, pyro."

"Do it then," he hissed. "Damn monster, do it."

"Do what exactly?" she mused.

"Kill me already. Make it quick."

"I've no intention of killing you. Though if you keep attacking vampires like this, killing you now would be a mercy." She hit him hard on the side of the head so that he fell unconscious in her grasp.

"Is he all right?" Sarai asked.

"Out cold, silver needle in his shoulder, but he'll be fine. Let's get him up to Setanta, before human cops come running from the explosion."

"What a way to end a date," Sarai mused as her lover hoisted the witch over her shoulder like a sack of potatoes.

"At least dinner was good... for both of us." Marcelle pulled Sarai closer by her waist. "Can't go walking around with a body. Ready to move fast?"

"Wait!" Sarai picked up the bow that had been dropped. "Okay, now we can go."

"You want to bring his weapon?" Marcelle asked.

"It could be his focus," Sarai said with a shrug.

"If you say so. Hold on tight."

With that, they sped through the dizzying streets of New York City, captive in tow.

Chapter Twwenty-One: They Eat People

"And this is…?" Setanta asked as he watched Marcelle dump the unconscious witch on his couch and zip-tie his wrists together.

"Witch attacked us trying to 'save' Sarai. He doesn't work for the Vasi. I thought he might be useful."

Setanta nodded and looked at Sarai. "You're both unharmed?"

"Didn't even singe me," she said. "I mean, he was more mad at Marcelle. But we're both fine."

"Can you wake him?"

Sarai blinked. "Uh, I do healing. I guess I can do a spell?"

"Please. My focus stands out too much for traveling, so I'm currently spell-less."

Feeling a bit of stage fright, she took a deep breath and took the slumped witch's head between her hands. She could feel with her healing magic that he had a slight concussion from how hard he'd been hit and healed it for him before focusing on a single word, pushing her power and intent through her focus for the spell.

"*Lehitorer.*"

His eyes fluttered, and he frowned in confusion at the sight of Sarai's face.

"What…" The grogginess from the healing was heavy on his eyelids and in his speech, but the moment he saw Setanta, he was snapped out of the stupor. He jumped to his feet, wincing and trying to grasp his shoulder, only to realize his wrists were bound in front of him.

"It's okay; they won't hurt you," Sarai assured him.

"The pain in your arm is from a silver needle," Marcelle informed him. "It breaks off under the skin so that an opponent can't fish it out in a fight. You can get it out with tweezers once you get back to your home."

"Where the hell am I and what do you leeches want with me?" he snarled.

"You're in my apartment," Setanta said calmly. "Are you by chance from the Ellis Coven?"

He tensed and gripped Sarai's hand and she noticed his fingernails were blue, the same exact shade as his eyes. "Get behind me. You run. I'll try to keep them busy."

"No," she said, yanking her hand free and stepping back. "It's not like that. Seriously, they aren't going to hurt you."

"They're fucking vampires! They eat people!"

Sarai rolled her eyes. There was a very good chance they weren't going to get through to someone like him. "Vampires drink blood. You're thinking of zombies." Zombies as the brain-eating, flesh-craving creatures of Hollywood legend weren't even a genuine danger to anyone. The closest to a creature like that would have been the dead she was able to control for a short period of time, and they didn't eat flesh.

"They eat people," he hissed. "Don't let them fool you."

"We don't eat people," Setanta interrupted. "In

fact, I have every intention of letting you go. Let's try to be civilized, shall we? Do you have a name?"

He clenched his fists. "Lochlan. Lochlan Kelly."

"Good to meet you, Mr. Kelly. Now, I would kindly ask that you answer my question; are you from the Ellis Coven?"

"None of your business."

"I'll take that as a yes." Setanta moved closer and gripped his hands, snapping the zip-tie. Sarai was distinctly reminded of when he had removed her collar. It had gotten her to trust him more... though as he released this other witch, she wondered if it was all a practiced method of manipulation, giving the illusion of control, power, or freedom.

No, there was more to it with Lochlan. Setanta hadn't just released him to let him have some semblance of freedom, he'd broken the bonds with ease, let the man feel the force of it close to his skin. He was asserting dominance.

"Don't touch me."

Setanta let go. "As you wish. I'll have someone escort you out."

"Just like that?"

"Just like that. Bear?"

The massive vampire who had been standing in the shadows unbeknownst to Sarai darted forward behind Setanta. "Yes, Your Highness?"

"See this young man safely to the street. Sarai, if you could return his bow?"

She nodded and handed over the weapon to the confused and angry witch.

"You're just letting me go," he said in disbelief.

"If you'd like to stay for drinks, we can arrange

that," Marcelle quipped. Sarai snorted in an attempt to cover up laughter, clapping a hand over her mouth and earning a glare from the other witch. He spun on his heel and stomped toward the front door, Bear close behind.

"Oh, and Mr. Kelly," Setanta called after him. "Tell your leaders to expect a visit tomorrow. I very much look forward to meeting the Ellis Coven."

****

Ellis Island, expectedly, had a decent crowd of tourists, though less than there might have been if it hadn't rained. People arrived wrapped in overpriced plastic ponchos with their hoods up, and Setanta kept a black umbrella up over Sarai's head.

Anxiety ripped through her as they got off the ferry onto the actual island, and she gripped Marcelle's hand tight. It was a slight reassurance to feel a squeeze back, but she still wished Marcelle could go with them into the interior. She could feel the magic rippling off the building in layers of protection, the kind only an established and powerful coven could produce. They would keep Marcelle from being even able to step foot in the human buildings of Ellis Island, let alone the witch coven.

"I can feel that from all the way here... just being on this land," Marcelle said, clenching her teeth, her fingers making indents into the plastic handle of her umbrella. "It feels like this is a... very uncomfortable place. That even the ground is trying to reject me. I shouldn't get much closer."

While not the oldest protection spells on a coven in

existence, they were a good hundred or so years old. Spells of that kind tended to strengthen over time; it made sense that the ground would feel that way to an undead vampire.

"Wait here for us," Setanta ordered. "I'll go with Sarai. Are you ready?"

Sarai shook her head. "But I don't think I'll ever be. I thought about coming here years ago, never made it to New York. It's just… surreal."

"Are you going to stay?" Marcelle asked.

Sarai froze, staring at her lover. She opened her mouth to reply, then closed it. How had she not thought of that? She'd assumed after all this she'd go back with Marcelle, back to her ridiculous French bedroom and ridiculous French bed. The day they'd spent together at the museum had been the best she'd ever had in her life, and her hand went to touch the amber bracelet around her wrist. But, at the same time, a witch living with vampires was unheard of, even if their leaders were secretly witches themselves.

"I, I didn't think about it," she admitted. She stood there a moment, then threw her arms around Marcelle, and gave her a lingering kiss, not caring at all that Setanta stood next to them, or about the water she'd splashed up onto her pants in her rush through a puddle. "I'll see you when I get back." Surely, she would have more time than just this one trip to decide where she would stay. Assuming she was allowed the choice. "Sir, I can stay if I want to, right?"

"I wouldn't force you to leave or stay," Setanta assured her. "The choice is yours, as long as you choose someplace safe."

Breathing a sigh of relief, she nodded, and gave

Marcelle another kiss. She could have stood there under the black umbrella kissing Marcelle for hours, if only they didn't have a mission to accomplish.

"I'll see you," Sarai said with confidence, before leaving with Setanta. It felt odd to be close enough that they were touching under his umbrella to avoid the rain, and she just kept her eyes down on her feet to try and avoid further puddles. The water that soaked into her socks from her misstep was quickly irritating her.

"You and Marcelle seem quite taken with one another," Setanta said as they walked with the tourists, a few glancing at him with confused looks since he had sunglasses on during such gloomy weather.

Sarai blushed. "Uh, yeah. She's nice. Is that, um… is that all right?"

"Of course." He said it as if it were common sense. "Why wouldn't it be?"

"Okay. Well, I guess, as long as we're cool."

Setanta chuckled. "Don't worry, Sarai. We're 'cool'." He wrapped an arm around her shoulders to pull her in to avoid a hurried group of tourists running past them to get out of the rain, and she trembled a little at how close they were. It felt… weird. But good weird. Safe.

They went up through the front past two sets of doors, into the large hall, where there was a display of luggage behind glass barriers being gawked at by noisy humans. Sarai wanted to stare too but was distracted by her gloved hand while Setanta closed the umbrella.

"I can feel… I don't know. Something. Calling to me," she informed him, holding up her hand. "This is why you needed me? My focus?"

He nodded. "Mine is a giant spear. It doesn't do

well in modern crowds or getting past security."

That made sense. "Get with the times," she teased him. "No one uses staffs and big things as focuses anymore. Even wands are kinda old-fashioned, you know, but it's better than a spear."

It made him smile. "If you please?"

"Right." She concentrated on her focus, feeling it connect to magic in the floor, in the ground. The air around them shimmered, and the human crowds and museum displays melted away. What took their place were a group of very angry looking witches, all holding some sort of elemental power in their hands, ready to strike.

Chapter Twenty-Two: The Ellis Coven

"He won't hurt anyone!" Sarai exclaimed, putting herself in front of the vampire prince. It had worked to protect Marcelle from the firestarter, so she had to hope that they knew enough to see that she was a proper witch, one they shouldn't kill on sight. She hoped.

"Miss, please move away from the vampire," said a tense, tan, black-haired woman in her forties with a hawkish face and a ball of lightning in her hands. Lochlan stood next to her, his bow drawn and arrow lit.

"No."

"If I wanted to attack you, I would have brought a larger army," Setanta said as he put a hand on Sarai's shoulder and stepped out from behind her. "I've come to talk."

"This the guy you told us about, Lochlan?" the woman asked.

"That's him." He pulled his bowstring just a touch tighter. "Just give the order, Captain."

Her brow furrowed, creating a deep "V" on her forehead.

"I assure you, there's no need for violence," Setanta promised. "You have a leader who discerns truth from lies and compels honesty, do you not? I request an audience with Danior Teli."

His words unsettled everyone, including Sarai. Witch leaders weren't the kind of people he should have detailed information about.

"How do you know that name?" Lochlan shouted. "How the f–"

"Lochlan," the captain snapped.

"You can't let him near–"

"This isn't your call," she said. She glared at Setanta. "How *do* you know that name?"

"We had a Vasi prisoner recently. He was very forthcoming in sharing their intelligence with us. I've harmed no free witches."

Right, of course, Sarai reassured herself. He wouldn't do that. But still, he could have warned her there was someone who could sense lies and force truth. They would ask her name, no doubt. It cemented in her mind that she didn't want to stay with the witches. The stares and glares from everyone who would know who she was and where she'd come from weren't something she wanted to deal with.

The captain nodded to one of the witches, who ran off to presumably go tell someone of Setanta's request.

The captain glanced back at Sarai. "You know, there's rules against bringing his kind here. How did you even get him past the protection spells? I don't think even an invitation would let one of them in, it's supposed to be watertight. *Fool*proof."

"It…" She paused, glancing at Setanta, who nodded. "It doesn't work on him because he's a witch. Like us. He's alive."

Stunned silence was replaced with murmurs of disbelief around them.

"But his eyes…" the captain said, shaking her head so that a few of her short locks flopped around like black octopus tentacles. "That's not possible."

226

"I know. Trust me, I know it's strange. But he really is a witch."

The captain's lightning ball slowly disappeared, though the others kept their floating weapons of various elements at the ready.

"I've heard of a few witches who've been turned. Is that what happened to you?"

"Not exactly," Setanta said.

Footsteps echoed against the solid floors, and a man in his late fifties, or possibly early sixties, appeared. He was olive-skinned and bald, clothed in a gray coat that reached his knees, and walked with a cane. His brown eyes darted between the two oddities.

"I am Danior Teli," he said. "You knew to ask for me by name?"

"I did," Setanta said. "I came here with peaceful intentions toward your people. I want to talk."

Danior narrowed his eyes. "And somehow, you're telling the truth. This is a first. I can't say we've ever encountered a vampire who had any interest in talking with us. Who are you?"

"As of late, I go by my birth name, Setanta mac Lugh. However, I'm more popularly known as CuChulainn of Ulster, if that is familiar to you?"

"No… you can't be him." Fire grew around Lochlan, blazing out of control like a solar flare. "Liar!" he shouted and flung flames at them. The heat enveloped the pair, and Sarai screamed. It burned from being so close, but not as much as she expected being roasted alive should. Setanta had stepped in front of her and cut the fire with wind caused by his speed, causing it to flow around them, only barely curling their hair.

"*Lochlan*!" Danior shouted. The firestarter stood

there, panting, sparks jumping from his fingertips. "Behave like an *adult*!"

"That name is–"

"I don't care what that name is. And you're lucky you didn't kill them."

"No harm done," Setanta said, though he patted out a few embers on his shirt as he spoke. "I'll accept that he does not act on your behalf and ignore this, for now. I am who I claim to be, and I will not harm anyone here." He looked squarely at Lochlan, ice in his gaze. "Unless I am provoked."

Danior nodded. "I see that. I believe you. And you, girl?"

"I-I'm just a witch his people freed from the Vasi. Sarai; I'm a healer," she said, being careful not to tell any direct lies.

"Do you have a family, a coven?"

"I'm on my own. My mother's dead."

That seemed to satisfy him, and she hadn't had to use a last name. "At ease everyone," the witch leader said, and the elemental weapons dissipated or returned to their originators' hands. Sarai breathed a sigh of relief.

"Thank you," Setanta said.

"Let's talk somewhere a little more comfortable. Captain Moretti, please inform the rest of the council. Shall we?" Danior gestured for Setanta and Sarai to follow. He led them to a large empty hall with arched and tiled ceilings, where there were rows of doorways, unattached to any walls. "This room is a place that is spelled to defend against any violence. I believe your intentions, but perhaps not your instincts. Should you attempt anything, the magic will render you unconscious." He opened one of the doors to reveal that it led into a conference room with a circular table and chairs. The enchantments were obvious, with paintings of sigils on the walls.

"I apologize about my son's temper. He doesn't care for vampires. That name... CuChulainn? I'm not familiar with it. Is it Irish?"

"Yes. It was once rather well known there, and though I haven't been back in some time, the mythology lingers so I imagine it still is," Setanta said, looking over the walls. "He's your son? There is no physical resemblance between you."

"Adopted, but he's still my son. I'd guess that's what bothered my Lochlan. He very much hates your kind, and his family was Irish."

The "was" wasn't lost on Sarai. There was little doubt in her mind that Lochlan had a personal grudge, likely a family dead at the hands of vampires.

"Miss... Sarai, you said it was?" Danior asked, his cane thunking against the floor as he walked to a seat and sat down. She nodded and sat down with Setanta across from him. "You haven't been harmed at all, have you? He hasn't been keeping you against your will?"

"No, nothing like that. Well, there was one vampire who tried to harm me, but he's dead now. These people saved me. They helped me escape the Vasi, and they've been letting me stay with them. Nice place, good food," Sarai assured him.

"And you helped him here... out of gratitude? Bringing an unusual witch to an unusual coven that might welcome him?"

"No, not quite," Sarai said, wringing her hands together.

"Let's not pretend I'm not a vampire, by your definition," Setanta said. "I am. While I am technically a witch, I have long since disregarded that identity and community to create my own. I come to you not as a fellow witch now, but as a vampire, and as a fellow leader."

"A fellow leader? I admit, we've never known much about vampire society. We've only done our best to avoid your kind. I know that you've divided the world up in your own way, with your own rulers," Danior said. "I hear it's like the mob."

Setanta laughed. "That's not inaccurate, though we would see it differently. I am to be the next king of northeastern North America," Setanta said. "My father is stepping down, and there are problems I intend to address more aggressively than he did."

"Problems?"

"I speak, of course, of the Vasi."

The atmosphere shifted. "Yes… they have been more troublesome in recent years. Five of my adopted children lost their families to the Vasi."

"Five?" Sarai blurted. Of course, the Vasi were a problem, but it was still a little surprising to her to meet someone with such a large family. It got a look from both the men. "Sorry… I didn't mean to interrupt. Just, big family."

"I can't expect my fellow coven members to open their homes to refugees from the Vasi if I as a leader don't do the same. I love all my children," he said with a slight smile. "Many of the families here welcome refugees into their homes while we create a place for them or adopt children who have no family. Our protective spells are some of the best in the country."

"Protective spells aren't enough against the Vasi," Setanta interjected. "They're powerful, I'll give you that. But they won't keep the Vasi out forever." He pulled a folded piece of paper from his pocket and slid it across the table. Danior opened it, his eyes narrowed as they darted from side to side, while Sarai wished she could lean over and read with him without being rude.

"Where did you get this?"

"It's intelligence we gathered from the Vasi. I consolidated some that pertained to you for convenience, but I do have a file in my office."

"This is the name of every protective enchantment on our coven," he said, looking up. Sarai gulped. Knowing what spells one was working against was the first step in undoing them.

"The amount of families and children seeking refuge with you has increased in the last decade or so, hasn't it?" Setanta asked. Danior nodded. "The advance of technology is a dangerous thing for anyone beyond the mundane. They're a bigger threat and more widespread than ever before, and they must be stopped. As such... the enemy of my enemy is my friend, wouldn't you agree, Mr. Teli?"

"I would agree more if your kind didn't have a habit of killing mine. From my perspective, a deer should let wolves and mountain lions fight until one destroys the other and hide from conflict as best as possible."

Sarai frowned. Pacifists, she thought to herself. Just like her mother's people. Sure, they wanted to welcome everyone, but only to hide.

"Your son, Lochlan, seems to think that hunting threats is the best course of action," Setanta said.

"His form of… vigilantism is not condoned by our coven, and he has been told to stop multiple times."

Sarai glared at him. "Excuse me, sir, can I say something?" The attention was turned back to her like a burning spotlight, and her breath constricted, but she didn't wait for permission. "You shouldn't compare yourself to a deer. We're not prey. *I* am not prey."

"I didn't mean to offend."

"Well, you did. I was hiding too, you know. Had myself a nice little warded apartment. All the protective enchantments I knew how to put up. And yeah, a ring of salt isn't the same as a one-hundred-year-old coven's wards, but it wasn't bad. They still got me. If Setanta's people hadn't come when they did, maybe I'd have signed a slave contract by now, or maybe I'd be dead. I don't know. I know if we don't stop the Vasi, they're going to keep doing this. They're going to keep finding our hiding spots, keep breaking past our wards, until we're all under their control or dead. And your coven has a massive target on their backs because they know where you are, and you've got a lot of witches here. They're going to come for you. Probably sooner rather than later. We need to take the fight to them instead of cowering. We are *not* prey. How many more kids do you want to have to adopt before you fight back?"

The older man's wrinkles deepened, but Setanta just smiled and leaned back in his chair.

"I concur with every word she said."

Danior sighed. "You realize I cannot decide something like this alone. I have two other councilmembers to confer with before anything of this sort can be considered properly. What exactly do you propose, Mr. Setanta? An alliance until the Vasi are defeated, and then what?"

"Ideally not just until the Vasi are defeated. But that would be our initial goal, yes. I want to crush them until their organization is nothing but a distant memory. That said, I do believe our people can coexist in a more peaceful way, and a common enemy could bring us together."

"And what about vampires attacking us?" Danior said. "I can't ignore that."

"There are laws against attacking free witches in my borders. My father hasn't been strict enough, but the ones who do act out are rogues and are punished if caught. I will be stricter during my reign. The punishments for harming protected allies are far harsher, and those would apply if we were allied and one of my people were to break the laws," he said.

"Your reign. And how long can we expect that to last?"

"Far beyond your great-grandchildren's lifetime, assuming the Vasi don't kill us all," Setanta assured him. "I won't give the crown to anyone who wouldn't honor our alliance. And, I do have significant standing among my fellow rulers. I could persuade other kingdoms in North America to join this alliance."

Danior sat deep in thought. "You've said nothing but the truth to me, so I cannot ignore your offer. I will speak to the rest of our council about you. Your name was Setanta mac Lugh and Sarai, sorry, I didn't catch your last name?"

She'd been so close to skating by without that revelation. She'd felt so confident, telling him off, standing up for witches, supporting Setanta. Any hint of that power drained with just that simple request, and she hesitated. Danior frowned, and she knew from his eyes that he realized something was off.

"I like to go by my mother's last name, Meir," she said carefully, her eyes flickering away from his.

"And, your father's last name?"

"I don't like it," she insisted. "Why does it matter? My father's no one."

The lie made Danior's eyes flash with a spark of magic, and he leaned forward.

"Who is your father, Sarai?"

There was a weight in the air, heavy on her shoulders, in her head, around her throat. Unbidden, the words rose to her tongue. "Alaric Reinhart."

Danior's eyes widened. "I... see."

"Her father has no presence in her current life," Setanta said. "It shouldn't concern you and is irrelevant to our discussion."

"Alaric Reinhart's coven concerns everyone," Danior said flatly as he stood. "Though I agree, this is unrelated to your request. I'll go speak to the rest of our council now. I'll have to insist that you stay here for the time being. You as well... Miss Reinhart."

"That's fine," she said, as if it didn't bother her at all that she was seen as just as much of a threat as a vampire and had been called by the hated name she never wanted to hear again. As if anything she was feeling was actually fine. It didn't matter to her at all that she saw the recognition of her lie in his eyes, and her glare dared him to challenge her on it. His expression softened, but he said nothing as he left the pair alone in the enchanted room.

Chapter Twenty-Three: Age and Accents

"Witches," Sarai grumbled, and kicked the chair next to her harder than she intended, causing it to fall over. She glanced at Setanta, then looked down guiltily and picked up the chair, putting it upright. "Sorry."

"You have nothing to apologize for. It's not my furniture."

"Just the name!" she exclaimed. "Just that name, and they keep me locked up like I'm a, well, no offense, a vampire. They don't need anything other than that stupid name to treat me like a criminal. Every time. I just..." She got up and started pacing. "I'm not a bad person. I'm not my father."

"I know," he said calmly. "And, I'd like to say, I appreciate what you said."

Sarai shrugged and slumped back into a chair. "Just... needed to say something. They'll kick me out too."

"Too?"

"I tried to go to my mother's coven when I escaped my father," she explained. "They wouldn't let me through their barrier, to even talk. I could see them, but I couldn't... I scared them too much, was a disruption to their pacifist ideals because my existence was too violent. Who my father is, what my powers can do."

"So, your father's side wants to use you for the sake of his legacy and your mother's side abandoned you," he summed up.

Sarai winced. "Yeah, that's about it."

"I won't turn you away."

She hesitated, staring at the table in front of her. That was so... funny. A giggle bubbled in her chest, and she burst into laughter, tears filling her eyes. She wasn't quite sure why she was crying.

"Is something funny?" Setanta asked.

"Just... look, let's not pretend you want me around for selfless reasons, all right? You bribed me to be here. And maybe I owe you a bit for getting me away from the Vasi. Marcelle's nice, and while I think I could lo-really like her, she works for you. Who knows if she's just using me? You're just a nicer and richer version of the Reinhart coven."

"I like to think we're a little better than that. Less human sacrifice, I assume."

She shrugged. "I guess. I wasn't... I mean, he made me practice my power, but I wasn't slitting people's throats or carving out their insides like the rest of them."

"So, they are doing human sacrifice."

Sarai felt cold and uncomfortable under Setanta's red gaze. "What, you knew that already. Right?"

"I assumed. Thank you for confirming it."

"Whatever. It doesn't matter here. I got away so I wouldn't be part of it."

"Some things will follow you. I would be cautious of the witches here. If I were your father, I'd have spies in any large coven you might flee to. You're valuable to him in a way he cannot replace. You have no siblings with your dual powers, correct?"

"Older half-sister. She didn't get two gifts though,

and her mom's not a healer like mine was. She just does the dead people thing. My dad didn't hit her as much as he did me." She rolled her eyes. "Lucky me, right?"

"I'm sorry."

Sarai frowned. Why would Setanta care about any of that? "Does it matter? It's just more bullshit from my dad."

The way he looked at her told her it did. That bothered her.

"You know something you're not telling me," she accused. "What?"

His eyes grew sad, and he shook his head. "I'll tell you more when the grimoire is translated. Preferably somewhere with a few less listening enchantments in the walls."

Sarai pursed her lips and crossed her arms across her chest, but she understood. If it had to do with her father, she wasn't sure she wanted these witches to know whatever secret information Setanta knew.

The waiting was awkward, with Setanta sitting like a statue while Sarai shifted from position to position, trying to get comfortable. She pushed several chairs together and laid out on them like a bench, staring up at the ceiling.

"I feel like I should be talking to you about something," she said, breaking the silence.

"Anything in particular?"

"I dunno, it's just too quiet."

"Silence doesn't bother me. But we can converse if it makes you more comfortable."

Well, there was one burning question that came to mind. "We really are cool, about me sleeping with Marcelle? It doesn't bother you at all."

"Why would that bother me?"

"It would bother a lot of people I've known. There was this human guy I thought liked me once. Kept bumping into each other at the library, and he asked me out. Found out he was married when his wife tried to stab me in a hotel room. I'm not trying to be the other woman."

"You're not. For one, I don't think Marcelle is dating any other women. And as far as men go, right now it's just me. I consider Marcelle's sexual habits her business, not mine," he said. "Enjoy yourselves. Does it bother you that she and I are involved?"

Sarai shifted a little. "It's a little weird. Monogamy isn't her thing, I guess."

"It's not a very vampiric concept, no. Most of us aren't."

She didn't know what to say to that, and the silence settled back in, leading to her trying to come up with a new topic. As she did, she realized this was a good opportunity. He was a piece of living history, and she could quiz him.

"How old are you? I was reading up about your family in the library and the book just put 'unknown'."

"Older than Christianity. But beyond that I'm not certain due to the difference in calendars. There are some stories written about me that fit an incorrect timeline, but they were altered to fit the times they were recorded. I'd guess I'm around three, three and a half thousand."

Sarai rolled her eyes. He had to be messing with her. "There's no way you're that old. How the hell are you even alive?"

"I enjoy life." Setanta smirked. "And I'm very hard

to kill."

"That's the secret to living forever? Enjoying it and being stronger than the other guy?"

"Strength, cunning, and a dash of hedonism. It's gotten me this far. I intend to live forever and, so far, I'm succeeding."

"Cocky."

"Well earned, I think."

She laughed a little, still not sure if he was messing with her or not. Maybe he really was as old as he said he was? Not like she could disprove it. She moved on to fill the quiet.

"So, you're Irish, right?"

"From Ulster, specifically, but yes. I am Irish."

"How come you don't have an accent?"

"If you live anywhere long enough, you pick up the local accent along with general jargon," he said. Slipping into a thick Irish accent, he added, "I can revert, should the occasion call for it. And I am fluent in ancient Irish Gaeilge."

Sarai burst into laughter. "What kind of 'occasion should call for it?'" she asked, trying to mimic his accent.

"You sound closer to a drunken Scot than an Ulsterman."

"And you sound more like a 'wee leprechaun' than a vampire."

Setanta sighed, but she caught a glimpse of a smile. "I rather do take offense to that."

"Should I 'rather do' take offense to being told I sound like a Scot?"

"Absolutely." He chuckled, shaking his head. "You have just the slightest hint of an accent yourself, you know. The way you say the letter 'R', every once in a while. And the language you use for your spells. Hebrew, is it?"

"Yeah. It just always felt natural for spells. My father uses German, and I know enough to insult someone, but Hebrew feels more powerful and magical to me. Helps me channel my intentions better. I think my mother must have taught me when I was young, and it stuck. Don't really remember her though."

As she looked down at her own olive-skinned hands, a trait she shared with the late Sephardic mother she couldn't remember, a thought crossed her mind that made her uncomfortable concerning the fates of those who had darker complexions. Setanta was old, and he'd been a part of America for a long time.

"When did you come to America?"

"My family came before me, but I arrived in the early seventeen hundreds."

"So you... were around for the Civil War?"

"Are you asking me if I've ever owned slaves?" he said, cutting through the surface of her question. She bit her lip and nodded. "Not in America."

Well, what the hell did that mean? It was possible he'd been in the Caribbean somehow, maybe even been in some way responsible for the trans-Atlantic slave trade directly. Or had he been in Europe at that time? She couldn't remember enough history to know much about Ireland and whether the Irish were a significant part of that time in history for the Americas, though she knew at some point they hadn't been considered a favored group.

"You, uh, you want to tell me more about that?"

"I'm an Iron Age warlord, Sarai. We captured

slaves from neighboring clans and tribes. Raided the coasts of England, Wales, and Scotland for slaves. They did the same to us. It was standard at the time. That, and the first made vampires were all considered property. The dead are dead, and their bodies were controlled by our commands. That made all vampires slaves to purebloods."

"Wait, is Marcelle your…"

"She is not a slave, nor has she ever been. But had she been made two thousand years ago, she would have been. And it is a fact that I can control her with my words." He leaned forward. "I helped rid our society of the practice. I admit I did not start out with this mindset, but I learned to abhor slavery. By the time the practice was at its peak in America, New Ulster supported the north. You can ask Lilly for details of that experience if you like. She was a conductor on the Underground Railroad. I promise you, I took no part in perpetuating the Civil War era injustices."

As Sarai nodded in satisfaction, the doors opened, causing her to sit up straight and brush down her skirt. Danior had returned, flanked by two serious but curious looking witches. One was an older Native American woman, smartly dressed in a black pant suit, wearing white lace gloves, and her white hair braided to her waist with an eagle feather tied into it. The other was a tall blond man a little younger looking than Danior, but with prominent worry lines on his wide forehead and a much less put-together appearance with his untucked button-down top sporting more than one stain.

"These are my fellow coven leaders," Danior said.

"Hannah Little Hawk and Tobias Kroll," Setanta said without pause. "It's a pleasure to make your acquaintance."

"You know our names too then?" Hannah said. "And do you also know what gifts we have?"

"You do astral projection. I'm not sure what Mr. Kroll does, that information was missing."

"Let's keep it that way," Tobias said in a gruff voice.

"We've considered your offer. It's bold," Hannah said. "Our people wouldn't accept this easily. I heard you already had a fireball thrown at you."

"I believe in your ability to keep a handle on your own people," Setanta said. "And in the ability of mine to prove themselves."

"We don't control our people," Hannah said. "We represent them, assist them. Maybe someone like you can't understand that."

"I do understand. But I also think that masses can be guided into new eras by the strength of their leaders. We need each other."

"Perhaps. We'll need a little time to consider your alliance. And we'd like to ask you questions." She turned to Sarai. "Dear, you can leave if you wish. Someone can get you settled with a room, but don't wander. You understand if we need to take precautions given, well…"

"Given that you're Alaric Reinhart's daughter," Danior said bluntly.

Sarai glared at him. Of course, her reputation preceded her. That was fine. She didn't need this.

"Don't bother," she said, hopping to her feet. "I'm not staying."

"Not staying? Dear, this is one of the safest covens in the United States," Hannah insisted, her voice kind like a grandmother, but more condescending.

"Great. I'm staying with the vampires."

"But you can't be serious!" Danior exclaimed.

"I'm dead serious. Or undead serious." She laughed, but no one seemed to appreciate the joke. "Oh, come on, that was funny."

"We can't abide vampires holding a witch," Danior said to Setanta.

The prince shrugged. "Does it look like I'm holding her? She has free reign to wander our halls, and I personally released her from the silver the Vasi had her collared in. She is free to do as she pleases, within reason, and she is under our protection."

"And I 'please' to stay with them," she said, crossing her arms. "Are you going to stop me?"

The three exchanged glances.

"Our coven does not keep witches against their will," Hannah said, then glared at Setanta. "If she's harmed in any way…"

"I have no intention of allowing harm to come to her. One of my subordinates is waiting for me outside. If you wish, return to her, Sarai."

"Gladly."

She stepped out of the protected room, leaving the witches flabbergasted so they could have their conversation about whatever politics they needed to discuss with Setanta. She did her part, and now she was out.

The captain was waiting outside. "So, when we get new witches, they usually stay—"

"I'm not staying," Sarai cut her off. "If you want to walk me out, that'd be great. I'm going back with the vampires."

"I'm sorry, what?"

"Did I stutter?"

"No, just–"

"Your bosses said you don't keep witches against their will. I want to leave. Are you going to stop me?"

"Well, no, but…"

Sarai strode past and used her focus to merge back with the human world. She noticed a few eyes on her and assumed a few of the witch guards were keeping watch.

But they didn't matter, and it felt good that they didn't matter. She didn't *need* other witches. Sarai had made her choice, and it felt fantastic. Even the sun had come out, gleaming off the large puddles like gold. Though, it was only clear over the island; the rain had moved to pour over the water and the rest of the city, obscuring much of it. She stepped out to run through to where she could see Marcelle waiting.

"*Stop.*"

Sarai froze in her tracks, halfway to her lover's embrace. Liora's voice had been silent for so long, ever since she'd shouted at her for the singing and the nightmares. Immediately, she was on high alert.

"*Turn back.*"

She turned to go back into the tourist spot, but the rain began to pour even harder around her, drenching her as if buckets had been poured over her head. Sarai tried to move forward, to get back under shelter, but the water sloshed under her feet, hydroplaning her steps so that she couldn't move the direction she wanted. Panic gripped her. It was magic, and an attack. The witches weren't going to let her leave.

She couldn't see much but saw a figure who must

have been Marcelle moving forward, slowed by the protective spells like a woman forcing her way through molasses rather than water. Yet, she managed, and the vampire gripped Sarai's wrist, pulling with her supernatural strength to yank Sarai from the trap. The water surged after her but wrapped around Marcelle instead.

There was a flash of blinding light, and the rain disappeared. Sarai was alone, her protector ensnared by a trap meant for her.

Chapter Twenty-Four: The Gun

Marcelle didn't have time to recover from her disorientation before a pain unlike any she'd felt in recent memory encircled her neck. It burned like fire and she screamed, dropping to her knees and trying to pry it from her skin, her hands protected by her gloves. She could smell her flesh, hear it as it sizzled. Her ears rang from the pain, and she tried in a panic to calm herself, to figure out where she was, what she could do to stop the pain.

"Holy shit, it's a vampire!"

"Is-is that Sarai?"

"Of course it's not, you idiot. Sarai doesn't look anything like that."

"Well, where the hell is Sarai?"

"I don't know. Who the hell is *this*?"

Voices surrounded her, and she tried to breathe through the pain as her skin cracked and turned black against what had to be a silver collar, the blood both burning and dripping down her neck. More pain shot through her scalp as someone gripped her hair and forced her face up as tears and blood streamed. Two confused and angry men looked down at her in the dim, windowless room. Even in her state, she had enough training to make note of every detail she could.

There was a small scar on the blond man's chin, like a scab that had been picked on too many times and healed. The other, an auburn-haired human, had distinctive eyebrows, a nose that had been broken too many times, and a prominent Adam's apple. Their faces were burned into her memory as assuredly as the silver burned into her skin.

"Who are you?" she said through her fangs.

"Who are *you*?" the blond one countered.

"Don't talk to it, just dust it," the other said, looking down his hawkish nose at her.

"That would be a bad idea," she told him.

"It's a vampire, just kill it."

"I'm not getting near it. You kill it."

"It's silvered. You're scared of a silvered vampire?"

"If you're not scared, then you step up and kill it."

Neither of them killed 'it', so while they argued, Marcelle took her chance. She pulled out her gun from a hidden holster at the small of her back and fired off a shot at each of them. The blond one was struck in the head and fell to the floor, the other blinked away as if he'd never been there in the first place. A teleporter. She heard breathing behind her and spun around to shoot again. The teleporter grabbed her wrists and wrestled her down to the ground. Disorientated from the pain in her neck, she forgot for a moment that it robbed her strength and tried to brute force her way up. It was a stupid mistake, and she paid for it. The witch pulled the gun away from her.

"What the fuck," he said, shaking as he pointed the gun at her and stepped back, looking down at his dead companion. "What the fuck!"

"Don't kill it just yet."

A rustling behind them alerted Marcelle to the rest

of the room as she tried to focus through the pain, and through the engulfing scent of witch blood. A stern woman with wildly teased, short, blonde hair leaned forward in a tattered leather armchair, a frown deepening lines in her overly tanned forehead. She was a memorable woman, physically speaking. Not only was her hair distinct, but the twinkling jeweled gold that hung like an ox ring from her septum stood out too, as did the tribal eagle tattoo on her muscular bicep, shown off by her sleeveless, black leather vest of a top.

Despite being certain that Marcelle had never seen the woman before in her life, she looked familiar. Her eyes were different colors, one angry green and the other warm amber, a rare trait Marcelle didn't recognize. But something about her jawline and the angle of her nose... she must have seen her somewhere before. But where? A battle, perhaps. A whip rested at her waist and Marcelle's trained eyes noticed daggers hidden in her boots. The woman was a fighter.

"What kind of vampire carries a gun?" she asked, apparently more concerned about the presence of a gun rather than the dead witch.

"This kind," Marcelle said as she sat up from the floor, her fingers twitching to reach for her other hidden weapons. She was watching her now though, and she needed to be careful without her powers. She'd learned to rely on them too much. Talking could be a good distraction, and she needed information about these witches. "You're after Sarai Reinhart, aren't you?"

"How perceptive," the woman said. "So why are you here instead of her, killing my men?"

"Because Sarai Reinhart is under my protection. She is my ward, so I sprang her from your trap."

Her eyes narrowed. "And you are?"

"Marcelle de Sauveterre," she said. "Now why don't you take this collar off and we can talk like civilized people?"

She barked a laugh and strode over, staring down at her. "You're the one who killed my cousin. Is that civilized?"

Marcelle looked her up and down, reading her body. She wasn't mad about the loss of life. That meant nothing to her. She was mad Marcelle had stolen one of her possessions by ending the witch's life. "Yet, you don't care."

When their eyes met, she could feel the power struggle in the moment, feel her trying to assert dominance. Despite her agony and position on the floor, Marcelle met her with an equal gaze, one that did not submit. A dark scowl clouded the woman's expression, and she struck Marcelle across the face. Blood welled in her mouth where fangs scratched her tongue, and her bottom lip split. It felt strange, for the wounds not to heal.

But even in silver, Marcelle was still a vampire. The slap caused her to turn her face, but she held herself firm, preventing herself from being knocked to the floor as intended. She knew what sort of person this was. She'd known her kind too often in her human life, though they were usually male. They were the ones used to seeing women and lower-class unfortunates meekly whimpering, groveling, or sobbing at their feet. She wouldn't give the witch the satisfaction.

Marcelle spat the blood on the floor and looked up at her without a hint of the pain she was in on her face, not a shred of fear. "That's no way to treat a lady."

The witch glared. "You're not really a lady. You're a corpse."

That face, Marcelle recognized the glare. She'd seen a similar glare, though with less hatred. There was even a similar smell in the air, a hint under the scent of her own burning skin and the blood of the dead man on the floor. She knew who this was.

"You're Sarai's sister," she said. The recognition brought a smile to the woman's face.

"Alma Reinhart. Pleased to make your acquaintance. Is it obvious? I didn't think we looked alike."

"You and your sister share a frown."

"Half-sister." Alma walked around her, large boots landing heavy and slow. Marcelle suppressed the urge to roll her eyes. Amateur. Did she think she was frightening? "And where is the beloved Sarai?"

"Not here. I have to say, you're not what I expected, Alma. Sarai called you a good person."

Alma laughed. "Silly girl, isn't she? Good, bad. It's subjective. You're a vampire, isn't that your whole persona? Finding reasons why bad things are good if they help you survive?"

"Probably why I can smell it rolling off you in waves."

"It?"

"Your bullshit. It stinks."

Alma's eyes narrowed, and her pierced nose wrinkled. "Why don't you just tell me where Sarai is?"

"She is protected."

"At the Ellis Coven?" she said. "Our spies contacted us from there. They wouldn't have triggered the trap spell if they weren't certain they could have caught her. Yet here you are. A vampire, of all things."

Marcelle made a mental note that she used the plural form of the word, rather than referencing a single spy. The Ellis Coven needed a little purging, it seemed. She'd be more than happy to let them know and help if they let her in the door.

Alma knelt. "So, what is a vampire doing in the Ellis Coven with my sister?"

"Your spies haven't told you?" she mused. She didn't answer, which was an answer in and of itself as far as Marcelle was concerned. If Alma didn't know about Setanta and the presence of vampires on Ellis Island, then either her spies weren't high up enough to know, weren't part of the guard, or had been caught and prevented from transmitting further information. Marcelle hoped it was the latter.

Unimpressed with her response, Alma reached out and pressed her finger against the black, bleeding, cracked skin of Marcelle's neck as it sizzled against the silver. Pain shot through her, and she hissed, fangs bared.

"Why were you with my sister?" she asked and pressed the collar against her skin harder. Marcelle winced, but she'd had enough time to adjust mentally. She could handle pain. "Why are vampires at the Ellis Coven?"

It was a good thing. As long as Alma wanted something from her, she wouldn't kill her. But if Marcelle knew mortals and the behavior patterns of people like her, it would not be fun. She had to keep an eye out for an opening, a way to turn the tables. She did have weapons on her person. Hidden silver needles, a blade. They assumed that the silver had her bound as thoroughly as she could be, that she was helpless without her speed and strength. That would be their mistake.

"We had business," Marcelle said. "Thinking of buying a condo on the island."

Alma sighed. "Kurt, tie its hands and frisk it."

Marcelle found herself shoved to the floor, her hands yanked behind her back and cuffed. She tested the metal. She could break it if the collar were to be removed, but she needed to figure out a way around them without her strength. Given the opportunity, she could contort herself to bring her hands to the front, which was a start to making them useful. Unfortunately, she was searched, and the silver daggers and needles were pulled free. She was forced up into a chair, her ankles cuffed to the legs. That made things more difficult.

"Well, well, you are someone important," murmured Alma as she examined one of the daggers. It had the crest of the royal family on the hilt, and other markings indicating her rank. Though Marcelle doubted the witch knew enough about vampire society and politics to know anything other than that the wolf on the crest belonged to a pureblood, if she even knew that much.

"Are we… are we doing anything about Hugo?" Kurt asked, glancing at his dead partner.

Alma didn't even look up. "We'll take care of it later." She unsheathed the dagger and touched the blade. "Silver. You know you could hurt yourself with this."

"Usually, I hurt other people with it."

"Like this?" She pressed the bare silver against

Marcelle's cheek, and the pain was immediate, like rubbing her face against hot coals. While the vampire had mentally adjusted to the pain around her neck, more was far from welcome, and elicited a tortured shout. The scent of her own burning flesh permeated the air, turning her stomach. Alma pulled the blade away, black flakes of skin sticking where it had melted against the metal.

"That is really something to watch."

Marcelle glared, not stifling her whimpers. Her cheek wasn't healing with the silver suppressing her abilities. Depending on how far Alma went, that could be very dangerous. She made up her mind not to bother attempting to suppress her screams. The more intense her reaction, the more chance Alma would linger on less painful torture longer before escalating. That particular technique worked more often on male torturers than female, but it was always worth a try.

"Wow." Alma leaned closer. "I can see your muscle. You're just sitting there with your cheek all out."

She tossed away the silver dagger and held up her hand. Her nails grew like claws, long and sharp, and without warning she pierced the skin of Marcelle's untouched cheek. For a moment, nothing happened. Then Marcelle felt the pain, her eyes widening. She felt a crawling sensation spreading from the scratch, eating away at her face. She screamed again, this time in genuine fear as well as pain.

"Do you know what little baby Sarai can do?" Alma slashed across Marcelle's collarbone, and the pain radiated across her skin where the witch cut. She shrieked, straining against the metal encircling her wrists and ankles. Oh, it would feel so good to kill this witch. Marcelle knew right then and there that she wanted to kill Alma, to feel her beating heart and taste her blood. "I'm better at it. Now, we can play this game until you're nothing but blood, bone, and guts, or you can tell me what the hell vampires are doing on Ellis Island."

"Why are you so concerned?" she gasped. "Tell me why it matters, and I'll consider it."

Alma's eyes narrowed. Apparently, she was used to getting her way quickly. She could see why the witch would get answers fast, considering her power, but most of those answers had to be worthless. Victims would say anything to make the torture stop. If it wasn't for the fact that Marcelle was certain Alma would kill her the moment she didn't have a use for her, she'd have told her some sweet nothing lies to make the torture stop too.

But her life now depended on how long she could make the torture last, so that she had more time to break free. If that was even a possibility.

"How about you tell me what I want to know, and I'll let you have a little blood from your murder victim?"

A tempting offer if Marcelle had been about four hundred or more years younger. She smiled to show off her fangs, feeling the pain in her necrotic and bleeding cheeks from the strain.

"I'd prefer yours. Lean in a little closer, I'd be happy to take some."

Alma glared and gripped her prisoner's shirt, yanking it open to expose more pale skin. One of

Alma's claws drew down her breast, decay blossoming like a butterfly unfurling its wings.

Marcelle screamed.

Chapter Twenty-Five: Missing

The moment Sarai realized what had happened, she shifted back to the witch's side of Ellis Island, ran back into the coven, and pushed past the guards. Hyper focused, she ignored their questions as she burst back into the conference room, still dripping what felt like gallons of water into twin pools at her feet. Setanta sat there with the other three witches, hands clasped on the table.

"Dear, why are you dripping-" Hannah began, but Sarai cut her off.

"There was a trap," she gasped.

Setanta stood. "What trap?"

"There's no trap," Danior said. "We didn't even know you were coming. We couldn't have prepared one."

"Well someone set up a water trap right outside your damn front doors and Marcelle pushed me out of it, and now she's gone!" Sarai shouted. "Where did you take her?"

Danior shook his head. "I do not lie. But you... you think you're telling the truth."

"I *am* telling the truth!"

He frowned. "Show me where this happened."

She led the group outside to the front doors, Danior gesturing for some of the guards to follow, and pointed to the spot on the ground that was still a puddle.

"Right there," Sarai said. "The water was all around me, and trying to trap me, then Marcelle got close enough to push me out, and it teleported her out instead."

Setanta rounded on the witches, and while he didn't have any magical spell-power, Sarai could feel anger radiating from his body. It was satisfying to see it directed at the witches.

"Where is my commander?" he said in a quiet voice that made her tremble.

"Sir, please calm down. We've done nothing to your commander," Danior said. "Captain Moretti, what do you know about this?"

"If anything was here, it wasn't placed today." She frowned, and knelt by the puddle, touching her fingers to the water, letting her fingers spark. "This was put here a while ago. I'd say even years. Two, maybe?"

"To... target vampires? Who put this here?" Tobias said. "That's not one of our safeguards as far as I know."

"Water, teleportation..." Moretti stared, deep in thought. "We have a few members with related powers. Water is good for holding spells, letting them soak into a place. If they worked together, they could set up a trap like that."

"Anyone who joined in the last two years?"

"Captain?" piped up one of the guards. "Kurt and Hugo... they're not guards, but they help with processing new witches. I haven't seen them since the vampires showed up. Kurt does teleportation. Hugo works with water."

If these witches hadn't set the trap, if this unknown duo had set a trap years ago and it triggered for Sarai when she passed through on her own… Then Kurt and Hugo had been placed in the coven with a mission.

"My father put them here," she whispered. "It's the kind of thing he'd do, put spies in other covens, to keep an eye out for me. And get information, but he's looking for me. And he got Marcelle instead." An uncontrolled tremble gripped her body. "Marcelle's with him."

Setanta put a cool, strong hand on her shoulder, but his expression was far more stern than reassuring as he looked at the three witches.

"I want my commander found."

"I can help with that," the Native American woman said. "I can astral project to her, find where the teleportation took your commander. I'll need to know a little about her. If you have something of hers, that would help."

"She's got long black hair, bright blue eyes, porcelain skin, she's pretty, a little taller than me, but not much, I think she uses a rosewater perfume, and she likes bright red lipstick and…" Sarai paused, feeling everyone's eyes on her. She was babbling like a lovesick teenager, and she knew it. But their judgement didn't matter. "And you need to help her."

"We do happen to have something of hers," Setanta said, and held out his hand to Sarai. She stared at him in confusion.

"What? Me, I don't…" She looked down at her hand, at the antique gold ring there. She nodded and gave the ring to Hannah. "Here. It's her ring. Well, it might have been some French king's first, but it's hers now. She gave it to me."

"That's quite a gift," Hannah said as she took the

ring and examined it. "I need somewhere unenchanted to sit so I can project myself. Come."

They followed her back into the building and an office room, different from the one that was spelled against violence. Sarai briefly wondered why there was such a normal looking room without enchantments she could sense but was more bothered by how slow the old woman moved. It was an emergency, and she moved at the pace of a snail. All Sarai wanted to do was to yell at her to hurry up.

"Is there anything I can do to help?" she said instead, anxiety clear as broken glass in her voice.

"Quiet and calm," Hannah murmured with a stern glare as she pulled off her delicate lace gloves. She closed her eyes, cupping the ring in her hands, and slumped in the chair a little, looking almost as if she were sleeping.

"How long is this going to take?" Sarai whispered.

Hannah shot up, as if she'd heard her. "Do you have anything else of hers?" she said, holding up the ring. "This is powerful from age, but it led me to Versailles, and I don't think she's there."

Setanta thought for a moment. "That's the best link to her we have. She's kept it since the Renaissance. The only other thing I can think of without going back to our haven is my blood. It runs through her veins."

Hannah looked visibly uncomfortable. "Well, between you and the ring, I may be able to pinpoint her. But just how many vampires are there with your blood?"

"Many. French ones from that era... fewer, but more than just Marcelle," Setanta admitted.

Hannah sighed. "This will take a little time. Give

me your hand." She held out her hand, and Setanta gave her his. She frowned, no doubt confused by the strange temperature of the pureblood's body, and then closed her eyes again.

It did take longer for Hannah the second time around. Every minute felt like an hour, though she wasn't sure how long had actually passed, and Sarai found herself pacing. Setanta was still as a statue, and it was unnerving, so she almost felt as if she were balancing out his stillness with her motion.

Suddenly, Hannah's eyes opened, and she once more sat upright, but her eyes were different. Glassed over and white, as if she were blind.

"I see her," she said in a distant voice, as if speaking from the far end of a tunnel. "I think. The one your blood and the ring call to in harmony. She... is it a she?"

Setanta tensed. "You should be able to tell."

She screamed, pushing away and blinking rapidly as her eyes returned to deep brown. "Good god, I've never seen..." She looked up at the surrounding faces. "You need to find her, now. I'm not sure what will be left if you don't. She's in an abandoned building. No, I can do better. Give me a map."

"I got it," Moretti said. She ran off, then reappeared slightly out of breath with a folded tourist style map of the city. "Will this do?"

"Perfect, perfect, bring it here."

Captain Moretti laid out the map in front of Hannah, who put the antique ring into Setanta's hand, her bony digits shaking as she focused and touched her other hand to the feather in her hair. Sarai recognized the surge of power as coming from the item. It had to be her focus, like Sarai's glove. For a moment she wondered how something as fragile as a feather had withstood the test of time, but that didn't matter. What mattered were the words the old woman murmured. Sarai couldn't quite catch or make sense of them, but the map folded and crumpled before their eyes, twisting itself until a paper bird arose, flapping its wings.

Sarai's eyes widened. She'd never seen such an intricate spell before. The use of the craft and the spell involved was so beyond her ability, it seemed ridiculous in that moment that she'd ever thought to evade more powerful witches. It was a miracle her rudimentary wards protected her as long as they had.

"This will lead you to her. They loosely warded their location with salt as an afterthought against most scrying, but no such paltry magic will defend against my astral eyes," Hannah explained. "You must hurry. They aren't expecting company, but I don't know how much longer..." Her voice trailed off, and a lump formed in Sarai's throat.

"What am I facing?" Setanta said, slipping Marcelle's ring back onto Sarai's finger and lifting up the paper bird in his hand.

"Three witches in the room with her. One seemed to be dead on the floor. I didn't see the rest of the building, so I don't know if there's more."

"One... one is my father, right?" Sarai said, feeling cold sweat and nervous numbness creep through her body. "His gift... he destroys people. He has Marcelle. That means he's destroying her piece by piece. I've seen- he has my Marcelle."

Hannah's eyes filled with sympathy. "I'm not sure if I saw your father, but there was a man there. Stay here, child. We'll look after you."

Sarai clenched her teeth. "No." She looked up at Setanta. "There's at least two of them. Two of us. You don't have time to get Angela, Bear, or Lilly. You need me."

"I can take down a handful of witches on my own," he assured her.

"One of them is probably my father."

"All the more reason for you to stay." He touched the tip of the paper bird's wing, and that small gesture, that looking away from her as she spoke, filled Sarai with fury. Even in her rage, she knew how to get what she wanted.

"He hurt me. As Marcelle's ward and a guest under your protection at your palace, I have rights, don't I?"

She could see him make the connection, and his eyes narrowed as he looked up at her. Good, she'd gotten his attention.

"As your protector's sire, it would be remiss of me to bring you into potential danger. And he is not a vampire. Neither are you," he reminded her.

"That didn't matter when it came to Dr. Stearne, did it? He was human. I'm a witch. You gave him to me. Are you going to break your own laws?" Sarai said, her voice higher than she remembered it being. When had she started shouting? "Alaric Reinhart has harmed me in more ways than you can imagine, so I want his life."

"If anyone has a right to his life according to our laws, it's Marcelle," Setanta said. "Dr. Stearne was an exception I extended to you, not a mandatory part of our law. It is up to the discretion of the highest-ranking pureblood to consider the matter. To me. You stay, end of story."

"I read your law books, so I know I have that right in your society," Sarai snapped. "Marcelle drank my blood." There was a collective gasp from the witches around them. "Twice. I gave it to her on my own. And that makes me part of your world. As, as a source. And since he acted against me, torturing me for years, I submit to you, oh wise vampire prince and highest-ranking pureblood to consider the matter, that no one has been more harmed by Alaric Reinhart than me, his daughter. On those grounds, I claim his life. I want to be there, and you are going to take me with you."

"Dear, we couldn't possibly…" Hannah began, but fell silent when Setanta raised his hand.

"You read our laws."

"I was bored."

The pair stared at each other, and once more Sarai could feel the power radiating off him not in a magical way, but from his sheer will. He wanted her to back down, to give up her claim. And she met his blood-red gaze firmly to tell him there wasn't a chance in hell. She was going to help save Marcelle.

"Enough talk," he announced. "You have a legitimate claim, and I will honor it." Sarai almost burst with relief but fear as to what she had gotten herself into replaced the fight instinct that had taken over. He gestured for her to follow and lifted the paper bird into the air. It took off, flying out toward the entrance. Setanta, Sarai, and Moretti gave chase.

"You can't just up and hunt down a witch," the captain tried to say as she opened the way out into the human world, and they followed the bird to the edge of the island. "You need to take me with you wherever this is."

"You have no claim," Setanta said.

"You're not going to be able to get across the water fast enough without me. Unless you plan on swimming? We have spelled boats, you need us with you," Moretti snapped.

"I can get across without a boat. Sarai, hold this for me."

To Sarai's surprise, he stripped off his shirt and handed it to her, revealing a warrior's muscular body, covered over almost every inch with intricate and ancient blue tattoos in a Celtic knotwork style, portraying animals and intertwining designs across his skin. Then, his back crunched, as if someone struck bone with a sledgehammer. His eyes closed in pain as his skin shifted, bones and muscle twisting and growing. Sarai and the other witch took a step back in shock.

When it was done, a large pair of pale, almost translucent and demonic bat wings stretched out from his body. They too were covered in blue ink. Sarai had never believed the rumors that vampires could fly, but here was a living vampire, one with magic beyond what she had believed possible.

He opened his bright red eyes and held out a hand to Sarai, but she hesitated, still trying to wrap her mind around the creature before her.

"How?"

"I'm a pureblood."

"But…"

"I don't want to waste time, Sarai. I would like to rescue my mistress. Will you be joining me to rescue your lover?"

She took a deep breath then, heart pounding, she accepted. He pulled her close against his strong body. She didn't have much time to think about it before he murmured, "Close your eyes."

Setanta jumped, and they were launched into the stormy sky, leaving the captain behind. Sarai didn't dare peek, shouting in fear as air lashed around them.

She could feel the power in his body, the beating of his monstrous wings. At least his body provided some hint of warmth, unlike Marcelle's. Otherwise, between the air and the rain, Sarai might have frozen.

"Won't the humans see us?" she asked close to his ear as wind and rain whipped about them.

"Not in this rain. They won't know what they saw."

They sped through New York City, voices and horns and traffic a whirl around them. Then, mercifully, it ended.

Chapter Twenty-Six: Alma

Upon landing well outside of the main city, Sarai vomited. She managed not to throw up on the vampire prince, but it was a near miss. Setanta didn't do well disguising his sense of disgust as he wrinkled his nose, and she felt guilty. To someone with a heightened sense of smell, she couldn't imagine very many worse things than being subjected to vomit.

"Sorry," she gasped. "Not used to flying."

"It's fine." He closed his eyes as his wings shrunk into his back, and he listened. "Six hearts beating below us. Two on the top floor, four on the bottom." He took his shirt from her and put it on.

At that point, Sarai realized they'd landed on a rooftop, and that her vomit was dripping down a storm drain like the world's worst precipitation. At least it was still raining, so there was water to cut the smell.

"Okay, so how do we do this?"

He knelt down and placed his hand against a relatively clean part of the roof, focusing. "Windows boarded up and spelled. Front door spelled. Back door could be an option. Come on. And stay silent."

Setanta gripped her waist once again, and they dropped off the side of the roof. Anticipating her own reaction, she held her breath to suppress a yelp, glad to be on solid ground. There was a thin line of wet, clumped salt along the edge of the doorway, which had already been broken by the sloshing rain. No wonder it was easy to get in; the protection was so clumsy it was ridiculous.

"Stay behind me and let me handle things," he said and reached for the door.

"Wait." She put her hand over his to stop him. "I should go first. They're looking for me, right? I can distract them, and you... do what you do."

"And they won't attack you?"

Sarai shook her head. "The only one who ever hurt me was my father. No one else would dare hurt me."

"If you insist. It's your people. We can try this your way." He stepped to the side of the door, out of sight of anyone inside if it were to open.

Sarai stepped up to the door and took a deep breath. It was terrifying, what she was about to do, and she hesitated. But at that moment, a horrible scream shattered the air and sent goosebumps erupting all over her body.

Marcelle.

She threw open the door and came face to face with four surprised male witches.

"What..."

"Tell my father I'm here," she said. Her body couldn't stop shaking. "He's looking for me, right? I'm Sarai Reinhart. I'm back all on my own, and you don't need to set anymore traps for me."

They all looked at each other, confusion obvious. The wind picked up around Sarai and the door slammed shut behind her. She glanced behind her for a moment, and when she looked back, gurgling came from the throat of one of the men, while Setanta held a beating heart in each hand. Two of the men dropped, and he tore his fangs out from the third's throat, as he also collapsed. Before the fourth had a chance to scream or attack, Sarai stepped forward and put a hand to his throat. Her power surged forth, driven by a new bout of screaming from the floor above them, and death consumed his body at a rate faster than she'd ever accomplished before. His arms fell to his sides, head drooping as it dripped oxygen-starved black blood onto the floor, and he waited in silence for orders from his new mistress.

Sarai let go, her hand sparking with deadly magic as her heart raced.

"I... I wasn't planning on doing that," she whispered. Setanta turned around and dropped the hearts to the floor. The image did nothing for the panic settling in her chest. He always seemed so... refined. So removed from the violence she'd seen when she'd met Marcelle. Yet there he was, the picture of a blood hungry monster.

"I'm not one to judge," he said as he pulled out a handkerchief and wiped most of the blood from his mouth. Should he be snarling instead of talking? He still sounded like himself. But she'd killed and puppeteered one of the witches herself, so maybe they were both monsters. "Let's move."

He darted up the stairs, and she scrambled after him, stopping for a moment to call back for the corpse to follow and protect her. It lumbered after her, barely a second thought in her mind. As she got to the top, she spotted Setanta waiting, listening at the door.

"Two hearts," he murmured.

Marcelle screamed again. Sarai thought she had mentally prepared, but until that moment, she didn't know the effect her father would have on her. She had always feared him; that was the reason she ran instead of ever confronting him. But it felt different, as she listened to him in the other room, torturing the woman she cared for. All fear drained from her body to be replaced with a burning rage that would make even mythical Greek furies tremble. The floor creaked under her feet as she felt her power well in the air around her, destroying what little life lingered in the water-damaged wooden floors beneath her.

Setanta took a step back and with only her frenzied wrath guiding her, Sarai threw open the door.

Alma Reinhart looked up from some sort of mess in a chair with surprise on her face and a whip in her hand that shimmered with death magic and dripped with blood. But she wasn't the Alma that Sarai remembered. Her hair was so different from the straight platinum it had been once, her skin much tanner as if she'd spent hours in the sun, and even the tattoo was new. It had been six years, but how could a person change so drastically?

Alma's expression melted into a smile that refused to extend to her eyes.

"Well, look who decided to join the party."

All of Sarai's rage evaporated, and the floor felt as if it dropped out from under her.

"Alma?" she whispered. "Where, where's Dad?"

"Daddy doesn't leave the coven much lately. So, I'm here to bring you to visit him."

Setanta stepped forward, the floorboards protesting under his presence as he stood behind Sarai. He stayed only a moment before darting forward and grabbing Alma by her throat.

"*D'anam don Gáe Bulg*," he snarled in what must have been Irish.

"Wait!" Sarai shrieked. "Don't kill her! Please, she's my sister!"

Setanta held her in the air as she gasped and flailed, then tossed her aside as he turned his attention to the mess in the chair. It was a person, or it likely was. Its scalp had been sliced off to reveal blood and bone, shirt removed for access to more skin that was covered in a mix of burns, cuts, and decay. The face had been mutilated beyond recognition, but the red eyes and the way the silver collar burned around its neck confirmed that the poor creature was a vampire.

"Oh god, oh…"

Setanta darted past the paralyzed and stammering Sarai to grip the silver collar in his gloved hands and yank it into two clean pieces. Marcelle's yowl of agony as burnt flesh tore brought tears to Sarai's eyes.

"Blood," she whispered. "You need blood. I can help." There was no doubt in her mind that the only reason anyone could survive such wounds was that they weren't alive in the first place. A mortal would have gone into shock. Or died.

"You want to feed it?" Alma said in hoarse disgust as she pulled herself to her feet.

"You did this?" Sarai asked through threatening tears. "How could you do this to her?"

"Just trying to find you, genius. I don't get peace and quiet until I drag your sorry ass back to make up for the mistake of letting you go in the first place," Alma snapped.

"Mistake? But you know how much Dad hurt me. Hurt us!"

"Because you can't just do what you're told! Do you have any idea how lucky you are? You just *get* everything. You have *two* gifts. You get Dad focusing on all that special magic shit for you. He stays up all night, thinking about rituals for you. If I could just crawl into your skin and have all those good things, my life would be perfect."

"But... but you helped me."

"I helped *me*. You made me miserable, every time Dad would look at you. When you talked about the lessons he gave you that I didn't get. You were that extra sister I didn't need around, and I got rid of you."

"Extra?" It felt like ice water had been dumped on her head. "I... I never saw you as extra. You're my sister."

"Half-sister. And even with you gone, he wouldn't even consider rituals for my future. Couldn't shut up about getting you back. And when mom read my brain and told him I helped, well. Here I am. Responsible for getting you back. So just make this easy and come with me."

"Alma..." Years of memories, of idealizing their time together, spun like a tornado in her mind. When Alma had been afraid of the dark, Sarai used her healing magic to make a glowing light in her palm. When Sarai had been starved for breaking rules, Alma would sneak her food. They'd been a team. They had loved each other; that had to be true. It didn't make sense otherwise. And if they loved each other, how could Alma ever even think badly of her, just for being born with two gifts and for attention she never wanted? "Alma, you don't have to go back to him. Come with me. With us. We'll keep you safe from him."

Alma laughed. "Your boyfriend wants to kill me."

"If you're referring to me, I'd love nothing more than to tear you to pieces," Setanta said with an eerie calm. "You took your pound of flesh from my progeny. But if you give your blood to heal her, I'll consider it a partial payment on your debt."

"They're good people," Sarai promised. "Listen to him. They've helped me, I live with them now in their palace. It's so much nicer than the coven, you'd love it. You can have my room, and–"

"Oh, it's so much nicer, is it?" Alma hissed. "You get the 'good people', get to live in a palace, and I get to share a lame house with my mom as long as we stay in Dad's good graces. But I don't need charity. I don't need your pity."

"It's not pity! If it's mine, it's yours. I want to be here for you, I love you."

"Fuck you, Sarai. And fuck your vampire boyfriend and his bitch, too."

Her whip cracked as it broke the sound barrier, and Sarai flinched, expecting pain. Instead, Setanta's arm reached out, the end of the whip wrapping around his wrist instead of Sarai's neck.

He grunted, and Sarai saw black necrosis spreading through his veins across his flesh, clouding away the blue tattoos. It was slower than it should have been, evidence of protection spells on his person, but dangerous. Setanta fell to his knees as his strength was drained by the life-robbing magic, red anger burning in his eyes.

"No!" Sarai covered his wrist with her hand, forcing her power through her red glove and back through the whip she knew was her sister's magical focus. The damage in the prince's skin reversed, and the tips of Alma's fingers began to turn black where she held onto the weapon. She yelped in pain, as if she'd put her hand on a burning stove.

"Oh, you'd kill me?" she said through her teeth. "You used to talk about how you wanted to do things together, but you'd hurt me with your power, after everything? You owe me."

"You started it when you skinned my girlfriend!" Sarai shouted, and her power surged forward. Necrosis spread upwards from Alma's hand, almost reaching her eagle tattoo as she screamed. "If you're surprised I'd fight back after everything you just said, then you never knew me. I fought Father when I could. I'll fight you."

Alma tried to force her own power back through the whip, but Sarai did her best to hold her at bay, even as pain began to twinge in her fingers. "Just give up! You're being so selfish, and you already get everything. You've had your fun. Now come home and think of someone else for a change. You used to say you'd do anything for me. Well, do this!"

Setanta's wrist healed, the necrosis gone, and he gripped the whip tight, digging his fingernails into his own palm hard enough to draw blood. As soon as it was drawn, Sarai could feel it amplifying her own power. Blood magic; of course, a vampire witch would use blood magic. "Don't stop," he told her.

"That promise is null now," Sarai said, her own black magic pulsing with every slow beat of the pureblood's heart. Fear filled Alma's heterochromatic eyes. "If I'd know how you felt toward me, I'd never have made a promise like that. I will always put myself over anyone who hurts me. Let him go now, or you'll lose that arm!"

But panic was settling in. If Alma didn't stop, if losing an arm and a little pain wasn't enough to stop her, Sarai didn't think she had the heart to finish her. She prayed Alma wouldn't call the bluff. That some sliver of sisterhood still existed, enough to make her stop and recant what she'd said. If she didn't... Setanta was already recovering. She didn't want him to kill Alma.

"Kurt!"

The cowering cousin Sarai had hardly even realized was in the room snapped into existence next to Alma, and then the pair blinked out of space along with the whip, as if they'd never even been in the room. Kurt, the teleporter. Sarai vaguely remembered him. And with his power, they'd gotten away.

She looked down at her hand, the pain throbbing like nothing she'd ever felt before. Her skin had turned black as charcoal, like she'd touched lightning.

A moan disrupted her thoughts, and she dropped to Marcelle's side, ignoring her own pain.

"Blood," she murmured, half in shock as she tried to process everything that had happened. "I need to give her my blood."

"This is not the same as a love bite," Setanta cautioned. "She may lose herself. Hurt you."

"I don't care. She wouldn't be here if it weren't for me. You can compel her to obey you with just your words, right? Stop her if she goes too far." Sarai brushed her hair out of the away and wrapped her arms around the bloody mess. "Drink, please. Please be okay, take what you need. Take everything you need."

The creature in her arms didn't hesitate. It went

straight for her vein, the sharp teeth in the front of its mouth tearing through skin just as the fangs pierced. It hurt terribly, the bite too vicious and needy for the mild numbing to make a difference, but Sarai forced herself to endure despite her eyes filling with tears. The pain was nothing compared to what Marcelle had experienced.

As her head began to spin, she felt a strong pair of arms around her, supporting her. Somehow, Setanta being so close relaxed her. Even his scent was pleasant, above the horror of burnt and raw flesh. He smelled of misty winters and a bit of the same rosewater as Marcelle. It was a nice scent to experience as she lost consciousness.

"Stop, Marcelle," he ordered in a soft tone, and the slurping Sarai could feel and hear at her neck ended as the vampire pulled away.

The skin had returned to Marcelle's face, though it still looked unhealthily thin, with the blue lines of blood vessels too close to the surface. Her hair was gone, from her eyebrows and eyelashes to the long black strands that usually graced her head.

"Sarai," she murmured. "You shouldn't have."

"Can you heal yourself?" Setanta asked.

Sarai nodded, which made her head spin. "It'll take me a little, I'm not at my best right now. Dizzy."

A pricked finger dripping liquid ecstasy was pushed past her lips and she sucked the drops she could before the wound closed. Immediately, she felt better, though felt a flash of guilt for drinking it when previously she'd preferred it applied directly to her wounds. Considering the situation, it was easy to forgive Marcelle for forgetting.

"Thanks. You shouldn't be giving me your blood though, Marcelle. You need all you can get," Sarai said.

"A few drops will be fine," Marcelle said.

"Still, Setanta could have maybe…" She blushed at the thought of sucking blood from his fingertips, but it was a better alternative than letting Marcelle spill her own.

"No," Setanta said. "My blood would kill you. Marcelle, *mo anam cara*, my soul mate, how do you feel?"

"Better. Much better." She stood, helping him hold Sarai between them.

"There are three fresh dead below. Still warm, if you need more. Don't take more from Sarai for now," Setanta said.

"I think what I took was enough." She closed her eyes and ran her hand over her head. Hair had started to grow again on her head, to Sarai's surprise. Soon, it was a long, wild mess, back to its original length as it brushed against the wooden floor.

It was as if she hadn't endured anything at all.

Yet, for some reason, even with the few drops of blood she'd taken, Sarai felt horrible. The pain in her hand had ebbed away, but as she looked down, she realized it wasn't from healing.

"Oh god," Marcelle whispered. "Sarai, your hand."

Sarai gingerly touched the withered hand; it cracked like shattered marble. She felt nothing as her fingers and palm crumbled away, but the shock was too much. Her head and the room spun, and she fell into a deep blackness that smelled of rosewater.

Chapter Twenty-Seven: Blankets and Blood

When Sarai came to, she found herself comfortably on the couch back at the penthouse, a blanket draped over her. She blinked a few times, staring up at the expensive light fixture above her. It was modern, like the rest of the apartment's features, made of interlocking circles like halos that emanated a white electric glow. It was so peaceful.

The peace didn't last long. The memory of what happened to Marcelle flooded her mind and she shot up, looking for her lover. Marcelle sat curled up against Setanta on the far side of the couch with his arms around her.

The image made her pause. She should be the one holding Marcelle, shouldn't she? She wanted to help her lover, yet, at that moment, she felt wildly inadequate. The two there had been together for so long, with portraits of their relationship framed in Marcelle's room watching them make love. This man had saved her from death, been there for her for hundreds of years. Sarai had just slept with her once and gone on a single date. She was nothing in comparison. Of course, Marcelle would want comfort in his arms, her head resting on his shoulder. Not the witch she had one encounter with. It was just for fun, their experience.

Just fun.

If it was just fun, then why did the possibility of losing Marcelle make Sarai panic like nothing ever had before in her life?

Marcelle lifted her head up from Setanta's shoulder, and what she'd been doing became obvious. Blood trickled down from a cut on his neck, soaking into the white collar of his undershirt.

Marcelle looked too... whole. It was eerie. Sarai knew what it was like to heal from wounds due to her ability, but with Marcelle, the wounds had been so severe. She'd never seen anyone endure something like that and come out fine on the other side.

"My blood isn't enough?" Sarai blurted. "I can give more."

"I'm countering your blood," Setanta said as Marcelle drank from him. "She took a lot from you. Mine will keep her from having side effects."

"Oh." That made sense. "Yeah, she had nightmares last time she took a lot from me." Even when Sarai wanted to help, she just hurt others.

Marcelle licked Setanta's wound as it closed, and all evidence of the feeding was gone as she rested her head against his chest.

"Is there anything I can do to help?" she asked the couple.

"You've helped plenty. You saved me." Marcelle's eyes softened. "Your sister didn't do those things to you, did she?"

"No, she... she was always nice to me but now I don't know. Maybe things she did I thought were nice, weren't? She helped me escape my dad. I used to think that was because she loved me. He was the one who hurt us. Like with you..." Sarai tensed and looked away. "I-I'll get you more blankets. Warmth makes you feel better, right? I can get you something warm."

"Sarai."

"I didn't think she could do that. Alma. I didn't think she could ever hurt someone like that. I thought she loved me."

"Does it hurt?" Marcelle interrupted with concern.

Sarai frowned. "What do you mean?"

Marcelle's eyes flickered down to Sarai's side.

"What..." Her hand. She lifted her wrist from under the blanket to see nothing but a smooth stub of skin. "Oh." She knew it was gone for good. Her power wouldn't grow back missing parts, but at least it saved her from the pain. She wanted to cry, but the tears were absent. All she could do was try to comprehend that she was missing a hand. "It doesn't hurt."

"There's bound to be some healing magic that can help, right?" Marcelle asked.

Sarai snorted. "That's not just healing, that's complex medical magic. Takes years and years of study. I don't know how to grow new bones and muscles and attach nerves." Sarai tried to breathe, but anxiety clenched her in a vise-like grip, her head spinning as oxygen became scarce. "Holy fuck I don't have a hand," she gasped.

"We can see if someone at the Ellis Coven can help," Setanta suggested.

They were a large enough coven that the chances they had a skilled healer were good. Still, it took a few moments for the panic to release her.

"I don't have the words to say how grateful I am. Thank you, both of you," Marcelle shifted to sit closer to Sarai and put a cold hand on her knee. "I owe you."

"You saved me from their trap. Consider it even." One hand for Marcelle's life was a fair trade. Even as she stared down at her wrist, Sarai felt no regret. Then terror gripped her. "My glove!"

Setanta pulled the red glove from his pocket and held it out. She snatched it with her remaining hand, heart still pounding at the thought of losing such an important item. But she couldn't put it on. The hand it would fit was gone.

"I guess I'll just hold onto it for now," Sarai muttered.

"How did you find me so fast?" Marcelle asked in an obvious attempt to distract Sarai. It worked when the witch remembered just how they'd gotten to Marcelle from the island.

"Setanta flew," she replied. "He has wings."

Marcelle smiled. "Oh. Yes, yes he does."

"Do you?"

"It's a pureblood attribute for my bloodline alone," Setanta said. "Made vampires can't fly. Other lines have other gifts, like witches do."

"Well, I appreciate you taking the risk, flying to find me as fast as you did," Marcelle said. "That was... it was pretty bad."

"What did she want to know from you?" Setanta asked.

"Where Sarai was and why vampires were at the Ellis Coven." Marcelle smiled. "They got nothing from me, don't worry. She's a terrible torturer, no technique or intelligence to her methods, moved too fast. But..." Her smile faltered, and she glanced at Sarai. "They're very concerned about vampires."

"I mean, you guys are a powerhouse. It's scary

when you show up on someone's doorstep," Sarai said.

The two vampires said nothing, and Sarai had the distinct impression she was missing something important.

"Flight aside, we found you thanks to help from one of the witch leaders. Hannah," Setanta said. "She used astral projection and an unusual spell. It's an interesting coven. I have high hopes for this turning into an alliance. I'll return tomorrow, but I think you two should go back to the palace."

"Wait, why?" Marcelle said, sitting up straight before Sarai had the chance to protest for herself. "I'm fine, I'm all healed up. Look at me." She threw her hair around as if that proved it.

"You were just tortured, Marcelle."

"Like it's the first time," she said, rolling her eyes. "I'm fine. I'm trained against torture, and that idiot was an amateur. Being in bed with you is more intense."

"It's not, and you know it. You're trained against breaking under torture, not against the effects afterward." He looked up at Sarai. "And I want you somewhere magically protected against intruders."

Both women launched into protest. The elevator in the hall dinged, and the argument stilled as Bear stepped into the room.

"Right now isn't the best time. What is it?" Setanta said.

"Sorry to interrupt." He glanced at Sarai's stump, causing her to shove it under the blanket. Why did she find the injury embarrassing? "You have visitors, downstairs."

"Someone important, I assume?"

"If you consider your potential witch allies

important, then yes, I'd say so. They seem… skittish. Well, mostly. They've got one guy who keeps making eyes like he's going to try and start a fight."

Setanta took a deep breath and let it out, almost in a meditative manner. "Thank you. I'll be there in a moment." He disappeared, then reappeared while buttoning up a new, clean shirt.

Sarai and Marcelle both headed toward the door with him, and he stopped.

"And you're coming with me now too?"

"Didn't the witches help you find me?" Marcelle said with crossed arms. "I owe them my thanks, don't I?"

"And I want to ask them about my hand," Sarai said.

Setanta sighed but didn't argue.

The four of them had the most awkward elevator ride Sarai had ever experienced. It almost made her think it might have been worthwhile to take the stairs all the way down by herself.

When the doors opened to the lobby, they found Lilly and Angela with the witch leaders: Hannah, Tobias, and Danior. Unfortunately, the temperamental fire witch Lochlan was with them. He did not look happy to see any of them, but the rest looked relieved to see Setanta, the most familiar of the vampires around them.

"I wasn't expecting to see you here," Setanta said cordially. "Welcome."

"Yes!" Hannah cleared her throat, glancing at the tall guard. "Y-yes, your people are… well, we're here to make sure you found your friend and to see that Sarai is unharmed. Lochlan led us, we hope you don't mind."

"He promises to behave himself," Danior said. "Were you successful then?"

"Yes. Please, Marcelle. These are the witches who helped us locate you," Setanta said.

"Then I thank you," Marcelle said as she stepped forward and bowed her head just enough to show respect. "I'm not used to turning to your people for help, but I couldn't be more grateful."

"Your people helped Sarai," Hannah said. "One of ours, even if she chooses not to stay with us. It's only fair we help you in return. Are you all right, child?"

"Well," Sarai reluctantly revealed her hand to a chorus of gasps. "I was kinda hoping maybe you would be able to help? I'm a healer, but not that good. I know we just met, and I was a bit rude, but if there's anything you can do, I'd appreciate it."

Tobias pursed his lips. "You shouldn't have taken her with you," he snapped at Setanta.

"No, I'm glad I went. It's worth it," she said quickly. "Just, you know, if there's something that can be done…"

"We have some healers, but I don't think they'd be capable of anything more than what you've done. If you have the hand still, we might be able to reattach it," Hannah said.

"It, uh, it disintegrated."

Hannah made a disapproving noise with her tongue. "We don't have anyone capable of growing you a new hand. But a functional prosthetic with an illusion spell wouldn't be out of the question. We'd gladly help you."

"Do vampires make it a habit to put others in danger like this?" Tobias asked, his tone rising. It caught the attention of a couple walking through the lobby at that moment, who gave the group an odd look.

Setanta put up a hand. "We do have humans staying here. Part of the cover. Perhaps we should go someplace more private to talk? Or are you just here to check on Sarai?"

"That's no small part of it," admitted Danior, keeping his voice lower. "But, considering the kindness you've shown Sarai prior to this incident, and the honesty I sense in all you've said, we've decided we want to know more about this proposed alliance. To let you know we'd like to enter negotiations between the Ellis Coven and the kingdom of New Ulster."

Chapter Twenty-Eight: A Start

The negotiations took a week. Sarai spent her time under heavy protection in the penthouse apartment with Marcelle, who refused to leave her side.

They didn't talk about what had happened. Sarai didn't bring up the subject out of fear Marcelle wouldn't want to talk about it and focused instead on keeping them both distracted with their games, and also with sex. She decided she liked strip-poker since no matter who won, they both won, and it was better than being beaten by Marcelle at chess. And less painful than dwelling on the sister she thought once loved her.

Aside from spending time with Marcelle, Sarai accompanied Setanta to the Ellis Coven several times to be seen by the witch medics and be fitted with a prosthetic hand. It was carved of wood and looked like something in a period-piece film. Once it was on, the enchantments woven into the wood took effect to preserve the polished material and to allow Sarai to move the fingers, though clumsier than before. There was unfortunately no sensation, but it let her have a place to put her red glove where she could once again use it as her focus for spells. To keep humans from noticing the blatant magic, an illusion spell was cast as a final touch that gave the wood the appearance of a proper flesh and blood hand. She made note to avoid shaking hands with humans. While it looked like a hand, the prosthetic did not at all feel like one.

When a treaty was accepted, the witches provided Marcelle, Bear, and Angela (Lilly had disappeared at some point, presumably on spy related work) with special necklaces of polished wooden beads to allow them passage as part of Setanta's entourage, which Sarai went over carefully to try and understand the spells on them. She concluded it was well beyond her abilities and gave up.

The group went together back to Ellis Island, and through to the witches' side where they were greeted by Hannah and their guard captain, Moretti. The elderly woman's eyes were noticeably drawn to Bear, and he smiled at her.

"Welcome back to our coven," she said to Setanta.

"It's good to be back. You've met Bear, Angela, and Marcelle."

"Yes, and the necklaces seem to be working?"

"Seem to be able to walk around fine so far," Bear said.

"They will prevent you from acting on any violent impulses," she warned. "If you try to hurt anyone, they will make you sleep. But they should make it so you can walk around on our side of Ellis Island."

"We appreciate you permitting them to accompany me. I assume that if they need to defend themselves, they will be able to?" Setanta asked.

"No," she said firmly. "However, no one with violent intent will be able to focus on them while within our coven, as an added measure of safety to the charm. Now, there is a large crowd we shouldn't keep waiting. Shall we?"

Hannah led them into the witch's side of the old,

stone building. This time, the main room was more crowded than it had probably ever been, even on the human side back when it had been a hub of immigration. Sarai had never seen so many witches in one place, let alone one building, and more kept coming through doors that opened to new locations with each swing. Half of them looked curious, and the other half looked angry. While all of the vampires got stared at, particularly Setanta in the lead, Sarai could feel far too many eyes on her. She knew what so many of them had to be thinking. She was the traitor who had brought one of their most feared enemies to their doorstep.

"I think I'm going to be sick," Sarai murmured to Marcelle.

"You're going to be fine," she replied. Sarai wanted the vampire to reach out and touch her, to provide some comfort, but there was no reason to give the witches any more reason to dislike the vampires. Then again, she wanted to hold Marcelle's hand and wasn't sure she cared what a bunch of witches thought. So, she reached back and gripped her lover's hand. She received a squeeze back, and a number of whispers around them as people noticed them holding hands. It almost reminded her of the glare they got on their date, the way it felt to kiss and make everyone uncomfortable. Kind of... good.

Sarai smiled at the witches who glared at her, and it made her feel powerful.

At the far end of the hall was a small platform that had been erected on which the other witch leaders stood around a table, waiting. They climbed up and for a moment, looking out at all the various faces there, Sarai was frozen. Thankfully, she was still holding

Marcelle's hand.

"You're all right," the vampire said.

"Friends!" Danior said. "We know that there have been many rumors in the past few days about our recent visitors. You have elected us as your council as—"

Sarai stopped paying attention. His words were like water washing around between her ears, and the stares of people watching made her feel as if she were in a fish tank. They were all watching her, staring at the vampires, and muttering to each other about the scandal unfolding on the stage in front of them.

After Danior stood back, Setanta stood up. He was a focal point at the center stage, attention following him like he had a gravity to his presence. His words brought Sarai out of the haze.

"I'm honored to be here," he said. "I know this is a difficult situation, that to many of you it seems as if our peoples have been at odds for an eternity. But I was born in a time when vampires and witches coexisted in peace with each other. We were more than just allies; we were friends, occasionally even family. I want to end the bloodshed, find a way to bring that ancient sentiment back into this era."

"We need each other. The hunters have enslaved your people and slaughtered mine for far too long. We are all magical beings, and the Vasi see all magic beyond their control as a plague to be eradicated. Together, our peoples can stop them. I come here in peace, offering protection and an end to the violence between our people. I swear that none loyal to my kingdom will harm any of you, and to do everything within my power to ensure that the Vasi's reign ends."

"I know many of you do not feel that someone like

me is worthy of your trust. And I know that for many of you, the mere sight of me is painful. I understand that pain. I too have lost many. Friends, family, loved ones. I refuse to lose any more. I come to you as a future king among my people—" He knelt before them, and put his hand over his heart, his head bowed. Sarai knew what such a gesture meant to him, the way it reminded her of how Marcelle knelt before him as his knight. It was a silent pledge, an offer of protection, and a statement that he would spill his own blood to keep others from harm. "—to humbly ask for a chance to prove myself. Divided we will die. Together, we can create a future beyond hiding. I simply ask for the opportunity. To that end, I gladly bind myself to this alliance, and pledge to serve not only my people as their ruler, but yours as defender and ally."

He stood and bowed his head. The crowd was deathly quiet. The silence was broken by a frantic clap coming from the front row. Sarai looked down, and saw a little girl held in a very unhappy looking purple-haired male witch's arms, clapping wildly. Slowly, others joined in. It wasn't an enthusiastic applause, but it was at the very least polite and appreciative. It was a start.

The treaty was signed, in a moment that seemed too important to be so short, and dreaded socialization followed afterwards, when they were invited to meet with the witches who helped run different aspects of coven life.

One particular fire witch pushed his way to the front of the crowd, to hand the girl in his arms over to Danior, then grabbed Sarai's arm. It took her a moment to recognize it was Lochlan, as he'd dyed his hair a deep purple, and must have used a potion to dye his irises to match. Looking a little closer at his brown eyebrows, she wondered if he had ever been a real red head in the first place.

"Can we talk?" he said sternly.

"I assume you can talk. Do you have something to say?" she replied, not letting go of Marcelle's hand.

"I mean, without that listening."

"No, we can't."

Lochlan scowled. "Look. I just want to say that if you need help, we can help you. You don't need to stay with leeches. They'll kill you. That's what they do. If you side with them… you're a traitor."

"*Lochlan*," Hannah snapped, surprising Sarai from behind. "That is no way to speak to our new allies. Either join and support your family or leave this gathering so that we may enjoy it in peace."

The witch glared at them all, then spun and stormed off in a fuss. Sarai could have sworn she saw smoke steaming up from his ears.

"I apologize for him," the old woman said, gently taking Sarai's hands. "And I'm truly glad to see you… the both of you, I suppose. But I wondered if we could speak? A serious matter, away from the crowd."

"I'm not leaving her side," Marcelle said.

"Oh, no, I wouldn't ask you to. But I do have something important to share, and we simply haven't had the chance to speak since I've been so busy with this diplomacy lately. Someplace quieter?" she said.

Sarai nodded. She trusted Hannah perhaps the most out of the witches she'd met so far, since she had been the one that led them to rescue Marcelle. The pair followed the elderly witch to the side of the large room and its echoing din, and she looked very seriously into her eyes.

"When I projected myself, I knew I had to find your vampire companion here. That was a time sensitive issue. But now that you're both safe, I need to say, there was something I saw with my astral eyes. With you, Sarai." She smiled. "You have a guardian angel. Your mother. Are you aware of her?"

"My… mother?" Sarai stared in stunned silence. "My mother died when I was little. I couldn't even tell you what she looked like. I don't even know her first name."

"You do though," Hannah promised. "She is tethered here by your fears, to protect you. Liora Meir."

Sarai tried to comprehend what she had just heard. "N-no, she… Liora is a part of my imagination. I made her up. To cope…" Her voice trailed off as she looked behind Hannah to see an olive-skinned woman with short hair and a white dress standing there, watching with sorrowful eyes. "*Ima?*" Mother, in Hebrew.

"This coven can help you. We have people here who can help you set your mother to rest."

Sarai stared at the figure watching and took a step toward her. They did have similar features. "But I… I can't stay here," Sarai said softly, and looked back at Marcelle. "I want to stay with you."

"My sire invited you to our home, for his coronation, yes?" Marcelle asked Hannah.

"He did."

"Then, you have a standing invitation to our palace. Perhaps someone can work with Sarai while she stays with us? Is there any harm in putting this off a little longer?"

Hannah sighed. "It is possible. There's no harm in it, as much as I would like to lie and convince young Sarai to stay with us. Danior would never forgive me for a fib, however well intentioned. You are a witch though, Sarai. You can't forget that."

"I won't." She looked back up at Liora, who smiled. Sarai couldn't remember ever seeing Liora smile. "I have my mother to remind me."

Hannah nodded knowingly. "I suppose... if you're sure then. Now, do either of you happen to know what tribe that tall, handsome fellow's from?" She jerked her chin up slightly, pointing with it in Bear's direction.

"Mi'kmaq, I believe," Marcelle said and raised an eyebrow. "Interested? He might be a little old for you." Sarai had to clap her hand over her mouth to keep from laughing.

Hannah scoffed. "Not in that way. It would be irresponsible of me not to pick his brain a little. Could I speak with him?"

"Of course. I'd be happy to introduce you."

****

It felt like coming home when Sarai returned to the vampire palace. The witches and the pressure of the situation were too overwhelming, and it felt good not to fear who might be a spy for her father. Vampires were one group he could never infiltrate. Their palace was the one place she was safe, under Marcelle and Setanta's protection.

When they asked her to meet in Setanta's office, she was certain they wanted to discuss the events having to do with her father or the alliance with the witches. There was so much to think about, after all. A new frontier was before them, or perhaps an old one from Setanta's perspective. Either way, Sarai was certain that the alliance signed between the vampires and the Ellis Coven was the start of something magnificent, the kind of history she could be proud of participating in rather than the plans her father had for her, and she wanted to be a part of it.

But yet, when she closed the door and stood in the room with Setanta and Marcelle, their expressions were grim, as if someone had died.

"Did something happen? Is something wrong, does it have to do with the witches?" she asked, looking between their stern faces.

"Yes, and no," Setanta replied.

"You may want to sit down," Marcelle said.

Sarai spotted the grimoire on Setanta's desk and itched to snatch it up. "What's this about?" she asked as she sat. "What's the grimoire for?"

Setanta opened the ancient book and held it out to her. There was a picture on the page he'd landed on, one that made her stomach turn. It depicted a man and woman, naked and clearly in the middle of sex. Around them were hooded figures, slitting the throats of other naked figures.

"What... why are you showing me this?" Sarai asked. "What kind of ritual is this?"

"It's the ritual that resulted in my father's birth. The first pureblood of my bloodline. Performed by witches in honor of dark spirits, using the blood of sacrifices to fuel the spell," Setanta explained. "There are different variations around the world, but they're all similar in that they require a couple with the correct powers and human sacrifices."

She traced the figures, and noticed her hand was trembling. Her father's clan was infamous for the occasional human sacrifice. "No one would do this now, right?" she said. "This is horrible."

"It is," Setanta said. "I told you this is my grandmother's grimoire?"

That made the picture feel more awkward, to know that it was Setanta's grandparents in the picture.

"Yeah... Uh, did you want me to close the book?"

"No. My point is that she had the same powers as you. That picture is a good depiction of her wedding night."

Sarai felt blood drain from her face, a cold chill engulfing her body. Her eyes darted around the picture in front of her as she shook her head. "No, but we're not the same. I wouldn't do something like that. I wouldn't..." She stood up, backing up as if putting space between the book could put space between her and the ritual itself.

"You wouldn't," Setanta said. "But I doubt that you would be given the choice to object, if this did come to pass. I believe your father chose your mother, created you, so that you could be the mother of a new pureblood line to make his coven stronger. So that he could raise a pureblood to serve his coven who would have control of their own vampires the way I do."

Everything clicked into place, and Sarai felt as if the floor had fallen away. To the Vasi, she was the cure to vampirism. To her father, she was the start of a pureblood line that he could use as an army against rival witches and any enemies. And to the vampires... both aspects of who she was and who she could be posed a threat to their existence and their power in the region.

"I don't feel well," she whispered. Immediately, Marcelle was by her side, and helped her into a chair. When had her cold touch become so comforting? "My father knows I'm here," Sarai said. "He's not going to stop until he gets me back."

"I'll protect you," Marcelle promised, entwining their fingers together.

She looked up, making eye contact with Setanta. "I'm not an idiot. I know the safest course of action for you is to kill me, treaty or not. Why am I alive?"

"I do not kill innocents except when I have no choice. You are not at fault for merely existing," Setanta said.

"There's a 'but' at the end of that sentence," Sarai accused.

"But I would insist that you remain within the bounds of the palace until a better solution is found. This place is magically protected. While it might not be as elaborate and aggressive as the spells on Ellis Island, they require that any non-vampire that enters has an invitation from a resident vampire. No witch or Vasi can harm you here. Your father included."

"So, no visits to the mall," she said sarcastically.

"No."

"I never got an invitation here. He could get in just as easily."

"I whispered your invitation to you when you slept in my lap, the day you arrived," Marcelle said.

"Oh."

"Due to the nature of the spell, it can be... adjusted with words from the reigning family. By someone such as myself," Setanta said. "As a precaution. I mean you no harm or ill will. Since we will be inviting other witches into the palace for the coronation, I would like certainty that no one can steal you away as they attempted at the coven. After they leave, you have my word that we will devise a better solution for you."

"What are you saying?" she said, her eyes narrowing.

"Sarai Reinhart, you no longer have permission to leave this palace."

Sarai's heart sank. As sure as she stood there, she could feel the magic present around her, his words shaping the spell that was already in place. For the first time, she cursed the fact that Setanta was a witch.

She was a prisoner once again.

A word about the author...

Evelyn Silver lives in Florida with her husband, their son, and their two cats. She has a BA in English and enjoys a variety of hobbies including belly dancing and singing opera. She is an Own Voices writer, spinning tales of polyamorous and bisexual paranormal romance at all hours of the night. Evelyn sews her own clothes (poorly) and somehow manages to kill every plant she ever tries to take care of.

Thank you for purchasing
this publication of The Wild Rose Press, Inc.

For questions or more information
contact us at
info@thewildrosepress.com.

The Wild Rose Press, Inc.
www.thewildrosepress.com